Ainsley St Claire

VENTURE CAPITALIST

Book 9

Fascination

A Novel

Venture Capitalist: Fascination—1st edition

Other books by Ainsley St Claire

Venture Capitalist Series (in order)

Forbidden Love

Promise

Desire

Temptation

Obsession

Flawless

Longing

Enchanted

Fascination

Holiday

Gifted
November 2019

Tech Billionaires

House of Cards
February 2020

Tilted
April 2020

chapter

one

CECE

SINKING INTO A BATH FULL OF BUBBLES that smells of lavender, feels so good, and I'm able to relax for just a moment. Today has flat-out sucked. Why do so many people feel the need to forward me the links and clips of the gossip rags?

I'm so mad at Frederic right now. If he wanted to break up with me, he should have grown a fucking pair and told me. He didn't have to take an eighteen-year-old porn star out to a heavily press-covered event and then get caught with her under the table on her knees going down on him.

His messages afterward were stunning.

"Please, baby. Savannah and I are only friends."

Yeah, right.

I guess I could own some of it. I haven't been feeling it with him for a while, and we were both just hanging on. Damn, it still smarts to be dumped on television.

Asshole!

With cucumber slices over my eyes, the stress begins to evaporate. My phone rings, and normally I wouldn't answer while I'm de-stressing in the bath, but my best friend, Emerson, is due any moment with her first child. This just may be it. Besides, Frederic's been blocked, so I'm pretty sure I don't have to worry about dealing with him.

"Hello?"

"Caroline, it's Evelyn."

Crap. Work call. I spent most of the day with Evelyn. I'm kicking myself for not checking the caller ID first. "Hi, what's up?"

"I'm here at San Francisco General Hospital with my boyfriend. We think he broke his arm. Umm… I just saw them wheel your friend Mason Sullivan in from an ambulance."

I sit up straight, splashing water all over the floor, but I don't care. "Are you sure?"

"I'm fairly positive."

"Thanks, Evelyn." We hang up, and I immediately call his cell phone. "Please pick up. Mason. Please pick up," I whisper to myself.

"Hello?" a male voice answers, but it isn't Mason.

"May I speak with Mason, please?"

"I'm sorry, who is this?"

"It's Caroline."

"This is Detective Lenning. Are you related to Mason?"

My mind is racing. "No. May I please speak with him?"

"Do you know how I can get in touch with someone who's related to him?"

"His mother lives in Ohio. I'm one of his best friends. Where is Mason?" I dread his answer, wondering, praying, hoping he's not at the hospital.

"Caroline, Mason is currently unable to speak. He's at San Francisco General Hospital. We need to reach a family member. Do you know his mother's name?"

"I can't remember right now. I'm on my way. Where is his girlfriend, Annabelle Ryan?"

"We can't be sure."

I don't have time to think about Annabelle right now, so I let it go. "I'm on my way," I repeat before ending the call.

I quickly throw some clothes on and call for a rideshare. While in the car, I call Dillon.

"Hello. Boy, do you have good timing."

"Dillon, Mason's at San Francisco General. All I know is that they wheeled him in on a gurney. No one knows where Annabelle is."

"We're on our way there now. Emerson's water just broke."

"Oh my God! I'll check on Mason and be right there."

I hear a loud groan in the background. Obviously, Emerson is having some serious contractions.

"I have to go," Dillon says in a rush.

"No worries. I get it."

"CeCe, let me know the minute you know anything about Mason."

Fighting back the tears, I tell him, "I will."

I disconnect the call and reach out to Mason's other best friend, Cameron.

He answers with "Did Emerson have her baby?"

"She's going in now, but the reason I'm calling is because Mason's at the hospital."

"What? Why?"

"I don't know, but a detective answered his phone when I called, and Annabelle can't be found. I'm on my way."

"Hadlee and I will be right there, too." I hear him tell Hadlee what's going on, and she jumps on the phone.

"What do you know?"

"Nothing, really. Just that Evelyn from my office called and said she saw Mason brought into the hospital by ambulance. And when I called Dillon, he said Emerson is in labor and they're on their way to the hospital."

"Okay. Cameron wants me to tell you he's calling Cynthia, Christopher, and William. I'll call Greer as soon as we hang up, and you call Trey. I'll call and use my hospital credentials to find out where he is, and I'll text everyone." Hadlee is a pediatrician and well known in the medical community for her work.

I can breathe a tiny bit easier. "Thank you."

I disconnect the call and phone my twin brother.

"Hey," he answers.

"Hi. Please let Sara know that Mason's in the hospital."

"Is he okay?"

"We don't know." I hear him call for Sara and tell her.

"We're on our way," he says, and I can't hold back my tears. "Ces, he's going to be okay. I saw the rags, and I know today has been terrible, but I promise a big hug when I see you." Trey is truly my best friend in the whole world. We've been through so much together, and he knows what I think often before I do.

"Can you call Mom and Dad? They'll want to know."

"Yep, I got that. See you in a few."

"Hadlee will send a group text out as soon as she knows something." The rideshare pulls up to the emergency room entrance. "I love you, big brother."

"I love you, too."

We're hardly at a stop when I open the door and race up to the information desk, pushing myself to the front of the line. "Hello, Mason Sullivan was just brought in?"

"You'll need to get in line. I can only help one person at a time," the tired-looking receptionist says.

As I step in line and take a few deep breaths trying to calm myself, my cell phone pings with a text.

Hadlee: Mason's in the surgical unit on the fourth floor. His doctor is Jordan Severs. She's an amazing heart surgeon. Everyone, let's meet at the fourth-floor surgical waiting room.

This hospital is huge. Where the hell is the fourth-floor surgical waiting room?

I see a janitor and figure he probably knows the hospital better than any lady at the information desk.

"Excuse me. I need to get to the fourth-floor surgical waiting room. Can you tell me how to get there, please?"

He smiles at me. "Yes. You take the green line on the floor to the elevators and head up to the fourth floor. Once you get out there, you need to watch the signs. It's about as far away from the elevators as you can get, but you'll find it. If you get lost, there are plenty of people who can help you."

"Thank you so much. I appreciate your help."

I race off, following the green line to the elevators, and he's right, the walk to the waiting room is as long as it can be once I reach the fourth floor. Once I arrive, I let the nurses know I'm here for Mason Sullivan.

A man approaches me. "You're here for Mason Sullivan?"

I turn and size him up quickly. As I begin to answer, Cynthia arrives with her fiancé, Todd, two steps behind her. "CeCe? Is Mason okay?" She turns, and her eyes widen. "Detective Lenning? What are you doing here?"

"Miss Hathaway? I wish we were seeing each other again under better circumstances."

"Did the Russian mob do this?" Cynthia was involved with the Russian mob a little over a year ago. I guess she knows him from her mess when they got involved with her former employer and she was a whistle blower.

He holds up his hand. "You must be the woman who called Mason not long ago."

"That was me. My name is Caroline Arnault." I extend my hand, and he takes it cautiously.

"What made you call Mason at that particular time?"

"I received a call from someone who works for me. She was here with her boyfriend in the emergency room and saw Mason come in."

"I see." Turning to Cynthia, he asks, "And who alerted you?"

We hear them before we see them. Up rush my brother, Trey, and his wife, Sara; Cameron and his fiancée, Hadlee; Greer with her husband, Andy; William and his fiancée, Quinn; and bringing up the rear are Christopher and his wife, Bella. They swarm us, all asking questions about Mason at once.

I focus on Detective Lenning. "I called Cameron, and between the two of us, we alerted everyone else," I answer.

"Did you tell anyone who isn't here?"

I look around at the group. "No… wait. Yes, I alerted Dillon and Emerson Healy first, but they were on their way here because Emerson's water broke."

The girls go crazy.

Detective Lenning is becoming visibly agitated. "Miss Arnault, when we spoke, you asked about his girlfriend—" He searches through his notes. "—a Miss Annabelle Ryan?"

"Yes." I don't know where he's going with this, but I'm not going to help him.

"Did you call her?"

I shake my head.

"Why not?"

I shrug. "I guess I figured she already knew."

"Why would she know?"

"Because they live together."

I begin to feel bad for not calling her. While she may not be our favorite person, she cares about Mason, I'm sure of it, and she should be told.

Me: Annabelle, Mason is at San Francisco General. We don't know much, but we're here. Come as soon as you can.

William speaks up. "Detective Lenning, why are you here asking questions? Is there something we need to be aware of?"

"No, nothing," he shares. Turning back to me, he asks, "Did you recall the name of his mother?"

"His mother's name is Janice Sullivan Harris of Canton, Ohio," I tell him, able to remember now that some of the panic has worn off.

He has Mason's phone in his hands and scans through the contacts. "Excuse me."

"Mason's going to be pissed if he calls her," Cameron mutters.

I know he's right, but she is his mother and should probably be here.

My parents arrive then. They're pretty close to Mason. "Any news?" my dad asks.

Trey tells them what little we know, and I try to collect myself.

My dad pulls me aside. "Do we know why Detective Lenning is here?"

I shake my head. "He isn't telling us. And I'm getting nervous that I can't find Annabelle."

"He's a strong man. He's going to be fine, and he has the best doctors in the country looking out for him."

"Thanks, Dad." I lean in and he hugs me tight. It sure is comforting he and my mom are here.

I'm a complete wreck as we wait. Sara and Greer take a seat on each side of me, holding my hands. All the things I've wanted to say to him circle in my mind, and if he dies, I'm going to be more than disappointed in him. I'm going to chase him down in hell and kill him again!

Hadlee has disappeared, and Annabelle hasn't responded to my text, so I decide to call her. I'm relieved when it goes right to voice mail—I don't want to explain why I'm calling her and not the hospital staff. "Annabelle, this is CeCe. Mason has been admitted to San Francisco General. We don't know anything. Please call when you get a chance or come down. We are in the fourth-floor surgical waiting room."

Cynthia puts her arm around me as I disconnect the call. "He's strong. He's going to be okay."

"Thanks. Annabelle's phone rings right to her voice mail. I should try the house."

She nods, and I call the main line at Mason's house. Fighting back the tears, I virtually repeat the same message on that answering machine. I hope she can get here soon.

It seems to take forever for Hadlee to return; when she does, she's in scrubs.

"They're unable to get Mason stabilized enough for surgery. He has an irregular heart rate and shortness of breath. His liver and kidneys seem to be shutting down. His EKG was bad, and they're trying to stabilize him and determine if they need to do surgery. It looks like they're going to induce a medical coma so they can run tests, and then they'll move him to the ICU." Hadlee looks at me. "Let's go get some coffee. It's going to be a long night."

My heart is beating triple time. *A coma? That seems extreme. What happened?* "I'm okay here. I can wait."

Cameron puts his arms around me. "Come on, CeCe, you look exhausted and in need of some food."

I paint a smile on my face. "I'll be fine."

Looking around the room, I see that everyone is as stressed as I am. Hoping they will follow my lead, I clap my hands together and say, "All right, everyone, Mason would not be happy to know that we are out here worrying about him. Let's head down to Labor and Delivery and see how Emerson is doing."

Everyone seems to perk up, and a few even smile as we walk to the other side of the hospital in search of our other friend and partner. Emerson is bringing the very first baby into our group.

When we arrive, the nurses recognize Hadlee but won't let the rest of us in. After a few minutes, Dillon walks out looking grim.

"How ya doin'?" Cameron asks.

"The baby is not moving into the birth canal. The docs are giving him a few minutes to figure it out on his own, or they'll begin prepping her for a C-section."

"I see the baby's stubborn just like his parents," Sara sympathizes.

"Maybe." Dillon grins. "Any word on Mason?"

"We don't know much, but Detective Lenning is here and investigating."

"Was it a car accident?"

I shrug. I'm following Cameron's lead and not wanting to stress Dillon about Mason's situation. I wish I knew why Detective Lenning was here and asking questions, but I'm not going to stress about this where we have something to celebrate. He needs to focus on Emerson and his new baby. "I'm hoping Hadlee can find out more from her side."

"You guys can wait here or, of course, with Mason. I can text you as soon as the baby arrives."

I give Dillon a big hug and whisper in his ear, "You tell Emerson we're here and cheering for her. We can't wait to see your little bundle."

We wander back to the ICU waiting area. The hours tick by even slower than normal. I stand, I sit, I read my social media. Everyone I care about is here with me, but I'm worried about Mason, and I'm mad at Annabelle for not being here. Where could she be?

Everyone's phone pings at the same time.

Dillion: When you can, come meet Liam Michael Healy, born at 10:22 p.m. at 7lbs, 8 oz. Mom is a rock star and doing great!

We jump up and cheer to celebrate the new addition to our team. I can't wait to meet the little guy.

"Hadlee, you go first to visit, and we can follow in less-overwhelming groups," Greer says.

"I think we can go in small groups of four," Hadlee informs us.

I stop listening to them. I'm sure Mason's doctor is going to be out any minute.

It's just Cynthia and me waiting when a petite woman steps out. "Caroline?"

I stand. "Yes, that's me."

"Hello, I'm Jordan Severs, Mason's doctor."

"How's he doing?"

"We can't be sure why Mason had a heart attack, but he seems to be doing well. We've put him in a medically induced coma for a few days. He needs to recover. Once things settle down, everyone can visit him. It will be good for him to hear you all talking to him."

"Thank you," I whisper as I fight back the tears. *Mason, you'd better pull through this. I have a lot to tell you, and if you think you can die, you'd better think again.*

"He's strong. This coma will only last a few days," Dr. Severs assures me.

chapter

two

MASON

"HEY," I RASP. "What happened?"

I watch CeCe sit straight up and smile at me. She looks so beautiful, but she's tearing up.

"You called 911 and told them that something wasn't right and you needed the ambulance and the police, and you specifically asked for Detective Lenning."

I remember now. I was finishing the dinner the housekeepers left me, and my heart began to race like a Formula One race car. "I remember a little now."

"Well, you most likely saved your own life."

I look around the room and see only CeCe is here. "Where's Annabelle?"

"That's the million-dollar question. We've all tried her cell phone, but it goes right to voice mail. No answer at the house and no response to texts." She reaches for my hand, and it feels warm and comforting.

"How long have I been here?"

"A little over a week."

A nurse comes in, and CeCe steps out of the room to give me privacy. I wish she'd stay. It makes my heart flutter—in a good way—that she's here.

The nurse asks me a dozen questions, and I lie there answering them all. She shows me how to use all the pumps and gadgets so I can self-manage my pain meds.

The nurse leaves, and CeCe returns. "I just texted everyone. They should be here shortly. Hadlee and Greer are down with Emerson, Dillon, and Liam. They're finally being released today."

"Who's Liam?"

"He's their giant bundle of love."

Of course, the baby. I'm so mad that I'm here and can't be there for two members of my team. I attempt to get up, but all I seem to be able to manage is sitting up. "I need to go see him."

"Don't worry, you will. Relax. We've all been worried about you." She grasps my hand again and squeezes it. The small gesture relaxes me. "Do you know where Annabelle is? I should let her know you're awake. She's going to have a fit when she finds out I'm here and she isn't."

I don't care if she has a fit. "Well, now I know what it takes to get your attention." I try to smile and I adjust to face her, but it hurts.

"A phone call is all it takes to get my attention," she says warmly.

"How did you know I was here?"

"Pure luck. Evelyn from my office called to tell me she saw you being wheeled in—"

"Hello, Mason," Detective Lenning says as he enters the room with a different doctor, who introduces himself as Dr. McMahon. CeCe and I both look up at him expectantly, hoping for good news.

"Hello, Dr. McMahon and Detective Lenning. What's your news today?" CeCe asks.

Looking at us both, he studies his notes. "We determined what happened. The good news is the numbness, tingling, and burning in your fingers and toes should reduce over time. Your shortness of breath should decrease, and we'll get you back with a physical therapist to help with some of that. The ongoing chest pain should go away as well. We still see an abnormal heart rhythm, so we'll have to watch that. We've confirmed your blood work indicated aconitine poisoning. We believe it was long-term poisoning by wolfsbane, so we're pretty concerned."

"Wolfsbane? What is that?" CeCe asks.

"It's actually a flowering plant that can be highly poisonous. Now we're concerned about long-term damage. We want to continue to look at your liver and your kidneys. We did a lot while you were in the medically induced coma to save those organs, and we'll want to watch over the long term to make sure we were successful," Dr. McMahon shares.

"How was I exposed to the wolfsbane?" I can't quite put together everything he's saying. What does it mean?

"We've gone through everything in your trash and refrigerator at home and your office, and we're not 100 percent sure. We've tracked your meals before you got sick, along with any pills you may have ingested, but we just can't be sure where you came into contact with it. What do you recall eating that night?"

I'm exhausted, and I have to concentrate on recalling what I ate. I don't really pay attention; I just eat what is left for me. "I had pork chops, if I remember correctly, rice, green beans, and salad, all made by my housekeeper."

"Tell me, what was in the salad? Were there any greens you were unfamiliar with or that you hadn't seen before? Were there flowers on it?" Detective Lenning asks.

"No, I don't think so. She likes these dandelion leaves and kale, which are always bitter greens and don't taste great."

"You still eat them?"

I nod. "As long as I smother them in plenty of blue cheese dressing, I can manage them."

"So much for eating healthy greens," CeCe snickers.

Her comment distracts me, and I want to reach out to her.

Detective Lenning tries to get my attention again. "Okay, can you recall what you had to drink?"

"Iced tea." I think about it a minute, my brain still a little foggy. "Maybe a beer. I don't recall exactly. Do you think someone poisoned me on purpose?"

"We believe so, yes," Detective Lenning shares.

"There was nothing in your stomach. You'd digested everything before we were able to figure out what had caused your illness," Dr. McMahon states with great authority. "You should know that it was your phone call when your chest pain and the dizziness started and you telling the paramedics that everything was purple that was the giveaway for the poisoning. But, we've no conclusive evidence how you were poisoned. Had you not called an ambulance, you would've been in really bad shape and probably passed away in your home."

"We're having problems locating your girlfriend. Could she have been behind this?" Detective Lenning asks.

"I can't believe Annabelle would've done that. We broke up a few weeks ago, and she moved out. We really haven't been talking. I know she was upset when she left, but I can't see her doing anything like this. Honestly, I'm surprised she isn't here. I wish I knew where she was."

"We want to make sure that we find how you were exposed so it doesn't happen again," Dr. McMahon says.

"How long do you expect to keep him here in the hospital?" CeCe asks.

"We don't know for sure. It will be several weeks. The tingling, dizziness, chest pain, and shortness of breath need to go away. He'll be weak for some time and will need some round-the-clock care for a while. But, before we can release you, we're going to have you go through a battery of tests," Dr. McMahon states.

Dr. McMahon leaves, and I put my head back and look up at the ceiling. I can't believe I got myself into this situation. I still can't buy that Annabelle is behind this. She hasn't been to the house for some time. How would she have poisoned me? But the question remains, where the hell *is* she? "I have no idea where Annabelle is."

"When did you break up?" CeCe asks.

"She moved out shortly after the trip to Vegas."

"Oh, Mason, I'm so sorry."

"There's nothing to be sorry about. She wanted to get married, but I didn't. I know everyone hated her, but she was sweet in a lot of ways. But we didn't love each other, and I feel that's important when you get married."

"I think that is a perfect description. But why would you live with her if you didn't want to marry her?"

"Because I liked her. But also because I was convinced she was the mole, and I wanted her right where I could see her," I admit out loud for the first time.

"Mason! What were you thinking?"

"I thought I could control the situation. I knew she wasn't the mastermind of everything, but I thought if I could get her to open up to me, we could figure out a way to double-cross the mole."

"Do you still think she's the mole?" Detective Lenning asks.

I hadn't realized that when Dr. McMahon left, Detective Lenning remained behind. "I'm not 100 percent sure. Maybe 75 to 80 percent sure," I hedge.

"That's still pretty confident. What makes you unsure?" Detective Lenning presses.

"It really hurt her feelings to watch others around her get married and not her," I answer simply, hoping it ends this line of questioning.

"That's good news, at least," CeCe muses.

I want to explain myself, not only to Detective Lenning but also to CeCe. "Someone else has my heart, and she knew that. She didn't know who it was, but she knew I'd already given it to someone else. Plus, I'm not sure she loved me. She loved the idea of being married to me; she loved the money and the access it provided, but she didn't love me," I assert.

"Who did you give your heart to Mason? Who—" CeCe questions.

"Oh my goodness! You're here, and you're alive. Thanks to the Almighty." My mother has arrived and in a full-length fur coat, dripping in diamonds, and wearing too much makeup. She launches herself across my body, and I cringe just as the nurse comes in.

"Mason, I'll have a few more questions for you, but I'll let you manage this." Detective Lenning motions to my mom and the chaos she brings with her.

"Mason! I just heard you were poisoned. Don't you worry, mommy's here to take care of you."

I'm struggling to breath with my mother's fur coat in my face and her laying across my chest. The thought of her taking care of me turns my stomach. I love my mother, but these days I take care of her, not the other way around.

"Get off my patient. You can't lie all over him with that rat coat you're wearing. It could cause him an infection. Get off him before I have to call security." The nurse reaches for the room telephone.

"It's okay. It's his mother. She just arrived and was very anxious," CeCe is quick to explain.

My mom looks at CeCe and scrutinizes her. Then her eyes register who she is, and she bubbles over in her best Valley Girl impression, saying, "Oh my God! You're Caroline Arnault."

The nurse looks at her. "You've now met his girlfriend. Now get off your son right this instant, or I'm calling security."

My mom stands upright, trying to reclaim her dignity. I watch her extend her hand to CeCe. "Hello, I'm Janice Sullivan Harris."

"So nice to meet you, but I'm not Mason's girlfriend. I'm one of his friends."

"Mason, you didn't tell me you knew Caroline Arnault." She turns back to CeCe. "You're even more beautiful in person."

Mortified. Positively embarrassed by my mother's behavior. I love her, but she has no understanding of discretion. I'm sure she's told every person she's met some inflated story about my company and me. I love and hate that about her. She's a proud mother, but maybe a little too proud. "Mom, thanks for coming."

"I should be running. Mrs. Harris, it was a pleasure meeting you. I'll be checking in on Mason tomorrow. I hope to see you again." CeCe gathers up her things and begins to leave. She winks at me, and my dick responds. Great, my mother's just layed on me, and now, I'm going to get a hard-on from just a wink. The blanket on the bed is thin and everyone is going to see it. Can the earth just open up and swallow me whole?

"Wait, you don't have to go." My mother's begging. Lovely. "I was reading on the plane about your prince boyfriend. What a loser. A porn star? She obviously has no problem with public sex."

"Yes, well, it wasn't really a shock. We'd been on the outs for a while."

"Well, he missed out."

What the hell is my mother talking about?

"Have a good night." CeCe leans down and embraces me and kisses me softly on the cheek, and I smell her subtle Chanel No. 5 perfume. Classic, just like CeCe.

"Don't be a stranger." I squeeze her hand.

"Never." She waves and leaves. I'm sad to watch her go. I wanted to tell her all about Annabelle.

I look over at my mom, and she has tears in her eyes.

"I can't believe I almost lost you."

I'm convinced if she could crawl into bed with me, she would.

"I'm here, Mom. What did you mean about Caroline's prince?"

"It's in all the gossip rags. I don't usually read them, but it was a way to pass the time on the plane. He dumped her for that porn star, Savannah something. I guess she got caught going down on him under a table at some fancy New York event."

"Thanks, Mom. I'm not sure I needed that visual."

"Why didn't you tell me you were friends with Caroline Arnault?"

"Did I tell you I was friends with Greer Ford?"

"No. Who's Greer Ford?"

"She's another one of my friends. It doesn't matter who they are; it matters how we treat one another."

"Well, Caroline is loaded. I remember when she and her twin brother, Trey, inherited billions when their grandfather skipped their father because he didn't go into the family business."

"Charles did go on to start Sandy Systems with his wife, and they are self-made billionaires, so I think they're doing just fine."

"Have you met Trey? Do you think he likes older women? I'm a great MILF."

I think I'm going to vomit. "Mom, he's happily married to Sara Arnault, our company attorney, and a partner. *Happily*," I stress.

"I'm exhausted. The flight took forever," she whines. "Can I crash at your place?"

"I don't know, Mom. I just woke up. I need to call the police to see if that's possible."

"Well, I can't stay just anywhere." She's become too spoiled. Growing up, staying at the Holiday Inn was a step-up for us because they had a pool; now, anything less than four-stars is slumming.

"For all I know, the police have it locked up because it could be a crime scene."

"Why would it be a crime scene?"

"Because I called them as my heart attack started."

"Are you telling me someone made you have a heart attack?"

"Mom, the poisoning presented as a heart attack." I don't want to tell her anything, and while I have no idea if my apartment is open or closed, I don't want her there. "Call the Fairmont. Tell them you're my mother and get the

Presidential Suite. They'll take good care of you, and I'll pay the bill."

"You mean it won't come out of my allowance?"

"No. I've got you covered." It's just easier giving in to her than fighting.

She leans down and gives me several quick kisses. "I was so worried about you. I'm glad you're okay. I'll be back tomorrow morning."

"Thanks, Mom."

After she leaves, the nurse comes back in. "I'm sorry about that, Mr. Sullivan. I was just worried about her lying all over you."

"Don't worry about it. I love her to pieces, but she can be a little overdramatic."

"I don't know if you want to know this or not, but Miss Arnault was here every day and rarely left your side except to go home to sleep each night. She read to you each morning and would just work sitting here by your side."

I'm a little surprised by this. "She's a good friend."

"And a pretty one. According to the tabloids, she's single, too. If I were you, I wouldn't wait around for an invitation."

I laugh. "Ouch. That hurts." I rub at my chest. "I'll try to keep that in mind. We've been friends for a long time."

"I'm pretty certain she likes you as more than friends." With that comment, she turns to leave. "I'll check on you at the end of my shift. If you need me, just hit the call button."

Once she's gone, I sit here thinking about what my mom said and what my nurse said. Could our timing actually work this time?

Me: Sorry my mom ran you off.
CeCe: Don't worry about it. She's a delight.

Me: You're very generous. The nurse tells me you were here all day, every day. Thank you for staying with me. It means a lot to me to know you care.

CeCe: I do care. I'll stop by in the morning.

Me: I'm sorry but not sorry about the prince.

CeCe: I'm not. We've been struggling for a long time.

Me: I want to take you out for a nice dinner when they free me.

CeCe: I'd like that. See you in the morning. Let me know if I can bring anything. We need to figure out how you ingested the wolfsbane.

Me: Agreed. Good night.

CeCe: Good night.

I don't sleep well in the hospital; there's so much noise, and it always seems like someone is in my room checking my vitals. I mean, how does anyone get any rest around here?

CeCe stops by when I finally fall asleep. Figures. What crappy timing for me to finally get some rest.

"Hey, are you going to sleep the day away?" I open my eyes and see Dillon standing over me. "You're awake."

"Hey. Congratulations." I struggle to sit up, and the small movement makes me feel as if I've climbed two flights of stairs. "I understand you named your son after your dad."

"Emerson insisted on it." I see her standing behind him holding the baby.

"You came to visit me?"

"We couldn't let you be awake for long without introducing you to your godson."

"Really?" I've never been a godfather, but I'm going to be the best one there ever was.

"There's no one else we'd ever choose." Emerson smiles. She extends her arms to me, offering me the baby. I hold him next to me, and he's awfully tiny. He coos at me, and I'm in love. They're both taking time off, so they're out of the loop about what's going on at the office. We have a few closings coming up. I have no idea who's handling what. It gives me a headache and my heart races—and not in a good way.

I'm really frustrated lying here in the hospital. I'm beginning to think that they're putting meds in my IV to make me sleep. I feel like all I do is sleep when the nursing staff isn't checking my vitals and interrupting me for one test or another. I have appointments with a dietitian, a physical therapist, and multiple doctors to do all sorts of activities to get me back to my life.

I struggle to explain to them why I need to get out of here, but they don't listen or try to understand. I know my health depends on these things, but I also have over a hundred people who depend on me for a paycheck. I need to return to work for them.

My phone keeps ringing and pinging with texts, asking work-related questions. Mason, what do I need to do about this? and Mason, so-and-so wants to know X. If I don't respond, it becomes overwhelming.

Sitting in this low-lit room, I marvel at how much I deal with in a day. I know it must be stressful for the team to be missing their leader. It doesn't help that Dillon is out, too. That only leaves Cameron and Sara, who are swamped with their jobs of keeping us going, but not great with dealing with the day-to-day. Thankfully, we have Quinn in place who's really acting as my number two.

Quinn recently joined the partnership. I dated her years ago when we were in grad school, and I've always thought she was the smartest person in our class. She worked for one of our competitors and knows this business better than anyone. She has tremendous instincts, and I trust her to keep the boat afloat.

chapter three

CECE

MY PRIVATE LINE RINGS. Few people have this number, so I answer. "Caroline Arnault."

"Hello, beautiful."

My stomach drops. My ex-boyfriend Tim Carpenter always crawls out of the woodwork when my love life crashes and burns on the gossip rag pages. It's taken him a week to call me. I was hoping he'd lost interest. I'd block his calls, but he's also CEO of the world's largest cosmetics company, Cosmetics, Inc., and I sometimes need his help.

"Hello, Tim. What's up?"

"No need to get grouchy since your man went off with a porn star."

I so want to hang up on him. He's a true lesson in patience. "I'm okay with it. We'd been limping along for a while."

"He was limp, huh? You know I'm happy to take care of you. I'm never limp when I'm with you."

Gross. I shake my head and roll my eyes. No, he wasn't limp, but he was best at getting himself off and then rolling over and leaving me to finish myself. "I'll keep that in mind." If I don't change the subject, I know I'll say something I'll regret. "How are things at the big cosmetics conglomerate?"

"We'd still love to have Metro Composition Cosmetics under our umbrella. Think of all the doors we can open for you."

No more than I can open for myself. It may take me a bit longer, but I still have control, and when they made their last offer, they were going to phase out the nonprofit work we support. That was a no go for me. "That's certainly tempting, but we're busy getting ready for our fourth year at Fashion Week."

"You don't need anyone do you?"

"Apparently not." I do, but I'm not going to admit that to him.

"I say this because you know I adore you, but you need to be more vulnerable. What can a guy offer you that you don't already have? You've got your shit together; you're a billionaire; you run a wildly successful business—don't tell my board I said that—and you have parents who adore you and shower you with support and a twin brother who is your surrogate boyfriend."

"Trey's a surrogate? I'll be sure to tell him." That's actually really funny.

"When you need a male perspective, you call him."

He's right, I do. I know Trey will always be honest with me, and he knows my business and truly knows all the weaknesses and insecurities I have. Plus, I trust him. I don't trust Tim. "You're right, but I also have a cadre of men I talk to, and you're one."

"You always know how to sweeten someone up. We need to have lunch soon. When will you be in New York?"

"Fashion Week is in four months. I'll see you then." I know he was hoping I'd ask him to fly in, or that I'd move heaven and earth to go see him. I did that once, but he's too selfish a friend and a lover, so I'll never do that again.

"Fine, but if you need an itch scratched, I hope I'll be your first call."

I chuckle. Not a chance. "I'll let you know. Have a great day."

"You, too, beautiful."

When I hang up, there's a knock at my door, and it's Evelyn, my vice president of operations, my number two, as I think of her. I know that if I were to go hide away for months or even years, she could manage things just fine here. "Do you have a minute?"

"Always. What's up?"

She tosses a group of ad slicks on my desk. They are designed and sent out to prospective editorial staff for coverage, the industry's version of a press release. I quickly see they're from a Chinese competitor. My stomach drops. It is their fall line of colors complete with eye shadows, nail polish, and lip colors. I look at Evelyn in shock. "Where did you get these?"

"They were sent to my contact at *Desire* magazine." She crosses her arms in front of her, looking defiant and upset.

I study the names of their colors, and they are exactly the same as our names for our fall line we're on the verge of launching. I look up at her. "Holy shit!"

"Exactly. Who the hell leaked our information to them?" Evelyn demands.

"This can't be. This must be a hoax. Are you pranking me?" My heartbeat accelerates and perspiration drips in my cleavage.

"I wish I were. What do we do?"

How is it possible that SHN has a problem and now we do? I'm not 100 percent sure what I need to do, but I do know a few things. "We need to get the FBI involved. This is espionage. Trade secret theft." I continue to shuffle through the ad slicks, looking at what they have. Their logo and cases are eerily similar to ours, so they'll be going after our customers and our small but growing market share. *Holy shit.* My mind is racing, and I can't help but see my company circling the drain. "I want you to pull all our research and our meeting notes. I want a list of who had access to what. I want to know who left us and when. And damn it, anything else you can think of."

She nods. "I've started that. I'll get it all to you quickly." She gets up to leave. "We can recover from this."

I nod. Evelyn can recover. She'll be nabbed up by Tim and one of his cosmetic companies. For me, it won't be quite so easy.

I fight back the tears. I won't go down easily. I'm going to fight this.

I pick up my phone and text my brother.

Me: 911. Call me when you can.

It's seconds later when my personal line rings. "Is everything okay?" Trey asks when I pick up.

"No." I tell him about what we got from *Desire.* "What do you suggest I do?"

"We need to reach out to the FBI. Is Mason able to string a good conversation together? He might have some great ideas for you."

"Excellent point. I was thinking the same thing, but his mother is in town, and needless to say, she's a force unto herself."

Trey laughs. "Good luck with that. I've heard about her. Mason is the center of her universe."

"As I understand it, he's all she has."

"Doesn't matter. Call him and see what he says."

"I was going to head over in a few hours anyway. I can go now."

"Baby sister, I know this is devastating, but you are going to come out of this just fine."

"Thanks. I hope so. Love you." It doesn't feel like it right now. Everything is flashing before my eyes. Financially, I'll personally be fine, but I worry about my team. The majority of cosmetic companies are based in New York, and most of my team won't be able to move. My stomach turns somersaults. How did I not see this coming?

"Love you, too." We disconnect our call.

Tim was wrong. I am vulnerable, and I do need people—I just don't need him. I bring up Mason's number and call.

"Hey," he croaks.

"How are you doing today?"

"I'm doing okay. My mom hasn't arrived yet. I'm so sorry she ran you off yesterday."

"She didn't, and I know she'd just flown in. I'm sure she was worried about you—we all were." There are a few beats of silence. "I've had something come up here at Metro Composition. Can I stop by and talk to you about it? I need some of your expertise."

"Of course. I don't think my mom will be here for a few hours, but even if she is, I can set her up with a personal shopper at Nordstrom to keep her busy."

"Would you mind? This is a big deal."

"Is everything okay?"

"I'm not sure. Can I come over now?"

"Absolutely. Mom's staying at the Fairmont. I can have a car pick her up for a day of shopping. She'll be thrilled."

"I have a personal shopper at Nordstrom who I highly recommend. I can get that set up."

"Okay. They won't let me go anywhere, so I'll be here. You can save me from the daytime soap operas and talk shows."

"Thank you, Mason. Can I bring you anything?"

"I'd love a real cup of coffee. But, I meet with the nutritionist this afternoon, and I have a feeling that caffeine and salt are no longer in my diet."

"We'll find something you can enjoy. I'll call Jennifer at Nordstrom and get something set up for your mom. See you soon."

We hang up, and I quickly dial Jennifer's personal cell phone.

"Hello, Caroline. Will I be seeing you soon?"

"You always send me the best things; I don't even have to come in."

"Well, I've seen some of the things you've been photographed in, and they didn't come from me, but they're amazing pieces."

"It helps to do the makeup of some pretty awesome designers at Fashion Week."

"One day I'll get to Fashion Week. That would be Mecca for me. How can I help you?"

"I need a favor. I need to meet with a friend who's stuck in the hospital, and his mother has arrived. I was wondering if I could send her over to you this morning and you could take good care of her."

"Of course. I'd be happy to. What time would she be coming in?"

"She's staying at the Fairmont. I know you're close enough that she can walk, but I'll arrange a car to take her over to you. How does eleven sound?"

"Perfect."

"I'll call you back if it doesn't work for her, but her name is Janice Sullivan Harris."

"I'll be waiting for her arrival at the Market Street entrance."

"Thank you, Jennifer. I appreciate your help."

I call the Fairmont. "Janice Sullivan Harris, please."

I'm put through quickly. "Hello," a muffled voice answers.

"Hi, Janice. This is Caroline Arnault." She's silent. "We met yesterday in Mason's hospital room?"

"Oh, yes. I remember. I took a sleeping pill, and my brain's not working well. Is everything okay with Mason?"

"Yes, he's just fine. Maybe a bit cranky since he can't have coffee, but he's doing okay. I thought you might enjoy spending the day with my personal shopper at Nordstrom, so I set that up for you today."

"You set me up with your own personal shopper?"

"I did. Her name is Jennifer, and she'll be expecting you at eleven. Would that work for you?"

"Yes, of course."

"She'll meet you at the Market Street entrance. I'll send a car to pick you up, and you'll be well pampered today."

"Thank you so much! My Mason is single, you know. And he's crazy about you."

"I'm crazy about him, too, but I think we're good as friends right now." Before she can go on trying to play matchmaker, I say, "So I'll confirm that you're going to meet Jennifer at eleven."

"Yes, thank you, Caroline."

"Enjoy your time. She has an amazing eye."

I end the call and text Mason to let him know what I've set up and that I'm on my way.

I grab the ad slicks and head out the door, calling out to my assistant as I go. "Christy, I need to run out. Please cancel my meetings today. I'll be on my cell phone. I'm not sure when I'll be back."

"No problem."

I take a rideshare across town to the hospital, and just as I arrive, I see a woman in colored scrubs walk into Mason's room. I hang back outside the door and listen.

"Hello, Mr. Sullivan. My name is Wendy, and I'm your nutritionist."

"Nice to meet you."

"Mr. Sullivan, your cholesterol is slightly elevated, but your weight is… perfect."

She's flirting with him, and the hair on the back of my neck stands straight up. I stand outside the door and listen to the conversation while checking emails on my cell phone. Emerson has sent me a fabulous picture of her with Liam curled up on her shoulder. She's titled it "Exhaustion." I love it, and I tell her as much.

"Mr. Sullivan, you must work out a lot," the nutritionist coos. "You're so muscular. I bet you have a washboard stomach, too."

Oh good grief. I roll my eyes.

"You're quite young to be having a heart attack. You need to eat vegetables, whole grains, fruit, nuts, and seeds every day. Aim for two to three servings of fish and other seafood per week. No more fast food for you."

"I don't eat much fast food and already do all that you're suggesting. I drink a lot of coffee, and my afternoon snacks tend to be peanut butter crackers."

"Maybe you should trade out the peanut butter crackers for some raw almonds, and please limit your coffee intake. No sugar drinks."

"Okay. Thank you."

"Here are some helpful pamphlets about how nutrition affects your heart. If you ever need any help, here is my card. I've put my personal number on the back." She giggles, and now I know for sure she's flirting.

"Great. Thank you."

I use that as my cue to walk in. "Hey, Mason, how are you doing today?" I walk over and kiss him on the cheek. I know it's like a cat marking her territory, but does she really need to flirt with him while he's recovering?

She shrinks back, my point taken. She's cute, and under normal circumstances, I bet she'd be a great match for a single guy, but not Mason.

"Okay, then. I guess I'll be going," she says and waves, but Mason doesn't notice. I hate that she makes me jealous.

I watch her walk out. "Washboard stomach?"

He shakes his head with a grin. "Do you want to see? I didn't show her."

"Hey, you already told me you're single. Go for it."

If he agrees, I'll be crushed.

"Why would I go there? I told you someone already has my heart."

"You did, and you were ready to spill the beans when your mom came in."

"She always had impeccable timing." He smiles at me but doesn't continue.

"Well, let me tell you why I'm here." I hand him the Chinese company's press slicks and then our mock-ups.

"I like these. I particularly like the packaging. What's the difference between the two?"

"Absolutely nothing, and that's the problem."

He looks at me, clearly confused.

"These are from a Chinese competitor."

He looks down at them again. "They have the same names?"

"Exactly. Someone has breached all of our trade secrets and has probably sold them to a competitor, making the last six months of work completely moot. This kind of theft could break Metro permanently."

He looks up at me. "Oh, Ces, I'm so sorry."

I fight back the tears. "What do I do?"

He looks them over carefully. "I think we reach out to the FBI and also start an investigation with Jim Adelson's company." I know that Jim runs Clear Security and has been running private security and investigations for us, the biggest being our mole and hacker issue.

"Does he work with companies other than high tech?"

"He must." Mason has picked up his phone and already dialed Jim. "Jim, this is Mason." He's silent a few moments. "Yes, I'm at San Francisco General." Mason reaches for the photos. "Jim, the reason I'm calling is that Caroline Arnault's company, Metro Composition, had someone take their entire fall line and sell it to a competitor. We need your help." He listens again and then says, "Jim, I'm going to put you on speaker. Mind you, we're in a hospital room and need some discretion."

Mason puts the phone down in front of him. I close the door to his room for a modicum of privacy.

"CeCe, I'm so sorry to hear about this," Jim says. "Tell me what you know."

I walk him through the comps we received from *Desire* and wait for his response. Mason reaches for my hand and gives it a comforting squeeze. That little move makes my heart race.

I told his mother the truth—I'm crazy about him. I know when he tells me who he's given his heart to, I'll be devastated, but until then I'll hold out hope for a future with Mason.

"Let's do this. Can you come into my office?" Jim asks me.

"Yes. I can come right now if that works."

"Give me an hour. I need to make a few calls."

We hang up, and I look at Mason. "Thank you. I'm sorry to burden you with this when you aren't quite 100 percent."

"Like I said before, you're saving me from the daytime talk shows and soap operas. They don't even have *SportsCenter*."

I cover my face with my hands. "You know this may very well close our doors, right?"

"You can fight this CeCe. I know you can."

I stand to leave. "I'll keep you posted. Your mom will probably spend most of the day with Jennifer. If she has a budget, we should let her know."

"No budget. It's the least I can do for her."

chapter

four

CECE

I TRY TO GO TO THE HOSPITAL TO VISIT MASON at least once a day. I love spending time with him. I always learn new things, and he's just comforting, a calm in the storm around him. I feel like he's all that and the bee's knees. Each day we spend together, I'm stronger in my belief that we can make a go of a relationship.

My car is waiting for me downstairs to drive me to the office. The FBI will be over later this morning to sit down with Evelyn and me, and I'm anxious to hear what they have to say.

My phone pings with a group text from Hadlee. I'm missing my girls. How about dinner and drinks tonight? We can meet downtown at Martuni's. Say 6?

Cynthia is first to respond. I'm in!

Sara: I can make it. Sounds fun.

Emerson: You're speakin' my language. I'll be there without Liam. I need to put clothes on that don't have spit-up on them, and it's a good excuse to take a shower.

Greer: Count me in.

Me: Can't wait!

Quinn: Forget the men! I'm in.

Today is going to be a good day. I'm sure of it. I go through all of my emails and things that have happened this morning since I checked last night at eleven thirty.

I think about my evening with Mason. He's absolutely the most handsome man I've ever seen. I can't help but think about what's underneath those shirts and shorts I see him wearing all the time.

My daydreaming is interrupted when there's a knock at the door and Evelyn comes walking in. "Are you ready?"

"I suppose. We're just going to listen to what they have to say. We can meet here in my office. Does that work for you?"

"Works just fine. They've arrived downstairs."

I look at the clock. I can't believe I've wasted my morning daydreaming about Mason. Boy, is that puppy love for you.

I let Christy know she can bring the two agents in, and then I wait patiently with Evelyn. We whisper about the gossip going around the office.

"I hear Nancy in accounting got engaged last night," Evelyn tells me.

"She did? That's great news. We need to order some cake this afternoon to celebrate."

"You just want an excuse to eat cake."

I smile—guilty as charged. Cake sounds like a perfect day. "You know me so well."

"How are we going to counter this espionage?" Evelyn asks.

She believes we should just go ahead with our release. This was her baby as well as mine, and I understand her not wanting to let go. I know she's probably right from the standpoint that this is a major loss for us and a way to save our line; however, I am concerned that it's going to be poorly received by the fashion world, given it would be a replica of something that's already out.

Vanessa, our public relations expert, thinks releasing our line would be a mistake. I'm not sure what to do. Vanessa's by all means the guru when it comes to public relations and the fashion world; that's her bailiwick. She'd have to bail us out if it went sideways, and one of the things I truly appreciate about her is that she only wants me spending money on things that make us money, not saving us from losing money.

I sigh. Why can't anything be easy?

My admin escorts a woman and a man into the room. Both are dressed almost identically in dark pantsuits and white dress shirts, although he's wearing a tie and hers is subtly opened at the collar.

They introduce themselves as Agents Leslie Winters and Alan Greene.

"Please have a seat." I gesture to the three chairs sitting opposite where Evelyn and I sit perched to listen to what the agents have to share.

"Ms. Arnault, we apologize, but we've not had any success in figuring out how your competitor might have accessed your information. We've reached out to the company in China. They claim they've been working on this for a year and that, if anything, you're copying them," Agent Winters says.

I'm stunned by this. "How the hell can we be copying them? We have six months of work that we've done. We've been using focus groups to determine the names of the colors. Meeting with over a dozen vendors to determine our packaging. Working with marketing experts about our logo. It took us three weeks to determine a small dot in the logo. It doesn't make any sense that they'd have the same information. They're notorious at trademark theft. It's pure and simple corporate espionage and trade secret theft."

"We understand that, but it's only makeup, not proprietary computer data. What's the big deal?" Agent Greene asks.

My blood pressure goes from zero to five hundred, and I'm going to lose it. I can see Evelyn doing the same. "Makeup is my business. It's a very big deal. I appreciate that you are not a user of our products, Agent Greene. However, it's important that you understand this is a $40 million business in San Francisco and a major employer in this city. This kind of theft affects not only my pocketbook but also thousands of others."

Wow. I know we're small potatoes compared to many in the cosmetics industry, but I have to believe this is a big deal to the justice department, regardless of our size. It's certainly a big deal to me, because this is my life and livelihood. "I'm hoping you're putting more into this than you're indicating," I finish.

"Well, we've had a few things on our plate, and we don't understand why you can't just release your line as you expected. Look, there are a thousand brands of running shoes, and they all play well together in the sandbox," Agent Winters says with indifference.

When they're done, they stand and shake our hands, but they've lost all credibility with me. I lead them out of my office with my brain going a thousand miles an hour. I'm not usually treated this way, and it burns me up.

"Christy, please escort these agents downstairs."

I shut the door behind them, my mind still racing. I expected more than hearing that the Chinese say they've been working on the makeup much longer than we have.

Evelyn turns and looks at me. "What the hell was that? Do they think that any industry loss to a foreign power is worth it? What would they have done had we sold sex toys?"

I laugh. "Probably ask for samples."

She begins to laugh. "What are we going to do?"

"I've got to think about this. Jim is doing a lot right now. I'll see what he's got going."

Sitting with my thoughts, I think about how this competitor could've come up with this much information before we did and got this to market quicker. How could they have come up with the names and the colors in the palette? Their palette isn't just similar to ours but exactly the same. Our competitors will have similar colors, sure, but not the same exact ones with the same names. More than anything else, I'm pissed that these two agents discounted my business.

I pick up my phone and call the next best thing to having the FBI on speed dial. "Hi, Jim. I just met with Agents Winters and Greene of the FBI's White-Collar Crime division in the local office. I was really disappointed. It sounds like all they've done is call the company that has stolen from us, were told they'd been working on it for months, and have now pretty much stopped investigating because they have so much on their plate. I'm having lunch with Walker Clifton today to see if I can get him to light a fire under these two."

"Metro Composition is a major employer in the city. What are they thinking?"

Jim says exactly what I'm feeling, and it makes me feel vindicated that I'm not overexaggerating their response. "That's Evelyn's and my thoughts, too. Any advice for me?"

"Let me do some research. I'll have some preliminary information for you in a few days."

* * *

chapter
five

MASON

I'VE BEEN IN THE HOSPITAL now for almost nine weeks, and I'm anxious to get out of here. My energy isn't back at 100 percent, and I still have a little bit of nausea and shortness of breath, but I'm ready to have a regular night's sleep in my own bed. My bags are packed, and I'm ready to go. My mother is nowhere to be seen. She's a night owl, so it's usually three in the afternoon before I see her. I always called it "Janice time." I love her, but she's a lesson in patience.

I look over at CeCe, who's been here every morning and has snuck me coffee on a regular basis. She's studying her laptop. I know Jim and the FBI are both busy working on her mole, and we've talked a few times about it, but she's understandably stressed. She can't stop the competitor's production, and the fact that they've launched already gives them the advantage of the color palette and names. I think she should just trade out the names of the colors and launch anyway; those who love her brand won't be interested in the knock-off. But she's unsure.

I'm anxious. Today's the day. Today they're going to tell me if I can finally go home. I've been warned by one of my nurses that they won't release me unless I have full-time care at home. I'd hate to hire someone for a short period of time, so when CeCe insisted I stay at her place, it didn't take me long to agree. I'm pretty self-sufficient, so a caregiver would only be there to make sure I get up and out of bed each day and to check on me anyway. If I were still living with Annabelle, that would have worked. I could invite my mother, but that would be more of me looking after her than the other way around.

Besides, being with CeCe is going to give me the chance to make my move. I'm sure of it.

Annabelle. I kept her close because I knew something was not quite right there. At first, I was convinced she was feeding information to the mole, but I could never be sure. But as time went on, she relaxed when she was with me. We had a comfortable rhythm. We didn't love each other, at least not in a traditional way. We were good friends. I ultimately told her that my heart belonged to someone else. It was nice to feel so well taken care of by her, and I feel really bad about being so blunt about it, but I didn't want to lead her on; I only kept her close because I really didn't trust her.

Turning, I look over at CeCe. I know I can trust her. None of the SHN team trusted Annabelle. I often questioned if I was driven by their suspicion or if my lack of trust stemmed from her behavior. I want to believe it was how she would act, as she always seemed to be up to something. Maybe at first, she sold information to the mole for money, but I think once she quit the company and moved in with me, the mole moved on to the legal assistant, who was caught and now sits in a federal prison in Lompoc.

"Are you thinking about Annabelle?" CeCe asks.

"Yes, I've been thinking about her a lot. More than I did before this happened. I just can't believe she could be behind this."

Janice arrives unexpectedly. "CeCe! So wonderful to see you. Thank you for connecting me with Jennifer. She's amazing."

"I agree."

She's so focused on CeCe that she seems to forget why she's here until I wave at her. "Oh, Mason, today's the day. After over two months in the hospital we're going to get you home. I'll feel so much better knowing you're no longer in the hospital."

"They haven't released me yet," I tell her.

She pats me on the arm. "They will. Don't you worry." She looks around. "I need to find out when your doctor is going to release you." And with a flurry, she's out the door.

"I don't want my mother to move into my place."

CeCe nods in understanding. "I've already talked to her and Dr. McMahon. I've made arrangements for you at my house. Misty is already there, and my housekeeper is there all day; she'll meet what you need. Jim has a team waiting to escort you, and they'll be set up in the guest rooms downstairs." She looks at me and pushes hair back from my face. "I don't want you staying alone. I hope it's okay that I've stepped in and taken over."

"As long as my mother is staying at the Fairmont, I'll be okay." I can't wait to see my dog, Misty. She's a beautiful golden retriever, and I've had her for many years.

CeCe giggles. I love that sound.

Mom returns. "Apparently we can't leave until Dr. McMahon arrives, and he teaches in the morning at the medical school. So we need to wait."

"Mom, I'm going to be okay. If you want to go back to Ohio, I'm fine. I'm out of the woods, and I'm not going home but to CeCe's place."

"I'm not ready to go yet. I still need to see how well you're doing outside of a hospital."

"You can stay as long as you'd like at the Fairmont, Mom." It's expensive at $1100 a night, but it's worth her staying there rather than in my house. I adore the woman, but she's nosey. She'll go through every single drawer, cabinet, and crevice, and there are things in my home that I just am not interested in explaining to my mother.

I'm convinced I'll be stuck with the turkey, stuffing, and potatoes the hospital is serving for lunch when Dr. McMahon and his trail of students arrive. "Mason, the time has finally come. Are you ready to go home?"

"I think I was ready about eight weeks ago."

He smiles. "All right. I will sign your discharge papers. Please note, you have an appointment with gastroenterologists along with a cardiologist." He looks at CeCe. "It's extremely important that he keeps these appointments. Aconitine poisoning will have long-term effects, and we need to monitor them."

"He'll be there if I have to drag him myself," CeCe assures him.

"You're good to go. Mason, it was a pleasure being your doctor. I think Miss Arnault has you in excellent hands." He winks at her, and she smiles.

They load me into a wheelchair, and I have a team of people following me out. Most people don't pay attention to me; they seem to be watching CeCe. She's easily recognizable, and people often ask for her autograph. To my dismay, these days several have been giving her the play-by-play with her ex-boyfriend. He's a true loser. But his loss will hopefully be my gain. I know she's always kept me at a distance, but this time I'm going to make my case. I've been in love with her since I met her, and it's time I told her.

CeCe has a grand home at the top of Pacific Heights. The front faces Alta Vista Park, and the back has stunning views of the Golden Gate Bridge, Alcatraz, the North Bay, Berkeley on a clear day, and downtown. Truly beautiful.

The car pulls into the back, so I'm able to get out without the pressure of cars passing. It takes me a while, as I'm easily exhausted. This is not how I want to live. When we finally reach the living room, I stop and park myself in a chair with a footrest.

"Wow, this is a beautiful home. And what a stunning view," my mother says.

CeCe smiles. "Thank you so much. That's very kind of you. I feel very lucky that the house came on the market just as I was looking to buy."

"Do you live here all by yourself?"

I think she's considering moving in.

"I have a housekeeper who helps and takes care of things around here, particularly as I travel for my work. She's been watching Misty this whole time and will keep up with Mason while he's here," she assures my mother.

"I grew up on a farm, and we didn't have dogs as pets, they had jobs. We never had a dog when Mason was growing up. I don't understand his fascination with animals."

I roll my eyes internally. My mother just says whatever comes into her brain, not thinking about who her audience is.

"I grew up with a bunch and love them. They never have a bad day, and they are always excited to see you," CeCe shares.

Misty slathers me with licks and nuzzles me, and her tail is wagging faster than most cars can drive. I missed her so much while I was in the hospital. I rescued her when she was a puppy. She'd been abused and doesn't like crowds, but who can blame her?

She leaves me and greets CeCe, almost equally as happy. I watch CeCe get down on her knees to give Misty the attention she's begging for.

"I'm not planning on staying very long," I tell her.

CeCe looks up at me sharply. That may have come out stronger than I intended. "You'll stay as long as the doctor says is appropriate."

I'm trying to think about how I can respond to that when my mother announces, "I have dinner plans tonight."

I look at her with a bit of surprise. "Dinner plans? With who?"

My mother ruffles my hair. She may be a bit overbearing, but she does love me. "There's a kind gentleman that I met. He takes me to dinner, and we enjoy each other's company. That's the other reason I'm in no hurry to head home."

CeCe grins. "I think that's wonderful. Go enjoy yourself. Angela and I will take care of Mason and make sure he doesn't get into any trouble."

I don't need any looking after, but I'm grateful for time with CeCe. "I'm just fine. No one needs to worry about me. Have a great time, Mom. What's his name?"

"He's a doctor here in San Francisco, and his name is Michael Frieman," she says with a look of triumph on her face.

"Have a great time." I'm going to have Hadlee check him out. She's a good friend and a pediatrician, well connected within the medical community here in the city.

Mom gives me a hug. "It's just fun to have somebody want to take me out to dinner for a change. Get some rest, and I'll be by tomorrow to check on you."

I can't help but be a little nervous about Dr. Frieman. My mom can be softhearted and takes in strays. I hope this is a good thing.

My mom leaves in the flair that she always comes with. I look at CeCe and shake my head in surprise that she hasn't run for the hills.

"What should we do for dinner tonight?" she asks. "Would you like to go out, or would you rather have something in?"

"I'm certainly open for whatever you feel you're up for."

"I'm not the one who spent the last two and a half months in the hospital, so you get to make the decision." She smiles at me, and right now all I want is to be with her.

"I could really go for… you know, this may sound crazy, but the pizza over at the Italian Restaurant sounds amazing right now."

"You're right. It's so good. Would you like me to have it picked up, or do you want to try to go?"

"I'd like to go out, but I need a bit of rest." I look at the clock and see it's still early. "How about we plan on leaving close to seven?"

"That sounds perfect. I can get some work done. Would you like a blanket here, or would you prefer to lie down in your room?"

I'd like to lie down with her, but I'm so tired, it would be a waste of a come-on. "Here's fine, and a blanket would be great."

I wake naturally. My stomach growls, and I'm hungry. I see CeCe studying her computer. She looks up at me. "You're awake."

"I'm hungry, too."

"Do you still want to go? I can have the pizza delivered."

"No. I need to breathe some fresh air."

"Let's go, then."

She walks over and helps me get out of the chair. I hate needing anyone. When I grew up, it was up to me to be strong. At the office, I'm the managing partner, and I'm the one who holds everyone up.

I manage things. I'm not managed.

We walk slowly to the car, and I'm a little out of breath, not feeling 100 percent, but I'm determined. I'm a man, and I'm not going to let anyone see me as weak. Plus, the thought of my favorite pizza sounds so much better than eating the congealed meals I would get at the hospital. Our security team helps to keep people back as we navigate to the restaurant and inside the restaurant so we're able to enjoy a quiet evening together.

Once we're seated and we've ordered, I look across the table at CeCe. She's positively beautiful. Her chocolate brown eyes, her dark brown hair I want to run my hands through, and her easy smile. Her beautiful, soft lips that I want to devour. My jeans are a little tighter than comfortable. I change the subject to distract myself. "Thank you so much for taking such good care of me and coming by the hospital every day."

"Of course, you're one of my best friends. I couldn't imagine not being there for you. I'm just really sorry about what happened. Any news about Annabelle?"

"No. She grew up down in Orange County, and Jim and his team have gone looking for her there and at her brother's and sister's places. Nothing yet."

"Have you tried calling them?"

"I don't want this to sound as bad as it does, but I've never talked to anyone in her family. She grew up in a foster home and never shared much about it. I would ask, but she would always deflect. It was rough for her, but I admired her… gumption. I know that's an old word, but she was determined not to let anything slow her down, and I liked that about her."

"Do you miss her?"

"No, not really. I was thinking about this before I got sick. I know we got along well, but I also felt like she was using me as a stepping-stone for something better. I deserve someone who wants me and all my imperfections and doesn't see me as her ticket to being invited to the right parties."

"I feel the same way."

"But you don't have any imperfections."

CeCe smiles. "You're the sweetest thing. I would say the same about you. I'm really sorry that you got so sick."

"What do you have to be sorry about? I feel confident we'll find out who poisoned me. I can't tell you how much I really appreciate you being with me and spending time with me. It really means a lot."

"Mason, I wouldn't have been anywhere else." Her comment makes my heart soar. I want to get a little healthier before I proclaim my feelings, but I believe we're heading in the same direction.

"Tell me more about what's going on within Metro Composition. I want to know what you're doing to capture your spy and how you're going to survive this breach."

She sits back and takes a large drink of her wine. "Corporate espionage happens. We aren't the first in the beauty industry to face it. We're not sure if the Chinese are behind it or if it's just an upset employee. The White-Collar Crime division of the FBI, Jim and his team, and my executive team are looking at all angles."

"It must be more common than people think if we're both being hit."

"I guess I thought we'd be immune. We're a small company with hardly any real impact on the international stage."

"I never thought we'd be dealing with a mole issue, either. I've been really surprised at how personal our mole has been. We're close, though, and I feel like this is going to get wrapped up soon." I take a drink of my water.

"Hard to believe that you've been dealing with this for five years."

The waiter puts our pizza down in front of us, and my stomach is so happy. "This looks perfect."

CeCe raises her glass. "To good friends and amazing pizza."

chapter

six

CECE

WALKING INTO THE KITCHEN, I see him sitting at the table. Angela's spooning scrambled eggs onto a plate for him.

"Good morning," he says.

"Good morning. You're up early. How did you sleep last night?

"I slept better than I have in months," he announces with a schoolboy all-teeth grin.

"That's great. You look good this morning." He's dressed in his work uniform of khaki pants and a blue plaid button-down shirt with the sleeves rolled up. His hair is wet, and he smells delicious—I swear I can smell lemon, green apple, a touch of vanilla, and cedarwood. I've worked in cosmetics for too long! "What's your plan for today?"

"I plan on heading into the office," he answers simply, as if of course that's what he's going to do.

I wait a few seconds before I respond. "That's not what the doctor wanted. He mentioned you should be home for a couple of days. Angela's here to keep you occupied and keep you out of trouble."

Mason looks over at her, and I swear he just winked at her. "Don't get me wrong, Angela, I adore you, but I'm not sure I can watch many telenovelas."

She laughs. "No worry, Mr. Mason. You're missing out, but I still like you."

"Promise me you'll take it slow today," I beg.

"I promise. Dillon is coming back to work today, too. He's going to swing by and pick me up. A shift change of bodyguards will be with me when I go in with him. They can bring me home if I don't feel well," Mason assures me.

He's an adult, after all. I'll keep an eye on him, of course, but I'm sure I slept better knowing he was here last night. I shrug. It isn't worth an argument. "All right. I'll check in on you in a little bit."

"I'd be disappointed if you didn't." He winks at me and gives me the cheeky grin again. His edge of irritation is gone, which confirms he's sleeping better. I know they had to check on him constantly in the hospital, so he's had no such thing as uninterrupted sleep for weeks now.

"Goodbye." I grab a piece of toast and walk toward the door, pausing to pet Misty on the way out, who gives me my morning kiss.

I have a big day today. I didn't want to resort to this, but the FBI has left me no choice. They aren't returning calls, and after our meeting, they pretty much blew me off. I pick up my phone and dial.

"US Attorney Walker Clifton's office."

"This is Caroline Arnault for Walker Clifton, please."

I wait a few minutes before he comes to the phone. "Caroline! What can I do for you?" Always the consummate schmoozer.

"I just wanted to call my favorite US attorney and see if he might be free for lunch today. I have a little problem I'd like some advice on."

"I'm always available to help such a generous supporter." Of course he is. He suckered me into a big check before, and this will come with a price, too. "How does one o'clock sound over at Waterfront Café?"

It's no surprise when he picks a place where everyone who's anyone will be seen. I roll my eyes internally, but I need his help, and he's out to garner some extra donations toward his next campaign, for which I'm sure I'll be high on the donor contact list. "I'll see you at the Waterfront Café at one o'clock."

I put a call in to Jim Adelson, my security advisor. The last time we spoke, he told me he had someone going into the Chinese cosmetics company and is hoping to have some information for me shortly. I'm hoping he has an update for me.

Before I can even say hello or announce myself, Jim says, "Caroline, how are you this morning?"

"Hi, Jim. Any news?"

"I just got the report in. I haven't fully translated it into English, but we can deduce that the Chinese company can't explain how they made the decisions for your color palette or names of the colors. You worked for several months on this, didn't you?"

"That's correct. They told the FBI they'd been working on this for months."

"I'm not sure that's the case. The Chinese are famous for their subterfuge."

"That's a nice way of saying it," I reply snarkily. "I'm having lunch with Walker Clifton today. I may not tell him all that you've learned, but I'm hoping we can light a fire under the FBI."

"Walker Clifton should jump if you ask him nicely. You can be assured that we're going through your team with a fine-tooth comb. If we don't see any movement from our background check, we can get further involved and dig deeper. I expect we'll have a few things to report to you shortly."

Jim has this commanding way of letting you feel like he'll take care of everything. I'm so grateful to have him on my side. "Sounds great. Call Christy when you're ready, and she'll make time for you on my calendar."

"Thanks. How's Mason doing?"

"He's staying at my place since I have a live-in housekeeper and he can't be left alone. Your team has bedrooms in the basement and are close by. If you can believe it, he went to work this morning. He hates being dependent on anyone."

Jim chuckles. "Sounds like me. He's lucky to have you."

"He's been a good friend for a long time." I'm not sure he'll tell me much, but I'll ask as an advisor to SHN. "Have you guys located Annabelle?"

"We think so, but right now my guys are staking the location out. It's odd that she's completely gone off the radar. She's had a pretty strict schedule for over three years and now this."

"That *is* strange, but sometimes we do silly things when our heart is broken."

We hang up, and I do a few things around the office before I need to meet Walker. As the time approaches, I gather up a few items, including the two cards the agents handed me, and stick them in my bag. I'm determined to get to the bottom of this.

As I leave my office, Evelyn walks up. "Where are you going?"

"To have lunch with a friend."

"Would you like company?"

"It's a personal lunch. I'm good. I spoke with Jim, and he may have something for us by the end of the week."

"Oh, great! Enjoy yourself, and I'll talk to you when you return. I'm still thinking over our options following this morning's meeting."

"I should be back by three."

"Great. If there's anything to report, just let me know."

I wave as I walk out, my mind distracted by the Chinese competitor. It wouldn't matter if I took Evelyn along, except that Walker may feel a little more comfortable talking to me alone. I just don't want to waste anyone's time.

When I arrive at the restaurant, Walker's already here. I watch him work the room. That's what happens with the late lunch crowd; it's more of a networking event for the who's who of San Francisco's politics and technology. As I work my way to our empty table, a few people wave to me. I know he picked this location because having lunch with me brings him some credibility—although my being jilted by a prince for a porn star may be a detriment for him.

I see my dad and go over to his table. "Daddy!"

"Sunshine! So good to see you. I didn't know you'd be here today." My dad is sitting with several of his friends; they are the true power brokers of Silicon Valley. I'll call him later and fill him in on what's going on with Metro and my lunch with Clifton.

Larry Ellison, the founder of Oracle, asks, "How is Mason Sullivan doing?"

"Believe it or not, he went to work this morning."

"That's the dedication I like to see. I was just telling your father that I want one of SHN's start-ups."

"If I know the team over at SHN, they'll listen to any reasonable offer," I assure him.

"That's what I'm counting on."

"I'll let Mason know I saw you today—that is, if you don't mind?"

"Not at all. You can tell him I'll call him next week," Larry says.

My dad winks at me as I say my farewells to him and his friends and wave goodbye.

Walker's watching me as I approach our table, where a beautiful blonde is standing next to him, and I spot his card in her hand. When I sit down, she looks at me sheepishly and says to him, "Talk to you soon, I hope."

I whisper, "Walker, she's a little young for you, don't you think?

He smiles. "Well, I can't get you to go out with me."

"If I thought you'd like me for more than my money or my name, I might consider it." I feel like I'm the bird and he's the cat waiting for me to get just close enough to capture me.

"Quite the group your dad is meeting with."

I look over at their table. No one in the restaurant dares to interrupt their lunch. They're old Silicon Valley, and they've made a lot of people in this town millionaires and billionaires many times over. "They've been his friends for decades."

He leans across the table and discreetly says, "You know, we'd make quite the power couple."

The thought turns my stomach. I don't want to be part of a power couple. I want to be loved and adored by someone who doesn't care what I look like, the amount in my bank account, or what my last name is. "You're probably right, but I'm interested in someone who loves me for me and not for the people I know."

"Romance and soul mates are all things for romance novels. Think about it. We could do some amazing things. Maybe even live in the White House one day."

I want to be rude, but I need him, so I must make nice. "Tempting, but right now, I have other plans. Should they change, I promise to let you know."

After the server takes our lunch orders, he asks, "What can I do for you?"

I pull the agents' business cards out of the pocket of my bag and place them in front of him. He looks at them, and I see his eyebrows rise in surprise which tells me he recognizes their names. "How do you know these two?"

"They stopped by my office a few weeks ago over an issue we're having. Since then they've not returned one phone call or given me any updates."

He studies the cards. "What's the issue?"

I walk him through what happened, where we're going, and what we've been doing. In addition, I share with him that Jim is doing a background check on my team and hint at what he's prepared to do if the FBI isn't interested in acting—even though he's already done it.

"CeCe, this is pretty serious stuff. This kind of trade secret theft could put you out of business."

Thank goodness someone understands. "My thoughts exactly, and it would absolutely affect the San Francisco economy. I employ over a thousand people in our management offices downtown and another four thousand down in South San Francisco in our manufacturing plant. Granted, I'm not the largest employer in San Francisco, but I am one of the larger single employers, and I feel like these two agents are discounting this theft because it's makeup. I run a good high-quality, independent brand, and someone has put my business at risk. I need help to find them and prosecute them."

"I agree. I'll talk to the head of the local FBI office and make some inquiries. I'll let you know what I learn."

"Thank you. That's what I was hoping you'd say."

"Good. So, let's talk personal lives. Rumor has it that Mason Sullivan's shacked up at your place. Is that why you won't consider any kind of commitment with me?"

"Mason has been in the hospital for the last two and a half months. He lives alone, and the doctor wouldn't release him without someone staying with him. I have a full-time housekeeper and assistant living in my home, so she's there to help keep an eye on him. Mason went to work this morning, so it won't be long before he'll be moving to his own home."

"The guy's a billionaire. It's not like he can't afford a caregiver to stay at his own place."

"True, but he's one of my best friends, and I absolutely adore him. Why hire someone when I already have Angela, and she loves catering to him? Now, what about your personal life? I heard you were playing with Dara Holiday. That's a big deal. Her grandfather owns half of Union Square."

"Dara and I aren't serious. She's a date when I need a pretty girl on my arm. Is there something going on between you and Mason?"

"Why are you asking?"

"I'm incredibly attracted to you. It isn't your money or your name. You're a stunning woman, and I have real feelings for you."

"Walker, please know that I adore you, and I promise to write you a very generous check for your reelection, but my heart belongs to someone else."

He doesn't even look disappointed. "Any chance you'll go with me to a fundraiser this weekend? Lots of photographers there to show that prince you've moved on."

While he may have a point, I don't care if Frederic knows I've moved on. "I'm sorry, I really wish I could join you. Unfortunately, I already have plans." Yes, I have plans. Mason may not know it, but I hope they're with him. If not, it's going to be with a container of Häagen-Dazs ice cream and popcorn, maybe watching something on television—anything other than adorning Walker's arm while listening to boring politicians talk. "Sounds like a job for Dara Holiday."

"That's too bad. I certainly would love for you to join me. You would know many of the people there."

We make simple conversation after that, talking about different people we know in common and what's going on. I'm careful what I say to Walker. I can't help but like him despite his being a third-generation politician and willing to use anything he can to his advantage.

After our lunch of lobster bisque, a salad for me, and some kind of fish sandwich for him, we part our separate ways. I give him a tight hug. "Thank you in advance for all your help with our issue. And , have fun with Dara. She's a sweet girl, and I have a feeling she may have more feelings for you than she lets on."

"You've broken my heart again, but I'm happy to help you. Maybe one day you'll agree to date me."

I walk out to my waiting car and think about what he said. He's a good-looking guy. Dara isn't right for him, but I may know someone who is. Walker's more interested in following in his father's footsteps to the Governor's office and then a bid for President. He needs a strong woman behind him, and I have an idea of who might be a good match for him.

I think about his comments regarding how alarming it is that we're a San Francisco business that employs a lot of people. The loss of the income generated by shutting down my company could really affect the San Francisco economy.

When I think about what the espionage does to SHN's clients, it has a different impact. The companies are smaller, so the impact is less noticed, but it is much more personal there, not only because they've said they're going after SHN's founders specifically, but also it affects them personally. Trade secret theft is a bigger deal than I ever gave it credit for.

I need a drink. It's still early, but I send out an SOS over text to my friends.

Me: I really need drinks tonight. I'll probably go early if anyone cares to join me.

It's very relaxing to know I have a great group of friends. I feel really lucky. I know I could call any of these women at any time and they'd pay to bail me out of jail. Of course, we're not actually that rowdy, but I can be myself with them. I don't have to put on any pretenses. I talk to Emerson almost every day, and I talk with the rest of the girls all the time.

I don't want to go back to the office for two hours of everyone needing me. I want to do something just for me. I could call up a rideshare, but it's only a few blocks, and I want to enjoy the sunshine. I call Christy and let her know my plan in case anyone is looking for me, then start walking.

Market Street is always hustling and bustling. On this end of town, the financial district begins on the north side of the street, the tech industry on the south side. It makes for an eclectic group of people. I love this city. It may drizzle most of the winter and sit under a dense cloud of fog in the summer, but the people here are vibrant and....

If I lose Metro Composition, I don't know what I'm going to do. It will be devastating.

I wander through the cosmetics section when I arrive at Nordstrom. I see the Metro Composition display and two of our employees both doing makeovers. We pay good money to be so visible here, but it's worth it. I love our cosmetics. Each season we launch a new palette of colors, and I like them better than the last. I watch them work, and eventually one of the women getting a makeover recognizes me.

"Oh. My. Gawd! You're Caroline Arnault!"

My makeup artists are always uncomfortable with me here. I hate to put them on the spot. "Hello. I'm here to just escape." I check the name tag of her artist out of the corner of my eye. "I see Alana is taking great care of you."

"Oh, I love your makeup. My friends back in Scottsdale are not going to believe I met you while getting a makeover."

"Well, we are glad you love the colors. You look fantastic."

"Can I have your autograph?" she begs.

"Me, too," the other woman says. This happens. I'm only famous because when my brother, Trey, and I were five, my grandfather passed away and gave us our father's share of his estate since they were estranged. We were the youngest billionaires on the *Forbes* list, and since then, people have been fascinated with our lives.

"I'd be happy to. Are you considering buying this powder?"

She nods vigorously.

"I can sign the lid."

Her eyes bulge, and she can hardly contain her excitement. "That would be incredible."

I scribble my name across the lid, then look at her friend. "You have the same powder. Would that work for you, too?"

"Absolutely."

I sign hers as well, and all of a sudden there is a large group of women crowding me for autographs. I feel someone come up and lightly take my arm. "Ladies, I'm sorry. I have an appointment with Ms. Arnault. Do you mind if I steal her away?"

There is a collective "Aw," but I'm relieved as we get away from the crowd.

"Jennifer, you didn't have to do that," I tell my personal shopper.

She laughs. "Whenever you walk into the store, security alerts me because they know you'll be bombarded at the Metro Composition counter."

"I don't mind, but I don't want to distract them from buying. My publicist in New York suggested that I start signing our makeup products. That way they'll buy them."

"You have a wise publicist." We take the escalator up to the eighth floor. "You're free to wander. If you want any help, I'll be right over there."

"I'm taking a me-afternoon. If you have anything you think I should try on, let's set up a room."

"I don't want to pressure you."

"Nonsense. Part of my me-afternoon is shopping." I don't know what it is about the racks and racks of beautiful clothes, but they always make me feel better.

She sets me up in her private rooms and brings in dozens of clothes. She knows my style incredibly well—conservative with flair. I always like almost everything she brings. She also brings me pretty and sexy lingerie. "Who cares about the prince anyway?"

I walk out of Nordstrom a couple hours later, several thousand dollars poorer. The clothes will be delivered to the house, and I have just enough time to catch a rideshare to the bar.

I walk into the large main bar complete with a long wood counter where various wise-cracking regulars banter with the bar staff. I see Emerson standing at the bar, preparing to order.

"What looks good today?" I ask her.

"I'm thinking a blueberry martini. It's fruit, right?"

I giggle. "Whatever your heart desires. I just want to head back to the piano bar, relax, and hope I can do today over."

"I do miss work sometimes. It really is easier than staying home with Liam all day. I love that boy, but he's not even mobile yet and he challenges me. I plan on having a drink or two tonight. I'll express my milk tonight and possibly tomorrow morning. Mama needs this."

I giggle. "How is my godson?"

"I can already tell he's going to be just like his father—stubborn and cute as can be."

"Getting the ladies to do his bidding at nine weeks?"

"Exactly!"

Talented local artists are tinkling Broadway tunes and scat specials on the piano. The bartender places a blueberry martini in front of Emerson and a dirty martini in front of me. Emerson and I look at him, surprised. He shrugs. "I heard that was what she wanted." Looking at me, he continues, "And that dog of an ex-boyfriend of yours doesn't know what he's missing."

I beam. "Thank you. That's very kind, and exactly what I would have ordered." I leave a forty-dollar tip—it's what the two drinks and a moderate tip would have cost—and we wander to a booth where we can visit without attracting too much attention.

Emerson looks at me critically. "Are you okay?"

"I'll tell you all about it when everyone is here."

"You sure?"

"Yes. I took part of the afternoon off and went shopping."

"Did you cause a scene at Nordstrom today?" Sara asks as she walks up and kisses us both on the cheek.

"How did you know?"

"Because you made TMZ again. Someone got it on video."

"I hope it didn't look like I was being a bitch."

"You never do, which is why everyone loves you. Me, on the other hand, they think I'm the ice queen."

I scoff. "They do not!"

"It's the resting bitch face they always get when they take my picture."

We're down to giggles when the server arrives. "What would you like to drink?"

"I'd like a pineapple-tini," Sara says.

"I'll take one of those," Cynthia agrees as she walks up and gives us all a hug.

"How about a dragon fruit-tini?"

"Oh, that sounds good. I'll take one of those," Hadlee says as she arrives.

"I'll take a classic gin martini," Greer announces, pulling up a chair.

Everyone is here, and we have a table in the back. Life is very good.

We have four conversations going at once. This is my posse, and I would be lost without my pack of great friends. My women who will support me through thick and thin.

"Where is Liam?" Greer asks.

"He's at home with Dillon. I needed a break. He's demanding and not sleeping. It's good for both of them." She gets out her phone, and we all swoon over the pictures. "He's getting to be quite the chubby little boy."

"That's because you don't produce milk, you produce cream. He's perfect," I share.

"As his doctor, I can attest that he is absolutely perfect," Hadlee says.

The conversation goes from there. We work our way around and learn everything going on with everyone. Cynthia shares her wedding plans. Sara and Trey are working hard on Trey's nonprofit for underprivileged kids who have an aptitude for science and computers. Hadlee and Cameron have found a new group to ride their Harley with. Greer is busy enjoying her husband's vineyard. We all have so many great things going for us.

"Okay, missy. Why the SOS?" Hadlee presses.

I look up, trying to fight the tears. Leaning in, I tell them, "Metro had our fall line stolen by a Chinese cosmetics company."

Sara sits up straight. Not only is she married to my brother, but she's a lawyer. "What do you mean?"

"*Desire* magazine sent over the ad slicks for a competitor, and they have the exact same palette along with the same names and packaging."

"What can you do?" Emerson asks.

"The FBI tells me the Chinese have records that they've been working on it for months," I share.

"That's bullshit!" Cynthia announces.

"I agree. Jim has looked into it, and we believe it's a lie. There's no way they're so similar by happenstance. I had lunch with Walker Clifton today, and he's going to light a fire under the team at the FBI," I tell them.

"I'm so glad you can do that," Greer acknowledges.

"How's Mason?" Emerson asks, trying to change the subject.

"He went into the office today. Sara, you probably know more than I do," I deflect.

"He left about an hour after he arrived. He looked absolutely exhausted," Sara answers.

"I'm sure he was. The doctors told him not to do much, and he ignored them." I shake my head with a bit of disappointment. I didn't check in on him today. I wanted to, but the day got away from me, and well, to be honest, I didn't want him to think I was stalking him.

"Why is that not surprising?" Cynthia asks.

"Now that you both are single...," Emerson nudges.

I shake my head. "I think that ship sailed a long time ago." These women are my best friends and until Mason and I get this figured out, I want to keep it close to my vest. They would put the pressure on him and if he's not there, it could scare him away.

"Have you jumped him yet?" Hadlee presses.

"What? No. Of course not." I'm shocked that they think I should get involved with Mason. They know as well as I do that if it were to go sideways, we would no longer have a nice and cohesive group of friends.

"Well, why not?" Cynthia asks.

I want to. I've wanted Mason for a long time, and knowing he's broken up with Annabelle, I'm open to the opportunity, but he's not given me any indication that he's interested. How do I tell this to my friends? The people who support me through thick and thin? They'd put pressure on Mason, and that would be a huge mistake in our group. It would divide us, and it would destroy the chemistry we've worked so hard to build over the years. "We're only friends. Plus, he just got out of the hospital."

The rest of the night, we talk in circles. Thankfully we avoid the conversations about Frederic and his porn star girlfriend.

Suddenly, Hadlee jumps up. "I have to go. I just looked at the clock, and it's after eight. I promised to be home by now."

Emerson looks startled. "Liam needs me. I should go, too."

Slowly but surely, we all make our excuses and head home. In the rideshare, I think about how much I love my friends. They're amazing. They're all coupled up except for me. I guess I could always fall back on Walker—no, not a chance. I want a marriage of love, not one of convenience.

I'm lost in my thoughts when the driver asks, "Isn't this your stop?"

"Oh. Sorry. Yes, I was just thinking about something else." I open the car door and exit. "Thank you."

He drives away without a word, and I open my front door. The lights are on timers throughout the house, so thankfully I don't enter in darkness. I can hear the television on in the media room.

Walking back, I see Mason sleeping in one of the reclining chairs. I debate on covering him with a blanket or waking him to move him to his bed, deciding on the latter. He'll sleep better in his own bed.

I turn the television off and jostle his shoulder. "Mason? Let's get you in bed."

"Huh? I fell asleep waiting for you."

"Waiting for me?"

"Yes, I wanted to know how things went today."

"I'll tell you about it tomorrow. Come on, you won't sleep well out here."

"Okay," he says, only half awake.

I lead him to his room and tuck him into bed.

"I wish you'd stay with me," he murmurs.

"Do you need me to stay?"

"No, I just want you to stay." He crashes on the pillow and breathes a steady rhythm.

I wouldn't mind crawling into bed with him, but unfortunately, when he woke up and didn't want me there, it would make for an awkward conversation. Turning the lights out, I head to my room and undress before crawling into my very empty king-size bed.

What a day. I'm just hoping to not see too many of these in the future.

chapter

seven

MASON

I ARRIVE AT THE TOP OF THE MARK RESTAURANT EARLY. It has a stunning three-hundred-and-sixty-degree view of the city as it sits atop the 104th floor of the Intercontinental Mark Hopkins hotel in the financial district downtown. It's a bit touristy, but it's one of the few places that's quiet, and I'll be able to talk to CeCe rather than yell across the table to be heard.

I've preordered the chocolate soufflé and brought along a dozen white roses. She thinks she's meeting a group of our friends, not just me. Emerson planted the idea in my head a few weeks ago, and I realized she was right. I owe CeCe this and so much more. I also plan on making my move. I'd rather she tell me to pound sand than to always wonder what could have been. I may not be an actual prince, but I'm ready to make my case.

I see her crossing the restaurant. She looks amazing in her emerald green pantsuit. "Are we first?" She looks around the restaurant, scanning for our friends. "That never happens to me."

"It's only us tonight."

She looks at me, startled.

"I wanted to thank you for hosting me for the last month in your home. I'm finally feeling good enough to go to work beyond lunch."

I hand her the roses.

"Oh my goodness, they're beautiful!" She draws in a big breath through her nose. "They smell amazing. You didn't have to do any of this." She smiles, and I see what all the tabloids seem to capture—a brilliant white smile full of honesty and caring. She rocks my world.

"I wanted to."

The waiter arrives to take our drink orders. Talk about lousy timing.

"I'll have a Jonny Walker Blue straight up," CeCe declares.

"That sounds good. I'll have the same."

The waiter leaves, and we're alone again.

"How are things going with the investigation into the Chinese company?" I ask.

"They're at least working on it. I don't think the FBI would've done anything if Walker Clifton hadn't lit a fire under them."

"I hate to think that's true. Those two agents were just imbeciles."

"Well, that's one way of putting it."

Our drinks arrive, and we toast to my health.

I lift my glass of amber liquid, suddenly anxious. "A toast. To you. You are beautiful, gracious, and generous. Thank you for allowing me to stay with you while I recuperated."

We clink our glasses and take a sip. "Thank you, though it wasn't any problem."

"You've watched my dog for the last three months. She isn't going to want to go home with me. Did you know Angela cooks her dinner each night?"

"I didn't know, but it doesn't surprise me."

"Well, I don't think Misty has any plans on moving home with me." I chuckle.

"She can stay as long as she'd like. And frankly, I don't think you should move home yet. I know you're anxious to sleep in your own bed, and we can easily move it over if it's important, but I still think until the doctor tells you otherwise, you should remain at my house."

The first course arrives: butter lettuce with pears, blue cheese crumbles, candied pecans, and a blue cheese dressing.

She looks at me, confused and happy. "What did you order?"

"They've made all your favorites, and we have a surprise dessert, so make sure to leave some room."

"Mason, this is too much."

"It's only the start."

We enjoy our salads, butternut squash soup, and the rack of lamb with scalloped potatoes while we fall into an easy conversation comparing our espionage examples.

When the soufflé arrives along with a glass of twenty-five-year tawny port, she wraps her arms around my neck and kisses me. I know it was supposed to be a friendly kiss, but I wrap my arms around her and don't let go, kissing her back with great passion. She's hesitant at first, but she eventually gives in and allows my tongue entry, and that's it. I'm a goner. Her kisses fill me with desire, and my cock stands on end.

When we break, she sits back. I can see her working through all the possible outcomes, and based on her expression, none of them are good.

Before she can get too far, I'm determined to lay it all out. "Look, I'm not sorry for having kissed you. I've wanted you since we met years ago."

Her eyes widen. "Mason, why didn't you ever say anything?"

"I was going to. We were supposed to play golf together, and I had it all planned, and then you sent your brother in your place."

"What?" Her hand goes to her mouth. "Are you kidding? I sent Trey to play golf with you because he needed to get out of his funk after Sara discovered her birth parents were still together and were married with four kids. Why didn't you say anything?"

"I figured you didn't want to spend time with me."

"Mason, I've wanted you since I met you, too. I don't know what it is, but you do something to me, and I compare every man I've dated to you. And we've never even dated! But why did you move in with Annabelle if you had any feelings for me?"

"As I saw it, you'd cast me away, and she was really into me. It really helped to mend my broken heart. But I also moved her in with me to keep an eye on her. I still think she may be involved with the mole issue, particularly now that she's disappeared."

She drinks her port, and I see conflict in her eyes, but I'm not going to allow her to push me away. I lean in and kiss her softly this time, and she immediately returns the kiss. "Nothing has ever felt so right, please don't over think this," I beg.

I hand the waiter my Black American Express card and quickly pay. I want to show her just how thankful I am.

We enter the elevators, and the doors close behind us. The enclosed space has electricity sparking between us, visible to the naked eye. I push her against the wall and show her how I really feel about her. My hands are in her hair, and her body is pressed against mine, her lips all over my mouth and neck. I'm sure she can feel how hard I am as I grind against her.

She gasps for breath and pushes me back. "What if this is a mistake?"

The doors open again, CeCe stepping away as a couple walks in. We never pushed a button, so the elevator never moved. They look at us curiously but don't say anything as they push the button for the ground floor. CeCe is flushed; I can tell she's as turned on as I am. There is nothing innocent about the way we look, and we're fooling no one.

The elevator stops and the door opens. Now is her chance if she wants to put a stop to this. She grasps my hand and squeezes it. My heart beats triple time and tells me she feels the same way I do.

When we get in our waiting car, I turn to her. "CeCe, we've had terrible timing, but the stars have finally aligned. I've had deep feelings for you for many years. Please, let's not overanalyze this. I don't think this is a mistake, but if you think it might be, let's talk about it. I'll do everything in my power to convince you otherwise." I lean in and slowly kiss her. It's like fireworks are going off inside me. My hand wanders to her breast, and I can feel her nipple through the fabric. She moans in my ear, and I'm a goner.

When we arrive at her home, we immediately walk in. Angela was in on my secret, and she left a bottle of white wine in a bucket of ice and two glasses. Pouring us both a glass, I gulp down a mouthful for courage, even though it's very cold. I refill my glass and put on some music. It's a cliché when Al Green's "Let's Stay Together" comes over the speakers, and it makes her laugh and relax a little.

I extend my hand. "Will you dance with me?"

She nods, and we dance slowly in her living room as I sing in her ear. My dick is hard, and I know she knows it, but I've pushed as hard as I can tonight. If she doesn't want me, then I need to move on. If she does, she can tell me.

We dance to two more songs. "I love being in your arms, I feel safe and secure." She stands on her tiptoes and kisses me softly.

I see this as a green light, but to be sure, I ask, "Are you okay with this?"

"I've never been so sure of anything. I promise, I'm not overthinking this."

My heart soars, and I know if I don't think of something else, I'll explode in my pants and ruin our night. I've wanted this for so long, I almost want to pinch myself to make sure this is a reality.

Our dancing slows, and I smell the Chanel No. 5 on her neck. I nuzzle and begin to slowly kiss up the side. Her breathing quickens and she moans softly encouraging me. Quickly we're making out like teenagers. I love the way her kisses begin tentatively and grow more urgent. Two more songs play and we're continuing to kiss. Nothing but our arms enclosing us and our bodies pressed against each other. I don't want to push her too fast. I've waited for this for years and if she needs to take her time, I will figure out how to do this. Her hands begin to explore and I'm ready to follow her wherever she takes me.

Taking me by the hand, she leads me up to her bedroom.

"I hope you don't think ill of me for moving fast," she says with a grin, "but we've danced around this for so long, I can't wait any longer."

"We're moving at the pace you need to feel comfortable." She moans as I kiss slowly down her neck, and it encourages me. She loosens my tie and unbuttons my shirt, running her hands over my bare chest. Her hands are warm, her breathing more ragged than before. She looks at me for permission to continue, and I grin.

"Then I think I'm ready to speed us up," she moans as she rubs her hand over my cock beneath my pants.

She turns around and grinds her hips into me and tips her head to the side, and I can't help but see it as an invitation. I kiss and nuzzle her neck as I slowly unzip her top. I don't notice she's unzipped her pants until they fall to our feet. My hands explore her taut stomach, and I can't help but press my desire into her backside.

She pushes me gently back onto the bed as she slips her top off and stands before me in a stunning black lace thong and bra set. "You are so beautiful," I rasp.

Her breasts are full and nipples hard. She has soft curves and smooth skin. I can't wait to smell, taste, and enjoy every inch of her.

I've lost my jacket, my shirt is unbuttoned, and my belt is undone, but I'm feeling terribly overdressed. I reach for her breast inside the fine silk and grasp it, taking a nipple into my mouth and circling it gently with my tongue. As she gasps, I suck harder on it, nipping slightly with my teeth.

Suddenly impatient, I want to climb on top of her and take it all. I push her down onto the bed and stand to hastily remove my clothes. When I'm naked before her, she says, "You're beautiful, too."

I work out, but to know that CeCe thinks I'm beautiful only excites me further.

She stands and runs her hands up and down my body. When she rolls my balls in her palm, I can't help but moan my pleasure. She lays me on my back and straddles me, rubbing herself against my body, needing to make contact. Her eyes are daring me to go further. I roll her over and position myself between her legs she pulls my face toward her hips. Her smell is divine, but I also want to see and taste. I shift her sopping panties to one side, my tongue makes contact with her wetness, and together we both groan in delight.

One hand holds me as she runs her other fingers through my hair. There is nothing shy or hesitant about this, and I eat her pussy with the enthusiasm of a starving man. It is heaven, and she moves restlessly as my tongue expertly dips in and out of her, sucking at her clit and pushing her closer to the edge. I can hear her heavy breathing, but she won't let herself go so she can come. I don't want her to feel any pressure, so I carefully remove her bra and admire her perfect soft pink nipples, slathering each with my tongue and playing with them until they're both hard as a pencil eraser. I hook my fingers into her thong and pull it from her. I'm ready to return to eating her pussy when she pushes me on my back. My cock stands at attention at the sudden turn of events.

She scrambles upright to get my cock in her mouth, greedily running her tongue along the shaft before taking as much as she can into her mouth. She licks and sucks, and I can tell she enjoys it as much as I do. As she bobs up and down on my hard shaft, I start moving my hips, fucking her mouth. I'm getting close. I grab her hair and hold her still so I can control the rhythm as I use her mouth for my pleasure. It's heaven, and I know I'm leaking precum.

Groaning in frustration, I have to pull away.

She wipes her bottom lip. "You taste divine."

"If you don't stop, I'm going to fill your mouth with my cum and watch you swallow every mouthful. But that's not enough. I want to fuck you so hard that you scream so loud the neighbors hear."

She reaches for the condom I've put aside and skillfully places it on my cock.

Once I'm sheathed, I move over her and look down into her eyes for a moment, watching her face. I nudge the tip of my cock against her, and she raises her hips slightly, searching for me.

"Wait," I growl, and with one hand, I hold her hands together above her head. "There's no going back after this."

I look over her perfect body. I need to imprint this permanently on my memory in case she tells me we're done. Her nipples are hard and a deeper pink now, as though they're blushing. Her skin is flushed, and there's moisture at the top of my thighs. There's a slight glisten at her slit, and it takes all my willpower to not lean down and lick it away. She's ready, but I won't move until she asks.

"Please," she begs.

That's exactly what I've been waiting to hear. I can't help but smile and thrust forward. There is no gentleness as I enter her, and her tight pussy feels stretched to the limit.

She cries out and moves her hips upward to accommodate all of me. "I've never felt so full. Holy cow, you're huge, and it is heaven."

I begin to move slowly at first, and it is exquisite torture as she grips me tightly and I fill her so completely. But the passion is taking control, and my movements become faster as I pound into her, driving her into the bed. She's matching my movements, her face telling me she's loving the rawness of it all, craving more and taking everything I have.

There is almost nothing now but pure carnal desire, and my breathing is broken. When she begins playing with her nipples, I know she's close. I can hear and feel that she's wet and hotter than ever. Her orgasm is building as I grind into her, and she urges me on. "Let it all go. Come for me. Take it all out on me." She's gasping for breath, and I'm getting closer and closer. She begins to moan, and her pussy grabs me like it's a vise, the pulsating waves of her orgasm soaking me, which sends me over the edge as she explodes with a scream of overwhelming release.

A primal cry erupts deep inside me as my own orgasm starts to build. I can no longer stop myself and thrust into her again and again as spurts of hot cum fill the condom. It seems like it will never stop. She's still rocking with the aftershocks from her own orgasm, and the rise and fall of her body accepts everything I'm giving her.

We lie there together until I soften inside her, then roll off her. I don't want to crush her. "That was even better than I ever hoped it would be," I tell her earnestly.

"Me, too. I'll tell you a secret: I've never been able to orgasm with a man before."

I stop and look at her. "Really?"

"I've gotten close, like I did when you were eating me out, but never able to tip over the precipice. That was fucking amazing what you did. Holy shit, you have twenty minutes, and then we're going to go again."

I smile. I'm in pure heaven. "Your wish is my command."

We go two more times, and then I'm completely spent. I've never been able to accomplish three times in one night.

We fall asleep with her in my arms. I know I want this forever. I don't want to scare her by moving too fast, so I've got to figure out how to play it cool. I've never been cool in my life, so this is going to be a real test.

We wake to my cell phone ringing. "Hullo?" I answer groggily.

"Masey, it's Mommy."

I shoot straight up as if I'm sixteen and just got caught with my girlfriend in my bed. "Hi, Mom. You're calling early."

"Or maybe it's late." She giggles. Oh goodness, I know what this means. She's gotten engaged again. My mom is amazing at getting engaged. She's been married four times and engaged at least twice that. I don't even want to think about how she does it.

"What's going on?"

"I thought maybe you and Caroline might want to join Michael and me for breakfast."

Caroline is sitting up now. She must have heard. I see some conflict on her face. "Mom, let me see what's going on here. Can I call you back?"

"Of course, honey." I can hear the disappointment in her voice.

"I'll check with CeCe and call you back."

"Okay. I'm on my cell."

I disconnect the call. "I'm sorry about that."

She pulls the covers up tight around her. I lean in. "You never need to cover up with me."

She blushes.

"CeCe, don't start overthinking this. Last night was amazing. Don't freak out."

"Are you sure?"

"I'm more than sure." I lean in and kiss her, my cock standing at attention. I take her hand and put it on my cock. "See?"

She smiles, and her eyes become hooded. I know she wants more just as much as I do. She strokes me, and I pull the sheet down to her waist and play with her nipples. "Are you still overthinking this?"

She shakes her head.

"You're absolutely beautiful."

Enjoying the afterglow of our fourth round in twenty-four hours, I finally remember why my mother called. "We've been asked to meet my mother's boyfriend for breakfast or brunch. Any interest?"

She shrugs. "Sure, why not?"

"I should warn you, she's giddy, which tells me she's engaged again."

CeCe stands and walks away from me. She looks stunning coming and going. I'm so excited that we've turned this corner, but I'm kicking myself that I didn't just ask her out when she gave her golf spot to her brother. Man, five years of wasted time.

I'm not going to waste any more.

We walk into the Fairmont and head to the Laurel Court Restaurant. I see my mother before she sees me. She's hanging on every word her newest fling says to her. I've spoken to Hadlee, and she tells me that he's a respected urologist here in San Francisco and has been widowed for a few years. I'm cautiously optimistic.

The restaurant dining room is large and bustling with people. A few patrons recognize CeCe, but she pretends she doesn't notice.

When we reach the table, my mother remains seated, but Dr. Frieman stands. "Hello, Mason." With a slight bow, he turns to CeCe. "It's so nice to meet you, Caroline."

"It's wonderful to meet you, too," CeCe says, which is always very telling. If he were someone she wanted to have a more personal relationship with, she'd ask him to call her CeCe. Because she isn't sure, she remains Caroline.

"Please sit down." He motions to the chairs at the table.

As we take our seats, CeCe reaches for my hand and gives it a reassuring squeeze. Nothing gets past my mother, of course, and she beams at the sight. "I'm so glad we're all finally meeting."

"How did you both meet?" I ask.

"I had a meeting here at the hotel and stopped for a drink afterward," Dr. Frieman begins. "Your mother was at the bar, flirting with the bartender, and I was immediately smitten."

My mother giggles. I don't think I've ever heard her giggle. I look at her, and she sits up straighter in her chair as if she's a little girl who's been reprimanded.

"I wasn't flirting for anything more than a free drink," she says defiantly.

"We girls need to use everything we've got sometimes," CeCe agrees.

"Exactly! I knew you'd understand."

"What kind of meeting brought you to a hotel in the city you live in?" I press.

"I'm an angel investor in a pharmaceutical company. They're working on a—" He leans in closer. "—penile enlarger." He shrugs. "I'm a urologist, and it's something men talk a lot to me about. It's an interesting concept, and if it were to work, it would be very important in my practice."

I suppress my own snicker. "I see. Did my mother tell you I work in the venture capital world?"

"She did. But only yesterday. I'd already pro—" He looks at my mother panicked.

"He'd already proposed to me when I told him who you were and who your girlfriend was."

I want to correct her version of our relationship, but it doesn't seem to faze CeCe. "How did they approach you?" I ask instead. I'm worried they'll take him for a ride.

"It was through a friend who was looking to invest, and he asked me to vet the medicine behind it. It needed some tweaks, but if it works, it'll be huge. If it doesn't, I didn't invest all my savings and I'll be fine."

I feel a little better now knowing he isn't trolling the Fairmont for wealthy single women to invest in fake businesses. I know Hadlee said he was a nice guy, but how often do a pediatrician and urologist cross paths?

"So you're a physician here in the city?"

"I am. I grew up out in the Richmond area and went to medical school across the bay. It wasn't until my late wife insisted she wanted to go to Paris that I ever left California. I was almost thirty years old."

CeCe smiles broadly. "I get it. California has all four seasons, and you're in driving distance of some of the greatest beaches and best ski slopes. The weather is near perfect year-round. Why leave?"

"Well, that's what I thought until I went to Paris, then Rome, then traveled throughout the Northeast. It's wonderful here, and I learned I love to travel. I will admit"—he looks at my mother affectionately—"I've never been to Ohio, but if my lovely wants me to move there, I'm close to retirement, and I'll go wherever she wants to go."

I like what he has to say, so I'm careful to not judge too harshly. I'll still have Jim Adelson do a background check on him before I'm completely sold, however.

The remainder of our brunch is my mother fawning all over CeCe. She's over the moon when some young girls approach the table. "Hi, Miss Arnault. We were, uh... uh... wondering if you'd give us your autograph?"

She smiles. "Of course."

I don't think we've had one meal together where we weren't interrupted, but she handles it with so much grace and style. I watch her sign the cards they present her with and even pose for a picture, which I take. My mother informs the girls that I'm CeCe's boyfriend, and they seem very impressed.

A few minutes later, an older couple stops by the table to tell her, "You don't need a prince that will drop his standards for a porn star."

She's kind and thanks them.

My mother leans over when they're gone and asks, "Is it always like this?"

I nod. "She's always kind to everyone." I put my arm around the back of her chair as a sign of possession when I see two gentlemen looking and probably taking bets on who she'll give her phone number to. They seem to back off immediately after that.

My mother loves the attention, but the rest of us are clearly uncomfortable. I pull my credit card out of my wallet, but Michael insists on paying for brunch. "It's the least we can do."

I like him a little bit more now. I see my mother is completely excited. I just hope he is what he says he is. She deserves someone who will love her unconditionally.

As we get in the car to head back to CeCe's place, she says, "That was lovely. They are so in love with one another."

"I'm going to make sure he isn't after her money."

"I thought you already talked to Hadlee about him?"

"I did, but really, how would a pediatrician know anything about a urologist? I'm just going to have Jim do a background check."

She grins. "And when it comes out good, what will you do next?"

"I don't know. My mom isn't without her flaws, though he doesn't seem to see them."

"And you see mine?"

"You don't have any flaws."

"Sure, I do. Everyone does. You saw the biggest drawback to me today at lunch. People think they know me and approach the table and give me their opinion on my life. Do you see how rarely Trey and Sara go out publicly? Sara will go out without Trey periodically with friends, but rarely do they go out together, and then it's only with protection. If my company, another flaw of mine these days, goes sideways, I may not even be able to live in San Francisco for a while. People will think I did something to sabotage the company, and over five thousand people will lose their jobs. That will be a nightmare."

"Those aren't flaws."

"They are, actually."

"Maybe because we've done so much socially for over five years, I just accept it about you." I lean in and kiss her. "There isn't anything about you that makes me want to run away."

"That's how Michael and your mother feel about one another," she reminds me.

chapter

eight

CECE

MY PHONE IS RINGING. I roll over and look at the clock. It's barely after six. Who could be calling me at this hour? "Hello?"

"Caroline? This is Philip."

I can't place who Philip is. I'll have to play along until he says enough so I know who he is. "Yes? What can I do for you? It's just after six o'clock."

"I'm... I'm sorry to call so early. We have a problem." I've figured out who he is. Philip is our IT person based out of New York City.

I sit up in bed, trying to shake the cobwebs away. "What is it?"

"People are posting about Metro Composition all over PeopleMover."

"What are they posting?"

"It looks like all these horrific animal photos that have been used for cosmetic testing." He's struggling to talk about it, so they must be awful and disgusting pictures. "They say they were smuggled out by an employee in our labs. People are saying terrible things and vowing to boycott our brand."

"We don't test on animals. I'm confused."

"Caroline, this is internet trolls pushing out fake information, and people read it as gospel because they saw it on the internet."

I look up, frustrated. Why have they targeted Metro Composition? "Thank you for letting me know. I'll reach out to the lawyer, and they can send a takedown notice to PeopleMover."

We hang up, and I immediately call my lawyer. He answers quickly, "Hello, Daniel Wilkins."

"Daniel, this is Caroline Arnault. I apologize for calling so early, but I've just been told there are several pictures that are circulating about Metro Composition on at least PeopleMover that are wholly untrue."

"We can manage a takedown notice, but chances are they're all over social media and soon will be all over your website and pages."

My stomach turns, and the waves of nausea hit me. All I want to do is cry. "Can you start issuing takedown notices to all social media platforms?"

"Of course, though it will take a few months for some to comply." He must be exaggerating. They must be able to take it down within a few hours.

"Thank you. I'll reach out to my public relations person and work on some messaging, so some people may be in touch on my behalf as we learn more."

I hang up and then call Greer. She doesn't work for me but is one of my oldest friends and is a goddess when it comes to public relations. She answers immediately, and without any preamble, she says, "I just spoke with Vanessa. She's reaching out to the crisis public relations company called Accurate

Communications. William just worked with them recently about his family's company. They're good at it. You *will* weather this storm, but it's going to be expensive, and it's going to be difficult."

"Thanks, Greer. We need to put out a notice to the employees on how to deal with the press."

"She's already on it. You don't have anyone in a New York office right now, but we can expect the press to be camped out at your offices here this morning."

"I need some coffee to deal with this." I can't hold the tears back any longer. "Why would anyone target Metro?"

"We're going to get through this. Don't worry." She sighs loudly. "I'm here for you."

I call my head of public relations, Becca, who manages press releases and getting the word out about our brand and our activities. She's always so flowery and upbeat, but this is going to be a real test for her. When it goes to voice mail, I immediately call back, since most cell phones that are in Do Not Disturb mode will allow a call through if you call it a second time. Unfortunately, it goes to voice mail again. "Becca, it's Caroline. We're under attack by internet trolls. I need to coordinate a meeting with you and a crisis PR firm. Call me back as soon as you get this."

My head is killing me. It's time to call Vanessa. She answers before it even rings through the line. "Hey, we have a call with Jeremy Padgett in twenty minutes. They're assembling their troops and are getting prepared. They have some information on us since I contract out to them in case there's bad press around Fashion Week."

"Okay. I've already reached out to the lawyer, who is issuing takedown notices to PeopleMover and all social media sites. I've told him he may hear more from someone on our PR team. I left a message for Becca, and hopefully she can join us."

"This will be expensive, but we will manage this."

"Thank you, Vanessa."

"You're welcome. You and Becca should have an invite for the con call in your email."

"I'm not out of bed yet. I'm going to need a lot of caffeine today."

"Talk to you in a few."

I pull the covers back and touch my feet to the floor. My head feels like a migraine is coming on, the severe throbbing pain and pulsing sensation on the side of my head, and I can feel nausea building. Light sensitivity is next, and then my day will be shot.

Why does everything have to go bad at the same time? I know this has shades of similarity to what's been going on at SHN, so I have a feeling they somehow figured out my relationship with SHN. They always say there is no such thing as coincidence.

I start my computer for the call and then wander in search of coffee.

My first view as I walk into the kitchen is Mason. I stop short. He's leaning into the refrigerator with only a pair of running shorts on, and all I see is his backside. My heart races as I see how tightly his shorts pull across his hips. I involuntarily shudder.

My God, he looks amazing. I need a fan.

I struggle to find my voice. "Good morning."

He turns around, his chiseled chest, with just a sprinkling of hair, glistening from his workout this morning. I need to hold on to the countertop to keep my knees from buckling.

He crosses over to me and brings me into his arms. "You're up early." He leans down and kisses me softly, nipping at my lower lip as he rubs his hardness against my belly. I'd much rather pull him back to bed with me right now and have a repeat of our evening activities, but I can't.

I pull back. "I just got a really disturbing call." I walk him through what I know.

"But Metro doesn't test on animals." He looks confused.

"No, they don't." I put my head into my hands as I grasp for reality. "First, someone steals all of our fall line and undercuts us, making the last six months of work a complete waste. Now there's talk of major boycotts. I don't know how we're going to weather this."

Mason walks over to the espresso machine, and I watch him make me a double espresso as he listens. "You'll need this," he says as he places the steaming cup in my hands. He kisses me on the forehead. "I don't see this as a coincidence."

I shake my head. "I know. I don't either."

"Would you like me to join your call?"

I'm both stunned and touched. "I'd really appreciate that, just in case we determine this is related."

We walk into my office and join the conference call. I still haven't heard from Becca. *Where could she be?* My head goes to twenty different places and begins to question everything she's done. Could she be the person who leaked our fall line? Did she target this mess at us?

I'm trying not to panic or overthink why she hasn't responded in the last twenty minutes. Maybe she's a sound sleeper, or in the shower, or at the gym with her phone in a locker.

Okay, I feel a bit better.

Everyone joins the call, and Vanessa begins by introducing me. "Jeremy, I'd like to introduce you to Caroline Arnault. Her mother is the founder of Metro Composition Cosmetics, and Caroline is now the owner and CEO of the company. Metro is based out of San Francisco and is a private and small independent cosmetics company. They've had rave reviews for their brand and usually fly under the radar."

Mason squeezes my hand, and I feel so much better knowing he's here.

Vanessa continues, "Caroline, this is Jeremy Padgett. He runs the best crisis management firm in the world. He's managed everything from Janet Jackson's Nipplegate, to all sorts of political scandals, the food-poisoning outbreak with Verde Burritos, to William Bettencourt's issue with the CEO and several members of the board and the executive team who were caught up in the human trafficking mess a few months ago. We will be in very good hands."

"Caroline, I won't confirm or deny anything Vanessa just shared, as we're under confidentiality agreements with our clients, but it's a pleasure to meet you," Jeremy begins. "I wish it was under better circumstances, of course. With me, I have fifteen people who make up the front line of your team."

"Nice to meet you. With me, I have Mason Sullivan. He's the managing partner of Sullivan Healy Newhouse. He'll be the link to the US attorney's office and the FBI. I sit as an advisor to them, and they've been dealing with a group of hackers. We think these may be related. We're concerned that it's too coincidental that both our companies are dealing with this in different ways."

"That will bring in some other questions, but let's start with where we are and what we're doing."

My phone pings, indicating a text.

Becca: I'm here on the phone, too. Sorry, I was in the shower when you called and didn't hear it ring.

"And Becca Bentley is on the phone," I share "She heads up our in-house public relations."

"Hello, Caroline, Mason, Becca, and Vanessa. My name is Adam Warner, and I'll be your project manager on this. My specialty is media relations. I've had the opportunity to see the photos posted on the Internet, and I'll admit, they aren't pretty. Do you do any testing of your cosmetics on animals?"

"None whatsoever. We decided when we were founded to not test on animals, and we're an environmentally and socially conscious company. It's part of who we are—not to mention we also like hip colors and were the company that was the first to come up with blue, black, and green nail polish colors. My mother has never been a fan of pink and wanted something else."

"This is Neil Rube in Research. I understand from Vanessa that a Chinese company recently stole your entire palette and fall line. What have you found out about that?"

"Unfortunately, it's slow going. They claim to have over six months of research in determining their palette and color names. They also had the same packaging we had designed."

"This is Mason. I wish I could say we knew who was behind it, but we don't know yet. The FBI is on it, as is Jim Adelson with Clear Security."

"I'm impressed you're working with Jim Adelson," Jeremy says.

"I work with him in my venture capital firm, and he's a friend," Mason replies.

"Caroline, this is Neil again. Did you decide to launch those same colors and packaging?"

"No, Vanessa said it would be confusing to the consumer."

"This is Liz Crown, in media planning, that is actually very good news. We can certainly deflect that it isn't your company but rather this Chinese manufacturer who did the testing on their products, and it's unrelated to you."

I sit back in my chair, and for the first time, I'm relieved. "Thank you, Liz. I think you just made my day."

"We aren't out of the woods yet, but we've scheduled you on four morning shows tomorrow here in New York. Can you be here by dinner tonight and we can walk through everything? That will give us about eight hours to pull it all together and be ready to go."

I look up at Mason, and he nods. "Yes, I can be there."

The conversation shifts to what information we're pushing out to our employees and how we're going to combat this mess. Mason kisses me on the forehead and whispers, "You're going to be just fine," as we wind down the conference call.

Once everyone's hung up, it's time to make the hardest call of all. I make myself one more double espresso and pick up the phone.

"Good morning, sweetheart," my mother answers. "This is early for you."

"Hi, Mom." I begin to walk her through what's happened, but she stops me before I get too far.

"Hold on a moment. I'd like your dad on the phone, too."

Once my dad has joined the call, I start over and walk them through the latest and what the plan is.

"Oh, honey, I'm so sorry. I'm glad Mason is dealing with the FBI and US attorney's office to take it off your plate," my dad says.

"Yes, he's been very helpful through this mess. I'm flying out later this morning and will meet with the crisis management firm for dinner in New York this evening. We'll go through what they've accomplished and the plan moving forward."

"Keep us posted and let me know if there's anything I can do."

"Thank you both."

"We love you. Stay strong," my mom says.

I was unable to get a commercial flight to New York. I hate flying private, but this couldn't be helped. I enjoy the ability to go when I want, but it's such an environmental waste to fly across the country for just me. When I land, Vanessa is there to meet me with her car service.

"This can't be good," I tell her.

"Nonsense!" She hugs me tight and kisses both of my cheeks. "I wanted you all to myself before Jeremy and his team have you."

"You'll be with me tonight and tomorrow, won't you?"

"I'll be with you as long as you want me to be, not only as your public relations manager but as your friend."

I can't help but love her even more. "Vanessa, I'd be lost without you." We get in the car and start speeding away into Manhattan.

"You have a reservation at the Four Seasons. They have your regular suite ready for you."

I stare at the sprawl of warehouses in the industrial area. The traffic is slow. "Thank you for all your help. I realized when we were talking to Jeremy that had I not listened to you and instead released our palette, knowing our customers would be loyal to our brand, we'd be in a different world of hurt right now."

"I know it was hard to walk away from all that work, but in the end, it'll be worth it." She pats my hand. "I have some disappointing news. I've learned that of your four contracts for Fashion Week, three are backing away. If we can salvage this, we might be able to get them back, but I'm not optimistic. I've explained to all of them that it's a smear campaign, and they understand, but they're worried that this is just the first. I still have Gap holding steady right now, though."

"Art's an old friend, but if this doesn't land well this week, we'll lose them, too."

I fight back the tears. This is so upsetting, but in the end, we'll rise above this and survive. I will personally float the company if that's what I need to do. I made that decision on the plane. I don't know who's gunning for me, but I won't be a victim. I'm ready to fight.

chapter

nine

MASON

LEAVING CECE THIS MORNING WAS REALLY HARD. I know she could really use some support right now. She plays like she's strong and doesn't want to show me any of her weaknesses, but I see how she can be vulnerable, too. As soon as she does the morning shows, she's going to have the tabloid press all over her. What a nightmare.

I wish she'd asked me to go with her to New York. I wanted to insist, but she was firm about my getting back to work.

I've been back for a few weeks, each day working a bit longer, and I believe I can finally make it a full day. It's a nice feeling.

I'm usually the first to arrive, but when I walk in the door, I see that's not the case today. The office is buzzing, and everyone is quick to greet me. I know I'm not supposed to really have any caffeine for a while, but I'm not sure I can make it without coffee. CeCe was amazing last night, and I didn't get a full night of sleep—not that I regret a minute of it.

I stop in the kitchen and see the breakfast buffet of french toast, various breakfast meats, and fruit. I pick up a banana and pour some coffee, then doctor it with cream and sugar. I hate anything artificial; I'd rather spend more time in the pool swimming laps than drink light cream or artificial sweetener.

I'm only going to have one cup. This throb has started at the base of my skull and works its way up to my temples and behind my eyes. I'm hoping the caffeine will help it go away.

There is a partners meeting this morning organized by the team. Normally we'd have them after dinner at Charles's home on Sundays, but since they're touring the world on the *Queen Mary 2,* we've taken a break from meeting as a group on Sunday evenings.

Joining the group in the conference room, I'm too busy thinking about who could be after CeCe to immediately notice there are balloons, a cake, and champagne. "Whose birthday?" I don't even realize a group of employees followed me into the room until they laugh.

Quinn giggles. "No one's, silly. We're just celebrating your official return to work today."

"Actually, we just wanted cake for breakfast," Sara jokes.

I look at the cake, which says "Welcome Back!"

"You guys are too much."

They erupt in applause. Quinn and members of her team pass around orange juice and the bottles of champagne to the standing-room-only crowd. I see Emerson standing there with baby Liam, and I know she was behind this. She winks at me, and I smile. What a moment. I'm overtaken by the thoughtfulness of this grand gesture.

"Mason, we are so glad you're back. While you were out the last four months, it showed us how much work you do for the company and each of us personally. You are the engine that keeps this jalopy of a company going. Welcome back," Quinn announces.

"Here, here!" everyone exclaims.

"Wow. I don't know what to say." I look around at the team, and all I see are smiles looking back at me. I know that sometimes being the managing partner is a thankless job, but I have to admit, this has me speechless.

"This is a first," William shares, and the team laughs.

I know I must turn a giant shade of crimson. "When Dillon, Cameron, and I started SHN, we had no idea that it would build into something like this. Everyone here is an integral part of our success, and if I don't say it often enough, we appreciate everything each of you does." I feel like I might tear up, so I raise my glass before my voice breaks. "To SHN and its continued success."

"Well, are you going to cut that thing, or are we just going to admire it?" Cameron eyes the cake.

It's placed in front of me, and I cut it into pieces for the partners to hand out to everyone.

Emerson gives me a big hug. "CeCe said she had to run to New York, so let's have dinner together tonight. You can come over, and we'll relax on the deck."

"I'd love that."

Once we settle down, and the last of the employees are back at their desk, I look around the table at the eager faces staring back at me. "Thank you for this warm welcome back. I can't tell you how much it means to me. I realize my absence wasn't easy, and I appreciate all you did to keep us going."

"Next time, can you plan to be poisoned and out of the office rather than just surprise us?" Cynthia says snarkily, but the giant grin crossing her face tells me she's joking.

"I'll do you one better," I reply. "How about I don't get poisoned again?"

"I like that much better," Sara retorts.

We walk through our agenda, and everyone gets caught up. As we're leaving, I hear Cameron ask Sara, "I sure do miss our Sunday night dinners with your in-laws. When are they due back?"

"Next week. I like those Sunday night meetings at their house. Not only is it the best and most nutritious meal I eat all week, but it really helps to set up my week," Sara shares.

"Me, too," Christopher chimes in.

"We can meet at my place this Sunday," I offer. "It wouldn't be as nice a meal, but it would be our typical Sunday night dinner."

"I can make that work," Dillon says. "Does anyone mind if Liam comes along? We don't have the nanny thing completely lined up."

"I think Bella would boycott if you didn't bring him," William says.

"Absolutely! It'd be great to have almost everyone together," Greer agrees.

"Sounds like it's settled. Sunday evening, my place, at six o'clock with your significant other."

Dillon hangs back once everyone goes their separate ways, and I can tell he wants to talk to me. "What's up?"

"Are you okay about being in your place again? We can certainly host at our place."

"I'll be fine. I feel silly that I'm at CeCe's and she isn't there."

"What's going on?"

I walk him through all that's been happening.

"You've got to be shitting me," he says when I finish. "Does Emerson know about the trolls?"

"I would think so, but I can't be sure. Right now she's hoping that the companies she's working with during Fashion Week don't pull out."

"Man, that really sucks. Let us know if there's anything we can do to help."

"Sure thing."

"Cameron and I were thinking we'd take you to lunch today," Dillon offers.

"I think that should work. How about we get a reservation at one somewhere?"

"I'll get that taken care of."

Walking back to my office, I hear a lot of greetings: "Welcome back to work full-time." "Great to see you." "So glad you're back. We missed you." It really makes my ego soar.

There's a line out my door with people waiting to see me. I talk with each of them and answer all of their questions. I have just enough time to get through a few emails before Cameron is standing at my door. "Ready for lunch?"

My head is pounding from a hunger headache. "Let's do it."

A rideshare is outside the building waiting for us. "We were going to get sushi; does that work for you?" Cameron asks.

"Absolutely."

In the car, the guys are talking baseball, and I keep thinking about CeCe. She should be close to landing in New York. I send her a text. Thinking of you. Enjoy your dinner and call me later.

We sit and order way more food than we can ever possibly eat. Our waitress asks, "You have other people coming?"

"No, we're just hungry," Cameron informs her.

As we wait for our lunch, we talk about things going on around the office. My phone pings with a text, and I'm guessing it's CeCe. My stomach tightens and my pulse races as I get excited about her response, regardless of how mundane it is. She's the woman I've loved for years, but I never thought she felt the same way.

"You're smiling. You don't usually smile. You're always so serious. What's going on with you and CeCe?" Dillon pries.

We haven't defined our relationship, so I don't want to say something until we do. "We're taking it slow."

Cameron asks, "You've been taking it slow for about five years now. At what point do you think you'll be speeding up a little bit?"

Dillon snorts.

I glance at my phone. The text is from her. We've just landed. I'm a stress-mess. Cross your fingers for me.

Me: Miss you already. Call me after dinner and let me know how it goes.

"CeCe has a mess going on right now at Metro. She's flown to New York last minute, and she'll be on all the morning shows tomorrow. I don't think I'm telling you any company secrets, but someone is going after Metro really hard right now, and it makes me nervous," I explain.

Both the guys sit up straight. When Emerson joined our company, with her came her three best friends—Hadlee, who is now married to Cameron; Greer, who currently does our public relations; and CeCe, plus CeCe's brother, Trey, who married Sara, our company attorney.

"What do you mean?" Cameron asks, looking like he's ready to defend a woman who is incredibly kind to all of us.

"I worry this is somehow related to our crap. Someone has posted false photographs and is spreading fake rumors about animal testing at Metro."

"Do they test on animals?" Cameron asks.

"No, they don't. I guess they've made a conscious decision that China is the only country that requires it if they are going to sell to any citizens there, so they won't sell to them." My cell phone pings again, and I look at it. I'm both shocked and surprised. It's from Annabelle. My heart stops, and I look down to read her message, then reply.

Our food arrives and the guys begin to dig in, but I can't help but be mesmerized by the car accident I'm witnessing in this text message exchange.

Annabelle: I understand you're out of the hospital. That's great news.

Me: Where are you?

Annabelle: I'm at my sister's. I'm really disappointed that you've chosen to move in with CeCe.

How does she know I moved in with CeCe? She's at her sister's? I need to let Jim know so he can locate her and she can be pulled in by the police for questioning, not only about the poisoning but also to determine if she's the mole and hacker. If she's the one who went after CeCe, I'm going to kill her myself.

Me: What happened to you?

Annabelle: Everyone was right.

Me: What were they right about?

Annabelle: That I was just a placeholder.

Me: Placeholder?

Annabelle: You never loved me.

This is the same fight we've had over and over, but for her to call herself a placeholder is new. I may not love her, but I do care deeply for her.

Me: Annabelle, are you okay?

Annabelle: I'm fine, but I can't say the same for CeCe.

Whoa! Did she just threaten CeCe? The hair on my arms stands at attention.

Me: What are you talking about?

Annabelle: She's trying to take what's mine. She'd better watch herself.

Me: Are you threatening CeCe?

Annabelle: ;)

I look up at the guys and they stop eating. I show them the messages, and Dillon reads the exchange out loud for Cameron. We all sit there dumbfounded.

"Holy shit! You need to show that to the FBI. Both the White-Collar Crime and Cybercrimes divisions need to see that. Particularly since they think she could be the mole and that she poisoned you," Cameron exclaims.

"I'm not sure she actually poisoned me."

"Come on. She's the only person who had access, and she just threatened the woman you're currently living with."

"Annabelle didn't have access. She left me about a month before I was poisoned. And CeCe and I aren't living together, I'm just staying at her house."

"That's only semantics. Where does her sister live?" Dillon asks.

"Southern California. She's threatened CeCe. We need to report this and put someone from Jim's team on her around the clock."

Cameron nods. " I agree. This isn't going to be good."

I look down at my half-eaten plate of sushi. "I'll reach out to Marci Peterson, our outside lawyer for these kinds of issues, and see if I can't see her before I walk over to see Cora and her team. If nothing else, we have an idea of where Annabelle is."

"Whatever you need to do. Let us know if we need to enlist the girls to rally around CeCe for protection."

I step away from the table and reach out to Marci, but she's in court until two. Her assistant says she'll call me back this afternoon. When I hang up, I text Jim.

Me: CeCe's on her way to New York, and Annabelle has resurfaced.

Jim: I've got two guys I can call that can cover Caroline.

Me: That's what I'm looking for. Annabelle threatened her. CeCe's had some issues since we talked—pictures on the internet with animal cruelty.

Jim: If Caroline pushes back, I'll let you know. I'll also beef up your team if Annabelle's making threats.

Me: I don't want to scare her off. I want her close enough that we can have the police capture her. She indicated she's at her sister's.

Jim: We've been watching her sister's home down in Orange County. No sign of her.

Me: Let me know if CeCe rebuffs your team in any way. I think between animal rights activists and the threats from Annabelle, she needs a team.

Jim: Agreed. I'm on it. And I'll also start my team looking into her animal cruelty issue.

I return to the table, though I'm not listening to the conversation as they talk about the Giants and the Twins before moving on to the Vikings and the 49ers. It's all a blur, and I'm not quite present at the moment. My headache that I thought was hunger is not going away. I haven't had a lot of coffee, so I know it's not a caffeine headache, but it's pounding, and I'm not feeling well.

Sara and I have a meeting right after lunch so I hustle back to meet with her. As our company attorney, she carried a big workload while I was out. When she steps into my office, she looks me over carefully. "You don't look like you're feeling very well. Are you sure you're not pushing too hard?"

"No, I'm fine." I show her the text messages from Annabelle. "I'm worried about CeCe and the mess she's dealing with, and now this only makes it worse."

"When is Marci out of court?"

"Any time now."

She nods. "If we need to go over this later, just let me know."

"No, it's fine. Let's get started."

Sara and I go through the issues four companies are facing with going public.

"DreamWeaver's financials are not in line with projections," she shares.

"Their competitor didn't do well when they went public a few months ago, so that's expected."

"I've heard they're ordering champagne by the case and sending it to all their offices."

"Let's see if Emerson or Quinn can't talk them out of that. Have Dillon do a current valuation, and if it's expected to be low, let's not be celebrating that we're worth less than we thought."

"My thoughts exactly." She looks at her list of companies. "Time Traveler's founders are arguing in the news."

I roll my eyes. Sometimes these owners are like small children. "I'll call and get them talking to one another."

"Better you than me. I just want to take my shoe off and knock them over the head with it to bang some sense into them."

"That might be fun to watch, but it probably wouldn't help."

"I know. That's why you get to work with them."

We go through two more companies with similar issues. Just as we're wrapping up, my cell phone rings. "It's Marci," I tell Sara.

"We're done anyway. Good luck. Let me know if I can help." Sara quietly walks out, leaving me to my phone call.

"Hey, Marci, how are you?" I greet.

"Are you back to work full time?"

"Today's the first official day."

"How are you feeling?"

"I've been going part-time for a while, working my way up to a full day. I won't be burning the midnight oil, though."

"Good for you! Any news on your ex?"

"Well, that's why I'm calling. She sent me a text today, and I have some concerns." I walk her through what's going on with CeCe and the need to go to the FBI.

"Let me make a few calls, and I'll see if we can't also involve the US attorney."

"You just want to invite all the cool kids."

She chuckles. "You know me so well. So, what time can you be here? I want to talk before we head over, and we have a little bit more privacy in my conference room. We still don't know what's going on at SHN, and it makes me nervous that now your advisor's company is having issues."

"I can leave now. My big afternoon meeting just ended, so your timing was spot-on."

"Well, that's a first."

"I should have some information for us by the time you arrive."

"See you shortly."

I stop by Dillon's, Cameron's, and Sara's offices and let them know what's going on. "Good luck," they all tell me.

When I arrive at Marci's office, her receptionist sends me back without announcing me. It's controlled chaos, with multiple banker boxes labeled with case names lining the wall next to a beautiful view of Oakland and the north bay.

Marci sees me at her door and motions for me to sit down.

"Great, we'll be by within the hour. Do you want us to alert SFPD?" She's quiet a few moments. "Great, we'll see you then."

She hangs up the phone and looks at me. "That was Cora Perry over at the FBI. She's going to assemble a group to meet us in about an hour. How is CeCe doing?"

"She's stressed. It's a company that was started by her mother, so she isn't going to go down without a fight."

"I don't blame her. Tell me about the issue with the competitor."

I show her a copy of the ad slick I brought with me and tell her how they got it.

"Everything was the same?" she asks.

"Everything. Not only the colors and their names but also the packaging and display."

"That's definitely creepy. She went to the FBI?"

"Yes, but they weren't too eager to help her because it's 'only makeup,' so she asked Walker Clifton to get involved, which he happily did."

"I can imagine, given not only is she a good donor for him, but Metro is one of the bigger single employers in the city." She looks at her notes for a few minutes. "Had Metro already started production of these colors?"

"I believe so, but on a small level. There is an expiration date, and they wouldn't have done too much beyond samples for photos and testing on models. I know that from previous conversations with her, but as I understand it, they debated moving forward despite the rip-off, figuring their fans would be loyal to them. In the end, though, they chose to not announce any new colors for the fall."

"That will hit their bottom line, I would imagine."

"I believe so, yes. We can ask her number two person to join us. Evelyn is amazing and knows a lot more than I do."

"Let's wait on that. For now, we're just reporting what you know while CeCe is away."

I nod. "Correct."

"Who alerted her about the animal cruelty?"

"She received a call shortly after six this morning."

"Where you there?"

Crap. Marci is good. "Yes, I'm staying with her until the doctor tells me I can live alone."

"You were with her, though?"

"Yes, but—" I take a deep breath. "Marci, this is new for both of us. We haven't even told our closest friends. I know I want more from her, but with everything going on, I don't want to jeopardize this in any way. Do we have to announce it to everyone today?"

"Honestly, I know this crowd. No one will catch it. If they do, I can direct them for now. If it goes to court, then we'll have to be prepared to talk about it, but hopefully by then, you two will be out to the world. That girl has been railroaded by the press and deserves someone who cares about her."

"I couldn't agree more. We've had bad timing for several years, and I'm happy we're on the right track."

"Back to this call...."

"It was her IT guy, and he alerted her to it. They don't do any animal testing. It's my understanding from them that if you want to sell in China, you're required to do animal testing, so they've decided to not sell there."

"Isn't it interesting that the competitor who ripped them off is Chinese?"

"Our thoughts exactly."

"And what's she doing in New York?" Marci asks.

"She's meeting with a crisis management firm in New York this evening. They've already told her she was doing the morning shows tomorrow. She'll be there for a few days dealing with this mess."

"The tabloids will be going crazy after this, I would think."

"She takes it as normal, but really she's a trooper when it comes to these issues."

"Let's start heading over." We stand and walk to the door and head down to my waiting car. Marci looks around at the guys who start following us. "I just realized you have a team with you all the time."

"Ever since I was poisoned, they've pretty much insisted on it."

"Do you have a taster, too?"

I laugh hard. "I guess that would be CeCe."

"That's a pretty high-value taster."

We drive over with my phone ringing like crazy. The sound is off, but it still buzzes. "What can we expect from these guys today?"

"I think you'll have a pretty big audience. You'll have Cyber, White-Collar, SFPD and, people from the district attorney's office, if not Walker Clifton and others from the US attorney's office. That's a big party."

As we pull up in front of the federal building, I follow Marci's lead as she hands the woman her driver's license. She chats briefly with Marci while she types our information into her system.

"When are you heading back to Philly?" the receptionist asks her.

"No offense, but I'm hoping not for a while. Though I sure could use a good cheesesteak."

"Girl, you can go to Jake's on Buchannan's for something close."

"I'll have to remember that. Give your cousin my best the next time you talk to her."

She hands us back our licenses, and we head through security. Once we're in the elevator with our escort, Marci explains. "I recently had a case in Philadelphia, and I recognized the family resemblance with the admin there. It happens to be her cousin."

"That must have been William's issue. What a small world."

She snickers. "Don't take this the wrong way, but you and your friends are my largest clients by far."

"Well, we're hoping that changes before too long."

"You cemented me for partnership, so thank you."

The doors open and we walk into what looks like the *Discovery*'s bridge on *Star Trek*. Cora crosses the room and gives me a great big hug. "You sure do look a lot better than the last time I saw you."

"It's been a few weeks. I was supposed to be back at work full time today, but it looks like this is going to derail me a little bit."

"I understand our mole may be going after CeCe, too?"

"We aren't sure, but someone's targeting her."

"Detective Lenning, his partner, and a person from the district attorney's office are in the conference room. Walker Clifton himself is coming, and he's always late." She looks at Marci, and they give each other a knowing nod. "Come with me."

She walks her way to a conference room where the walls are all glass. Attached to one side of the glass, I see a running timeline of our hackers. It's stunning to see it all laid out like this and how it all relates.

There is a flurry of commotion, and Walker Clifton walks in with Agents Winters and Greene. They're following him closely. So close, I wonder if their noses are brown.

Everyone takes their seats, and I notice Jim Adelson has joined us, too. He nods at me. "Mason."

"I'm glad you're here, Jim."

Walker starts our meeting. "Let's go around the table and introduce ourselves and our roles within our little group here. I'll start. I'm United States Attorney Walker Michael Clifton of the Northern District of California."

Each person around the room follows suit and introduces themselves. There is no self-deprecating humor; this is all formal, a bunch of dogs marking their territory. I know everyone through one scrape or another our team has dealt with.

Walker is the most senior in the room, so he takes the lead. "Mason, tell us what's going on."

"Thank you. I'm here sharing about what has happened with Caroline Arnault, the president and CEO of Metropolitan Cosmetics, as well as one of SHN's advisors and a shareholder. It could be unrelated. However, we feel that since it seems a little too coincidental, we should all be on the same page." I then walk them through the Chinese having Metro's fall line.

"Why wasn't this reported to the FBI?" Detective Lenning asks.

"It was," I respond but don't elaborate.

Detective Lenning looks at the White-Collar agents and asks, "Why didn't you send us the information?"

The two agents squirm in their seats.

"They felt it wasn't a big deal since it was only makeup," Marci shares.

Cora's eyes pop, as do Detective Lenning's. Everyone in the room is obviously surprised by this revelation.

"One of San Francisco's largest employers reports to you that her entire fall line has been stolen and is being released by a foreign competitor, and you dismiss her?"

Walker holds up his hand and interjects. "We've addressed this, and you will have the information promised by the end of the day."

Detective Lenning shakes his head, and I couldn't agree more.

"My team's been able to ascertain that they haven't been working on this for months, as was reported to the FBI, but rather a few weeks at most. We believe there is someone inside of Metro who fed them information as it went along. It went through heavy encryption and was outside of Metro's firewalls. In addition, the cosmetics company also is a known front for Chinese intelligence," Jim offers.

"How can you be so sure?" Agent Winters asks with pure disdain.

"Because Miss Arnault is a client of ours and we've investigated. We've done background checks on each person who had access to various parts of the process and narrowed it down to these five people: Becca Bentley, who heads up public relations; Christy Levin, who is Miss Arnault's admin; Evelyn Stevens, head of operations; Scarlet Lopez, who is Evelyn's admin; and Jordan Tyler, the project manager."

The meeting goes for the remainder of the afternoon. In the end, we all agree that the attacks on CeCe's company may stem from the same source, but nothing concrete is determined. "Is it interesting to anyone else that there were Russian hackers and now we're dealing with Chinese intelligence? Could this mean our hackers are selling this off to others?" I muse.

The White-Collar agents look at me in surprise.

"Our hackers did say they were close to you and indicated that we interacted with them regularly when they sent you that voice mail a few months ago," Jim volunteers.

"What voice mail?" asks Detective Lenning.

"I have it here." Cora works with her computer a bit, and then she plays the file.

"Good morning, Mason," a computer-generated voice drones on in a monotone. "I see you and your friends at the US attorney's office have indicted us. We want to assure you that we are not scared of you and your indictments. You should have figured out who we are, and none of you are smart enough to actually do that. We are everywhere, and you don't even recognize us. But we can assure you that we are not hiding. We are going to make a big impact, and you will regret the day our paths ever crossed."

"We've indicted Adam and Eve from that voice mail," Walker shares with the group.

We spend the rest of the afternoon making plans for our next steps. Most of the burden is going to be carried by the White-Collar team, but I'm not holding my breath.

As we walk downstairs, I make a point of speaking to the lackluster agents. "I appreciate any and all of your help."

chapter

ten

CECE

AS WE ENTER GRAN TIVOLI FOR DINNER, the paparazzi are in full force. I smile as they throw out questions about animal testing but don't answer any. When I see Jeremy, I know he'll be a good friend to help Metro weather this chaos.

"Caroline! So lovely to finally meet you. I just wish it was under better circumstances." He leads me to the back of the restaurant to a private room, where his team has gathered around a large round table. I notice there are noise machines. At first, I think it's to drown out the noise of the main dining room outside, but then I realize it's to make sure no one is listening to us here on the inside.

The team introduces themselves as they go around the table. Adam, the project manager and media relations expert, looks like he's twelve years old. I hope I'm in good hands.

Adam stands and begins a slideshow. I'm shocked at what they've put together in less than eight hours. He walks through some gruesome pictures and is able to show that they've been used before. I don't know why that comforts me, but it does. Then he talks about the plan to combat this nightmare. "As I mentioned this morning, we have you scheduled on all the morning shows. We have the questions they're allowed to ask and your answers, which we'll go through shortly."

"We know that some are going to go off script, particularly about your current love life," Vanessa reminds them.

I'm in shock. How would they know about Mason? We haven't talked about "us," and the last thing I want to do is talk about that publicly. I learned a long time ago that that was a simple way to destroy a relationship, and I've waited too long for him to get scared away by the press.

"We have some talking points about Prince Frederic," Adam assures her.

Oh, thank goodness. Frederic and his porn star. I'm just tabloid gold right now. "Do you really think they'll care about that at this point? We've both moved on," I say dismissively.

"Yes, they'll care. You're considered American royalty by all standards, and you were replaced by a porn star," Neil, the research guru, stresses.

"Well, the simple answer is that we didn't see much of each other before the big breakup, and we've both moved on," I patiently explain.

"They'll want to know who you've moved on with. Unless you're ready to share that juicy tidbit, I'd suggest we might want to adjust what you say," Adam kindly says to me.

"I'll take your advice on how to handle that, but be assured that I wasn't heartbroken over Frederic and his porn star. And I might add, despite what the tabloids write, I'm not frigid either."

The room laughs, which is what I was hoping for.

"You're going to do fantastic tomorrow. You've been managing press your whole life. You've totally got this," Jeremy exclaims.

He's right. I have spent my life managing the press. When my grandfather was upset with our dad for not coming back to work for the family business, he set his will up to give my brother and me our father's portion of his estate. He didn't understand how computers could make any money, but my father and mother were billionaires in their own right after they started Sandy Systems, which was the first company to figure out how to link computers together into networks. Our parents were very careful not to overexpose us, and we had a tight group of friends. I learned early on that when people shared our confidences, it would show up on the news or tabloids. We did many public relations junkets to downplay any drama.

It's nearly midnight when I get to my suite at the Four Seasons. My body clock tells me it's only nine, but I'm still exhausted. The car service will pick Vanessa and me up at six here at the hotel. I should be able to sleep at least a little bit before then.

I look at my phone and see a missed call and voice mail from Mason.

"Hey, beautiful. I'm thinking about you today. I hope you had a good flight, and I'll be watching you on the morning shows. You're going to do great. I'm here if you have the energy to call."

I smile. I adore that he touched base with me. Most guys seem to like to play it cool or see me as a way to up their profile. Maybe it's just as well that Mason and I started out as friends.

I pick up my phone and FaceTime him.

His hair is tousled, and I remember what those lips did for me just last night. "Hey, how was your flight?"

"It was good. Am I interrupting anything?"

"Absolutely not. Angela has fed me well, and now I'm watching *SportsCenter*. All my teams lost today."

"You're an Indians and Browns fan. You should be used to that by now," I tease.

"Ouch! You're harsh." His smile is as broad as the Grand Canyon.

I giggle. "Thanks for the message. It made my day."

"Well, it must have been a rough day if a simple message makes it."

"I've decided that I will personally float Metro if this goes sideways. Too many people will be out of a job, and I won't have that."

"That could be pretty pricey."

"I don't care. It isn't money that I made myself anyway. I've lost three of the four contracts we had for Fashion Week. Only Gap is hanging on for now, but depending on how things go this week, we may lose them, too." I sigh.

"I'm really sorry."

"The other thing I learned is that despite having the questions they'll ask on the morning shows tomorrow, we can expect them to go off script and ask about Frederic and his porn star. Accurate Communications didn't like my response."

"What didn't they like?"

"That we've both moved on and I'm not frigid."

Mason lets out a deep belly laugh. "Oh, I can definitely attest that you aren't frigid. Should I prepare a press release that I think my dick is going to fall off since we've had so much sex?"

I match his laughter. "Would you mind? Make sure you whip it out and show them and add that I give amazing blowjobs in private. I don't need to do anything in public for attention."

"Consider it done," he says while he continues to laugh. When we finally stop giggling, he asks, "Do you need to out us?"

"I did say we've both moved on, but they're suggesting that unless I'm ready to out us, then I should use different language. I'm not ready to expose you to the nightmare of the tabloids. You see what it does for Sara and Trey. Let's enjoy this for a while."

"Have you told Emerson or Hadlee yet?"

"Are you kidding? No way. You and I haven't defined what we're doing, so why would I let them do it for us? Have you told Dillon and Cameron?"

"No! I like having this amazing secret with you."

"I like it, too."

"Let's get away for a few days. We can even just hide in your place for the weekend. No plans with friends, and we'll send Angela away."

"I'd like that. Just the two of us alone all weekend. Our own little staycation."

"Can you manage that?"

"Believe it or not, I do it often just to recharge."

"A weekend hiding away with my favorite girl would be great."

My heart soars at the thought of being his favorite. "I should try to get some rest. They're picking Vanessa and me up at six tomorrow morning."

"All right. I understand. You're going to do great tomorrow. Good luck, and if you need me, I'll be there."

"Thank you, Mason. I can't tell you how much it means. Sleep well, because when we're in hiding, we're going to see if we can make your dick fall off."

"I can't wait."

The morning shows go without issue. Each one asks about Frederic, and my response is always the same, "I wish him and Savannah nothing but happiness." Thankfully, it pushes the paparazzi from me to them.

As we leave the last morning show, we drive back to the hotel for my press tour. When we arrive, Adam comes rushing out of the building to guide us through the hordes of press. I don't understand why people think they should be able to crowd me.

After thirty-seven interviews, six on television and the other thirty-one to online and newspaper journalists, I'm beat and ready for a break. The press is camped outside of the hotel, and they're not giving up. Hiding away sounds better and better.

I wrap up with Jeremy and his team, and Vanessa sends me home to San Francisco. I didn't think I could sleep on the plane, but after I cover my eyes with a sleep mask, I crash. It isn't until the flight attendant taps my arm to alert me that we're landing that I wake up. It wasn't a full night of sleep, but after six hours on the plane, I do feel more rested.

My car is waiting for me when I land, and I'm whisked home. My FaceTime rings, and it's Mason. "You look beautiful," he announces.

"Thank you. So do you." His chest is bare and glistening, probably from a recent workout.

"I wish you would have let me pick you up at the airport."

"It's a waste of gas, and I'll be there before you know it."

"Are you alone?"

"Well, other than the driver and thirty friends stuffed with me in the back of this Suburban...yes, I'm alone."

"Well, I thought you might want to see what's waiting for you when you get home."

He points the camera of his phone down, and his large glorious cock is there. My body unconsciously convulses. "It's beautiful." I can spot a small bead of precum leaking from the mushroom head. What I wouldn't give to lean down and lick it up.

"I just wanted you to see how much I missed you while you were gone."

I smile and unbutton my blouse, slipping my breast from my bra and play with the nipple. "I think I just came in my panties."

"I want so bad to stroke myself."

I point the camera at my breast. "I expect you to ravish me when I arrive."

He moans.

"You know, we've not talked about this, but after Frederic went off with his porn star girlfriend, I got tested to make sure I was clean. I'm completely clean, and on birth control."

"I'm clean, too. Are you good with going bareback?"

"Absolutely."

"How close are you?"

"Maybe ten to fifteen minutes away."

"I'll be here. Come find me."

He disconnects from the call. Seeing his hard cock and playing with my nipples made me ready to jump him. I can't wait. I love that his sexual appetite is as large as mine.

When I'm let out at the front curb of my house, I quickly walk inside and drop my bag. I'm a little disappointed that he isn't in the foyer waiting to greet me. Where could he be?

I peek in the bedroom, thinking Mason may be waiting for me there. Nothing. It's empty.

Curious, I continue down the hall. I see the glow of a fire dancing along the walls in the living room. It's not surprising, as it's a cool evening, and I know his recent illness makes him cold sometimes. Stepping into the room, I find him lying in front of a roaring fire on top of the soft faux fur rug. Wrapped in one of the large cozy blankets, he's watching the flames in the fireplace. "Are you hiding?"

"Not at all. I just thought that since you've been gone a few days, I might entice you so you remember me."

I smile and catch myself before I let out a soft moan thinking about his naked body strategically hidden. I pull my camisole over my head and palm my nipples. It's cold this far back from the fire, and they're aching. As I bite my lower lip, his eyes are glued to my ministrations. "Would you like some company in front of that fire?" I ask him breathlessly.

He nods and opens the blanket to show me his monstrous erection. I have on my skinny jeans that leave almost nothing to the imagination, but still I say, "I'm guessing you'd like to see me without these?"

"Please," he says hoarsely.

Hooking my thumbs into the sides of my waistband, I turn around and lean over, exposing my ass. I slap it, and he moans. "You're so beautiful," he whispers.

Turning back around, I slowly walk toward him like a lion stalking its prey.

I straddle his body with the blanket between us. My pussy is sopping wet, and I want him inside me. I missed him while I was away, and I want a soft kiss on my lips.

"Now, why don't you climb into this blanket with me so we can warm up together?" he says in a sultry voice.

I'm powerless to resist, the fight gone from me the second he lifts the blanket, inviting me to join him with a hint of his naked, chiseled body highlighted by the flames. Climbing off him, I slide in next to him.

Pressing himself tightly against my naked body, he wraps an arm around me, and I relish in the feeling of his fire-warmed skin against my own. His hands begin exploring my stomach before slowly gliding his fingers up my body. He lines his hips up beneath me, his cock hard and ready, sliding it up and down my slit. I can't help but let out a soft moan as his shaft caresses along my silky smooth skin.

His hand creeps ever higher, coming up to slip across my breasts. As he brushes along my nipples, I gasp.

"Did you get worked up playing with your nipples to tease me and drive me wild?"

"Yes," I breathe as he pulls and pinches both nipples, making the heat between my legs grow hotter.

"I missed you while you were gone," he murmurs.

I push myself against him, a flood of wetness growing between my legs. Leaning down, I place soft, passionate kisses along his beautiful bare shoulder. Working my way from his arm, along his collarbone, and slowly up his neck, my lips continue to explore his delicious skin. His head tilts up to make room for my mouth, getting higher up his neck. He snakes his hand away from my breasts, slipping between my cleavage to lightly place two fingers under my chin. With a gentle push, he turns my head to face him, meeting his fiery look and cocky grin. I dip my head to press my lips against his. What begins as a soft touch soon transforms into a deeper, lustful connection between us.

Our lips part, our tongues slipping through to dance around one another as my grip tightens on him, holding him close to me while our hands explore each other's bodies. I slip my arm under his neck, wrapping around him, while he tenderly massages my breast. At the same time, his other hand slides down, dipping his fingers into the wetness I know is growing between my legs.

I release a soft moan between us as his fingers creep across my skin and brush against my sensitive hard nub. His fingers part my wet slit as they go, coating them with my juices. Slick and wet, they easily glide along, beginning to explore every part of my sensitive pussy, hovering around my entrance as they move up and down my swollen lips.

I want him inside me, but he keeps teasing me, swirling his other fingers around my hardened nipples, sweeping across them to give them a quick pinch every now and again. As I let out another moan, he takes advantage of my open mouth and sucks my bottom lip, biting it and then tugging on it with his teeth before letting it slip away.

Looking down at me with a devious smirk, he suddenly slips his fingers deep inside my wet pussy. My eyes widen as I gasp from the pleasurable shock rippling through me. I feel them begin to slowly work back and forth, a slight curve making them touch the most sensitive parts inside me. My gasp turns to a low moan, and he looks at me with fiery desire, pulling me back to his lips so he can taste me once more as his fingers rock in and out of my wet pussy before his mouth salves my breasts.

The pulses of ecstasy he's creating make me want to lose control. I can't help it when my hips begin to gyrate against his hand, my body craving more of his touch. I reach down and take hold of his thick shaft, feeling him throb in my grip. "I need you inside me," I breathlessly demand.

He pulls away from my tits long enough to nod at me, desire written in his expression. I guide his cock between my legs, spreading them slightly to let his girth slip inside my sopping wet center. The tip presses against me, and slowly I feel him push inside me. God, he's so big. I arch my back to meet him, savoring the feeling of him finally filling me. His cock keeps going and going until I feel his balls press tight against me, his entire length deep inside me. I pulse against his thick cock, gripping him tightly, before he slowly slides his shaft out once more. Just before the head slips out, he pushes himself back in. Over and over, in and out, slowly letting me feel every inch as he goes.

I squirm against him, the ridge of the head of his cock hitting that spot inside me just right. I'm getting close, and I chase my orgasm like an addict must chase their next high. He smiles before moving faster and faster inside me as our lust grows. Then it hits me, and I let out a low growl against his skin.

Throwing the blanket aside, he pulls me on top of him. In an instant, his cock is back inside me as I lower myself down onto his shaft. I lean down to his lips, slipping my tongue into his mouth in a passionate kiss. He breaks away to gasp for air as I bounce faster and faster on his rigid shaft. His mouth finds my nipple, and he bites it. I shriek in ecstasy, and my pussy clamps down hard on his cock. A second wave hits me as we moan together, our primal roars overtaking the roar of the fireplace, its flames reflecting against our glistening bodies.

In perfect harmony, we let out a matched pair of moans as our orgasms explode out of us. My pussy tightens and gushes around his cock. His shaft throbs and pulses inside me, shooting thick warm ropes of cum deep into my pussy. He pumps against me and I thrust against him, loving the skin-on-skin contact. We come together in synced bliss, letting go of everything as we ride out our peak.

His legs and arms can no longer hold me up. Mine are no better. Together we collapse to the floor, me on top of him with his cock letting loose the last drops of cum into my already filled pussy. He kisses me over and over, across my back, my shoulders, my neck, until he turns his head and our lips meet, embracing each other in postcoital passion.

With our orgasms finally subsiding, he slips out of me, our juices leaking from my quivering center once he's free. I slide in beside him, tugging the blanket back over our naked bodies before he wraps me back up in his arms. I kiss his bare skin over and over, tilting my head to meet his eyes and giving him a quick, playful kiss on the lips before I look at him with a coy smile. "I'm so glad to be home."

chapter

eleven

MASON

I'M AWAKE LONG BEFORE CECE IS. I love to watch her sleep. The little crease between her eyes is gone, and she's so peaceful. I wish it was this way for her when she was awake. The aftermath from the animal testing accusation is hanging on despite her appearances on the morning shows. There are boycotts on PeopleMover and other social media sites. I watch how she pulls into herself and projects so much strength that she even fools herself. I wish I could just wipe it all away.

"Are you watching me again?" she asks sleepily.

"Guilty as charged. You're so beautiful that I can't help myself."

"You're too much." She stretches, and her features become very catlike. Out peeks her nipple, and I bend down and capture it in my mouth.

"We'll never make the meeting tonight at your parents' if we don't get moving."

She moans her satisfaction as my fingers search for her center. "I'm not complaining," she says breathlessly.

My fingers circle her hard nub and occasionally dip into her channel. I nibble on her ear.

She reaches for my hard dick, but I pull away from her. "This is all about you."

"You're spoiling me."

Her breathing quickens, and I know she's close. I pivot in and out while circling her nub with my thumb. I find that precious spot and rub it while sucking and biting her nipple. Her hips move and greet each wet pulse. I love how responsive she is.

When she finally comes, she smiles at me. "That's my kind of wake-up call." I lick her juices from my fingers and wink at her. "You go get in the shower, and I'll start the coffee," she tells me.

As I walk to the bathroom, I hear her say, "Damn, you look as good coming as you do going!"

I turn and look at her, and she's fanning herself with her hand. I grin. "Boy, you sure do know what to say to make a man blush."

"Margo, tell us about your cruise," Sara asks her mother-in-law.

"We were on the *Queen Mary 2*. It was beautiful and quite the luxury to get away from our phones and emails for a few months."

"We missed you guys," Cameron shares.

"I see a lot happened," Charles responds.

Margo, not to be deterred from sharing her vacation, continues, "We started in Vancouver and cruised through the outer islands of British Columbia up to Alaska. Then we went through the Aleutian Islands and down the Bering Sea into Southeast Asia, where we hit nine countries before we ended in New Zealand. It was positively breathtaking, and we had an amazing time."

"Wow. What was your favorite?" Cynthia asks.

Margo looks over at her husband. "We don't agree. I loved Japan and all the amazing temples, and I loved the culture."

"I loved the beaches we saw in Indonesia," Charles adds. "The entire cruise was a luxury. We had a wonderful stateroom and just enjoyed jumping from place to place. The restaurants were five-star, and the tours and activities on the ship and on land were first class. I highly recommend it when you have a few months to enjoy."

"Sounds like fun," Quinn says, looking at William.

"When Mason allows us to have three to six months off, I'll be ready," William responds, and the group laughs.

I look around the table. There are twenty-two people here—all of the partners and some of our senior staff, plus some of our outside advisors. This is a big meeting.

Margo serves an amazing feast of stuffed clams, rack of lamb, assorted veggies and salads, and homemade cheese ravioli in red sauce.

As Margo's team works their way around the table and serves everyone, Dillon claps his hands together. "We are eating so good tonight." He takes a big bite of a stuffed clam and moans his appreciation. "Don't get me wrong, Emerson is amazing at ordering food with Liam taking up so much of her time, but I really missed these dinners."

There is a chorus of "Me, too."

Margo and Charles spend dinner regaling us with stories of their trip. When the bell rings, several people get up to help clear the table while I set up a projector. "Tonight we're going to do something a little different. In the past, as partners, we sequestered ourselves in Charles's office to discuss SHN business. Well, since Parker, Constance, Jim, Cora, Marci, and Walker have joined us, I thought we'd open this meeting to everyone. Not everyone was a part of SHN as we started on this journey with our mole and hacker."

I bring up the slides while everyone enjoys an after-dinner drink. "I've been working on this for a while." Looking at Cora, I add, "This is nowhere near as impressive as your board, but I thought it might help to get some perspective on what's happened, and maybe some fresh eyes will point us in a new direction."

"Great idea. That's part of why we use the board," she encourages me.

The first slide comes up, and it's a picture we took of the partners not long after we started. Dillon, Cameron, and I are in the back row, and Sara and Emerson are sitting in chairs in the front.

"Wow, do I look young in that picture. Amazing what working here and having a baby do to you," Emerson exclaims.

"You look exactly the same. You haven't aged at all," CeCe admonishes her.

"We realized that someone was sabotaging SHN shortly after Emerson joined the company. We watched BingoBongo go to a competitor, and we lost Jamison Technologies, Page Software, and Accurate Software to Perkins Klein. At first, we thought we weren't getting the job done, and then when we realized there was a mole, we thought it was either placed by Perkins Klein, or the mole was feeding them information."

The next slide is Tom Sutherland and a PeopleMover logo.

"Our suspicions were confirmed when Tom Sutherland was looking for his last round of funding. He met with Emerson and me and presented us with all of our research and numbers. It was given to him by a competitor as an attempt to undercut us."

"That's right!" Cameron sits back hard in his chair, remembering the turmoil at the time. "Dillon was on his forced leave, and it was the four of us holding down the fort, and it was not pretty."

I nod. "Through Emerson's friendship with Quinn, who was working at Perkins Klein at the time, we learned that someone else was providing them with the information and they were acting on it."

"That's right. It was mysteriously showing up in the mail, and Terry Klein and Bob Perkins were already half checked out of the business, having cashed in over twenty years, and saw it as an opportunity to steal some business away," Quinn shares.

"Which they did, and it showed us some of our weakness in the market—we may come in early and want exclusive, but they aren't required. We need to treat our clients the same with angel and round-one funding through the entire process," I add.

I bring up the next slide, which is just a silly picture of three people dressed in black with masks on, looking like they might be ready to rob a bank.

"So, to ferret out our mole, we deployed a crafty strategy. The teams at SHN would work on several possible acquisitions that we believed to be faulty. Meanwhile, the partners were working on specific wins along with the help of Charles and his friends."

"What did that do?" Bella asks.

"We knew our mole had an inside person. By sending them companies that weren't good investments, they'd be looking at the shiny objects over there and not what we were doing quietly over here."

"Wouldn't they vet the companies, too?" Cora asks.

"Normally yes, but because our team had put them through our vetting process and our success rate is so high, our competitors went with the faulty material without vetting it," Dillon explains. "Our process goes beyond my numbers; Cameron and his team go through every line of code or product piece and make sure it's reputable and affordable. Cameron and his team can do math far and beyond many in the valley, and sometimes they're looking for him to figure this all out for them."

"Emerson's team will vet each member of their team, and often we walk away because her people don't think the leadership is right for the organization," Cameron adds.

"And, of course, Mason vets their business plan to make sure we can add value to the company," Emerson stresses.

"What we do is very different than all of our competitors, and our proprietary look at companies was sold and/or given to our competitors, who scooped up the information. Some adopted Dillon's numbers—"

"Which I've since evolved into something even better," Dillon boasts.

"—and in the end, our competitors invested in those companies. Perkins Klein invested the heaviest, but we saw investments from Benchmark, Argent Capital, and Carson Mills. But Perkins Klein was the biggest investor, and as we suspected these were bad acquisitions. Today none of the companies exist. We also believe these investments are what killed Perkins Klein and put some financial instability into some of the smaller VC firms."

My next slide is a list of company logos and which VC firm they went to.

"As we suspected, these were bad acquisitions. None of these companies are in business today, and the instability it caused at Perkins Klein made them fold up shop. It also put some financial instability into some of the smaller VC firms, as well."

"Thus the saying 'we're always one bad decision away from going under,'" William points out.

"Exactly," Dillon says. "But we also don't invest in just anything, and we've made a point to have a year's worth of salary we won't touch just in case something bad happens."

"Benchmark bought up several of Perkins Klein's struggling but successful companies, and Quinn came to work for us. At that point, we thought the mole was gone and it was over, but we learned otherwise."

I put up the logos of four of our client companies.

"Since our mole and hacker are still unknown, but we've figured out how to disable them, they took other measures." I point to each of the four companies and explain how each was sabotaged. "Initially we suspected that it was Russian mob involvement, but instead the Russian mob was interested in Cynthia due to her turning them in for money laundering at BrightStar Investments."

"Sorry I took you all off track," Cynthia apologizes.

"They were involved, they just weren't behind it," Cora emphasizes.

"But it did point you to the mole," Jim points out. "Your legal secretary had been feeding information to an unknown, and because of that, she is currently a guest at the Federal Correction Institution in Dublin, California—not Ireland, for eight more months."

"Very true, but we know the mole started before she did, so she was only the second person involved," Sara adds.

"We thought it was over, but we were wrong," I say with a sigh.

"We were at least hoping," Dillon adds.

I put up the logo of Pineapple Technologies. Our heartbreak.

"This is where the rubber meets the road. Pineapple Technologies was a big turning point for us. On the day they went public, someone had hacked in and stolen all their code and posted their confidential information on the internet. What was proprietary became public, and their stock plummeted. In a matter of weeks, they went belly up."

"That was really tough," William says. "That was my first day with SHN."

"Bet you thought you'd made a mistake," Emerson teases.

"Who says I've changed my mind?" William teases back. "That was a pretty crazy first week."

"Talk about walking into chaos," Sara sympathizes.

"It was a tough few weeks. But thankfully through Parker Carlyle, who was a member of Cameron's elite team—"

"Elite? Can I put that on my résumé?" Parker asks.

"No way. You can't update your résumé. Didn't you know? 'You can get in, but you can never get out.'" The group laughs at Emerson's quip.

"Well, Parker and Constance combed through over two hundred thousand lines of code and found several important things."

On the first slide, the threat. I read it aloud. "Dillon, Cameron, and Mason, you should have brought me on when you had a chance."

"Talk about a drop-the-mic moment," Cameron says.

"Agreed," I say. "This left open the idea that it was a candidate we had chosen not to hire at some point or a company we had not invested in—not a current employee."

"My team missed it. Pure genius to find that," Cora says with a broad smile. "I keep trying to talk Parker into joining my team, but nothing has tempted him yet."

"It was too exhausting," Parker shares.

"But you found that our hackers had signed their work. They were calling themselves Adam and Eve. They'd been signing their work as AM and EA, so when he found the words MacIntosh and Ambrosia, we made the jump that they were named Adam MacIntosh and Eve Ambrosia," I continue.

I then move to the next slide, where I have a picture of Ruben's painting of Adam and Eve in the Garden of Eden.

"With Sara's brilliant legal mind, we figured out the next step. We all agreed with Sara's theory that our hackers named themselves. With MacIntosh and Ambrosia being apple varieties and Adam and Eve being in the Garden of Eden, it pointed us to the fruit of the poisonous tree theory. We think the hacker believes that our gains through SHN are fruit from the poisonous tree."

"Sara, you really are a brilliant legal mind to have put that together," Walker says, obviously impressed with how she came to such a conclusion with so little information.

Sara shrugs. "I had recently been reacquainted with my birth parents, who are born-again Christians, and the ambrosia apple is my favorite."

"Don't let her pass it off. This really helped to make sense of who our hackers were," I stress.

I put up the logo of SketchIt.

"Quinn saved us again when she went to visit SketchIt and saw the beginnings of what happened with Pineapple Technologies. With her quick thinking, she called in Cameron, who alerted FBI Cybercrimes, and they inserted a Trojan horse into the hacker's system."

"It allowed us to monitor what they were doing, and we were able to identify several hackers and arrest them," Cora shares.

"I just wish they knew who Adam and Eve were," Greer muses.

"At least we were able to indict them *in absentia*, so no matter if it takes us two weeks or twenty years, they'll be going to jail," Walker points out.

"But our hackers know they were indicted and said as much," I add while I pull up the voice mail they sent me. "We have something big planned, and we are hiding in plain sight."

"That's so spooky," Hadlee says.

"It is, but it also tells us that we know who the hacker and mole are," Jim points out.

"Annabelle," William announces.

"Maybe, though we can't say for sure that Mason's poisoning and the hacking and mole are related."

I bring up a slide of the wolfsbane flower.

"That's pretty," Cynthia says.

"That is what I was poisoned with. We don't know for sure if Annabelle was behind the poisoning, but that theory has not been discounted, and many of you thought she was our original mole," I point out. "The jury is still out on that, too."

I look over at CeCe, and she nods. I bring up the logo of Metro Composition.

"CeCe is an advisor and investor with us. She's in our inner circle. Recently, someone has made a serious run at her company." I walk everyone through what they've heard on the news and in the gossip rags.

"But we can't be sure that your nutjob is the same nutjob Metro is dealing with?" Trey questions.

"We don't know yet. We've looked for listening devices throughout Metro's offices and Caroline's home. We're still working our way through the evidence, which continues to grow with each passing day," Jim shares.

Looking out at the group, I put my hands in my pockets. "This is our situation right now. I know we've commented along the way, but now that you're all seeing it in a more linear format, what do you think?"

"I want them found, arrested, and serving their life sentences in Lompoc and Dublin," Dillon volunteers.

"Amen," agrees Cameron.

"Well, as many of you know, my sister was behind a large theft ring in Napa right under my nose. They've said you know them. If you've figured out it isn't an employee, and this has been going on since before several of you joined the firm, who are some people who maybe you went to school with who you didn't invite into the firm?" Andy asks.

"We were pretty close in school, but each of us had other friends. If we're going to go that far back, the pool widens significantly," I say.

"That's not a bad idea. Why don't the three of you start a list of people? We can figure out what they're doing today and see who's doing well and who isn't," Jim offers.

"Is there anyone you've upset?" Marci asks.

"That list is pretty long. We gave a list of all the companies we chose not to invest in to Jim a while ago, and we continue to update it," I share.

"Sorry. I know we're looking for a needle in a haystack," Marci says while she studies the slide.

"Exactly, and despite the fact that we all think it's Annabelle, we also need to keep our minds open to others on the off chance that it isn't her and we miss something less obvious," Cora points out.

chapter
twelve

CECE

THE BARGES THAT SAIL BENEATH THE BAY BRIDGE on their way to deliver their goods distract me from the giant negative number sitting on my P&L. Good grief. The last year has essentially been a colossal waste of time. I gave my company all the love I had, and someone took it from me like a possession. My body's a shell of shattered remains of who I was: vivacious and high spirited. This betrayal has drained me better than a vampire. I hate the person who did this to us as sure as the sun rises and sets. It's just killing me. Someone in my own house has taken six months of work done by dozens of employees and focus groups and thrown it all out the window by giving it away to a competitor for a few measly dollars. I hope they can sleep at night.

My private line rings and I answer without looking. "Hello?"

"Hello, Caroline. This is Walker Clifton." I'm not in the mood to deal with him. He was professional yet friendly last night at the partners meeting, thankfully.

"Hey, Walker, what's going on?"

"Well, to start with, I'm absolutely mortified over the news that Jim Adelson brought to the table last night."

"What do you mean?"

"First and foremost, I want you to know that I have spoken to the head of the FBI's San Francisco office about how you've been treated, and I've also escalated a complaint to the Department of Justice over the handling of your case. I've forwarded the report Jim's team put together. Nothing was more disappointing last night to have no report from the agents assigned to your case, who personally assured me they'd jump on it, and then to hear a private security company has run circles around them. Shameful. Jim Adelson's report on each employee and narrowing the list down shouldn't be done by a third party. It should have been done by the FBI."

"Thank you, Walker. It's really disheartening to know they don't support—"

"I want to assure you that no matter the business, no matter the size, things like corporate espionage are a serious issue, and we at the DOJ, the state attorney's office, and the FBI take them seriously."

What a politician. I wouldn't be surprised if he asks for a campaign contribution at the end of this. "Thanks, Walker. I appreciate that."

"The next thing to share is that we discussed with both the head of the FBI and the DOJ, and we think we've come up with a way to bring out your mole."

The hair on the back of my neck stands at attention. "What are you thinking?"

"I think we should probably have lunch today. I want to discuss and flush out a solution face-to-face. There are still some pieces we need your perspective and buy-in on, and I think by meeting, we'll have the opportunity to go through our plan and figure it out together."

My stomach tightens. This is not what I want right now. "I appreciate the idea, but I'm not sure that I want to air my dirty laundry in public in front of so many people in a busy restaurant where people keep approaching the table."

"I get it. That's not at all what I'm thinking. I'm leaning toward the private room at the Baywater Café. We can sit down, just the two of us, and have lunch and brainstorm."

I keep my sigh of exasperation to myself. This will be a colossal waste of time. "Walker, you do know that I'm not interested in anything more than a lunch— "

"That does disappoint me on so many levels, but I do know that. Don't get me wrong, I hold out hope that you'll see the benefit of a relationship with me. Meanwhile, we do need to get Metro Composition through this. My feeling is that we should meet and go through this idea, see if we can make it work."

"Okay, I'll meet you for lunch today. What time?

"One o'clock. How does that work with your schedule?"

"That will work for me. Should I bring Evelyn or anyone else with me?"

"No. Absolutely not. We want the circle incredibly small on this. Besides, Evelyn is on the list of suspects."

I pause. "She's innocent in this."

"I hope so, but better to be safe than sorry."

"All right, I'll see you at one at Baywater Café."

As I look down at the sidewalk and watch the little dots of tourists, runners, bicyclists, and others making use of the San Francisco paths, my disappointment continues. I can't let myself fall into the pit of despair. The best remedy is a strong cup of espresso and to talk to my best friend. Luckily, I can do both. I call her and make a double espresso as it rings.

Emerson answers on the third ring. I hope I'm not waking her up.

"Hey, you."

"Hey, yourself. How's my favorite little boy doing?"

"Do you mean the little boy who doesn't sleep?" She laughs.

"An Energizer Bunny, huh?"

"You have no idea. Dillon has moved down to the basement at night so he can get some sleep before going to work. Liam had us both up every hour and a half last night."

"That little boy likes to eat."

"I just don't think I'm producing enough for him."

"I know I'm not a mother yet, but I've heard there's nothing wrong if you need to supplement with formula."

"I know, I know, but I'm trying… I'm trying my hardest to increase production, including drinking things that are supposed to increase my milk. I feel like I'm a fricking cow."

"You don't look like one, and that's all that matters. You look absolutely radiant and gorgeous."

"You wouldn't say that if this was a video call. You'd see that I have spit-up in my hair, I haven't had a shower today—maybe it's been a few days—and I'm sure the circles under my eyes are huge."

"Sweetheart, no matter what you look like, I'm sure you look spectacular."

"All right, I learned a long time ago not to argue with you, but I know you didn't call to hear about my losing battle with my four-month-old."

"You can call me any time, day or night, if you want. You know I'm here for you."

Her voice cracks, and I know she's on the verge of tears. "I know you are, and I can't tell you how much that means to me." Emerson clears her throat. "What's going on with you?"

"Walker Clifton just called asking to meet for lunch today."

"Is he still trying to talk you into a political merger?"

"Oh, I think he would always love that. He just isn't understanding that this isn't an opportunity in his future."

"You're so politically correct. Maybe you would make a good politician's wife."

"Right now, I'm not interested in anybody." I'm waiting to see where this goes with Mason.

"Walker knows you're not on the menu, so what does he want?"

"He was surprisingly upset that Jim's team has done so much work and the FBI has done nothing."

"No kidding! Who can blame him? The FBI looked like idiots last night, and so did he."

I smile. "It makes me feel better that he apologized. He told me he's reported the gaffe to the head of the San Francisco FBI office and to the DOJ."

"As he should. You're a huge employer in this town, and it's important that people recognize that. It's also important to note that you don't just do high-end jobs; you provide blue-collar work, and you provide white collar work. Plus, you pay well and offer great benefits to everyone who works for you. You've had the opportunity to take your manufacturing offshore. You could've done this a lot cheaper, but you don't. There's a reason you're consistently listed as one of the best places to work. You do a lot for San Francisco, and you also put money back into the area through the nonprofit work your company does. You're important to this community."

"But we won't be if we go under." I choke back the tears.

"Stop talking that way. This is going to turn around. It's going to be rough for a while, I get it, but you're going to survive this. I know you, CeCe. This is not going to stop you."

A tear falls, and I quickly wipe it away, knowing she's right. I'm just grateful to hear it from her. "Thank you."

"Hey, sister, I've got your back—always."

"I really needed to hear that today. Thanks again."

She artfully changes the subject; otherwise, she knows I'll be a giant puddle. "What does he want to talk to you about?"

"If you can believe this, he wants to talk about a plan to flush out the person who's behind the sabotage."

"Who do you think it could be?"

"It can't be any of the people they've narrowed it down to. Look at Evelyn. There's no way. She's worked her way up through the company. She's been with me for over ten years. She's had the job for the last four years. I find it incredibly difficult to believe she would do anything to sabotage the company when a major part of her compensation is based on profit-sharing. Besides, she lives and breathes Metro Composition."

"Okay, I can't disagree with that logic. What about Christy?"

"Christy? There's no way it could be her. Christy worked for my mother and has been with us for years. She knows where all of the bodies are buried. She knows all the drama that came when Trey and I inherited our trusts, all of my account numbers, my dating history, how to get rid of all of the creepy guys that come out of the woodwork each time I'm in the tabloids. There's no way it could be her. If anyone's going to take a bullet for me, she's jumping in first and pushing the rest of you out of the way."

"You're funny, but I don't disagree with that."

"And I would say the same for Evelyn's admin, Scarlet. She'd take a bullet not only for me but also for Evelyn. She's amazing, and if anything ever happened to Christy, she's who I would talk into moving over, but only if Evelyn would let her. She's very protective of her."

"You really are funny now if you think Evelyn would ever let her come work for you."

"I know. I'd be stuck. Then there's Jordan, the project manager. I don't believe Jordan would ever do anything to hurt herself in such a large way. If she were ever caught, it would preclude her from taking a job at any of the big fashion houses. This was a big step for her. When she's done with launching a full line like this, she could walk into L'Oréal, Maybelline, or Estée Lauder and get a huge six-figure salary. No way I buy that she would jeopardize her future like this."

"Again, I agree. So, what about Becca?

"I find it hard to believe she would do this either. She's not enjoying anything going on with this mess. She doesn't like crisis management, said it's too 'reactionary.' She wants to create something, not look like a hero. She's hating life right now. She's grateful to have Accurate Communications managing some of this, but for the most part, the day-to-day falls back on her. Trust me when I say she would much, much, *much* prefer to be working on new lines, Fashion Week, and things that are fun and exciting. I'm more worried about her leaving the company for something less stressful."

"Okay, so you know the only other person that's been involved from this since the beginning is you."

"I know, and it's a given it's not me. You know better than anyone that my mother drives me crazy, and there are plenty of times I consider selling it all back to her and walking away, but I really do love this business and what I do. It's a great reason to get up every morning."

"And you're good at this. So where does that leave you?"

"I don't know. And that's the scariest part of this whole thing. To have somebody behind this and we don't know who is what keeps me up at night."

"Well, hopefully you and Walker come up with something that will help you find your problem child."

I hear Liam crying in the background. "You go take care of that sweet little boy. Let's get together for lunch later this week."

"Love it, and I'll leave him with somebody. Joining you for a grown-up lunch is my perfect excuse to take a shower and become presentable."

Baywater Café is not the typical see-and-be-seen restaurant. It's high end and more for the discreet luncher. The traffic is tight, but I make it on time and am the first to arrive.

"Miss Arnault, may I show you to the room where you'll be joining Mr. Clifton?"

"Thank you."

I follow him to the back room. It's a little-known secret that this room exists. Rumor has it, it was originally designed for a man and his mistress to meet discreetly, but it's since become the place for private business meals. It overlooks the Bay Bridge and the water. I bet they get plenty of activity on baseball game days since the Giants play really close.

I stand at the window and watch the traffic on the bridge. So many people going in so many different directions, each with their own challenges. Maybe running away to a deserted island in the Pacific would be perfect. A cute cabana boy to entertain me—although I'm sure Mason has wrecked me for all men. We haven't been "together" long, but I sure do miss him in my bed when he isn't there. My trip to New York proved that, and he's said it was the same for him.

I feel the door open, releasing the pressure in the room. Walker strides over with his arms wide. "Caroline!"

I walk into his arms and give him a nice gentle hug, making sure it's more professional than personal. "Walker, thank you for inviting me to lunch."

"Sit down." He waves to the table set for two beside him. At least it's not a romantic setting, more business related.

As soon as we take our seats, a waiter appears. "Would you like some wine with your lunch?"

"No, thank you. Just unsweetened iced tea for me, please."

"I'll have the same," Walker tells the waiter, and he leaves as quietly as he appeared.

"You look positively radiant today, Caroline," Walker says. "No one would think you were dealing with what you're going through. You're certainly cool under pressure."

"Don't be fooled, it's definitely an act."

He chuckles. "I'd never guess. So, tell me how things are going right now. Give me a real understanding of what's going on and bring me up to date. I got the overview from the FBI team on Friday, but somehow I have a feeling that, given our meeting last night, they may have left a few things out."

"Sure. That's not a problem." I walk him through everything following the last lunch we had.

"Holy shit! That's huge. So not only did someone steal your line, but now they're plastering the internet with fake photos of animal testing? Why does anybody test on animals anymore? Knowing you've spent close to a quarter of a million dollars fighting this with a crisis management team is astounding."

"It's been a rough couple of weeks. The money just sits in bank accounts. I'm just grateful I have it to spend."

"What are your next steps?" Walker asks.

"We've determined that we're going to lose out on our fall season, and I've already lost my three contracts for Fashion Week. I have one remaining, but it's most likely to be lost."

"Who's it with?"

"Art Peck over at Gap."

"I know Art pretty well. I'm happy to reach out to him if you think that would help."

"Right now we're just waiting, but I reserve the right to take you up on that."

"Whatever you need. This all sounds pretty devastating," Walker sympathizes.

I nod in agreement. I don't want to tell him too much, because chances are it'll make it to the newspaper and local gossip sites, but I'm okay with sharing how much this has affected us and my determination to not let it sink me. "When I look at my P&L statements, I can assure you it is beyond devastating." I know we're alone, but for dramatic effect, I say in a very low breath, "Walker, the negative numbers on the P&L over this are astounding. Most people would shut their doors over this, but I'm not most people. I am personally going to pull out of my personal accounts to make sure every one of my employees keeps their jobs, can pay their bills, and keep their commitments. I won't lay people off, and I'm determined not to let this monster win."

He sits back hard in his chair. "Wow! That's pretty impressive. You're right, most people would just shut down, throw their hands up, and walk away."

"Yes, most people would, but I'm not most people, and they've pissed me off."

"Good. Now let's talk about our plan to catch them. I've spoken with the heads of Cybercrimes and White-Collar, and we have an idea for you to consider."

"Okay. Lay it on me." I sit back and drink my iced tea, prepared to listen carefully to their idea.

"We think that if you make movements as if you're going to launch the line you worked on, we might be able to ferret out the person behind this."

"I only worry that it'll bring the animal rights activists out."

"It would only bring them out if you really were going to do this. If your team is as innocent as they say, then this will go nowhere."

I raise a brow. "Fair point. How are you suggesting I move forward?"

"We think the first step is to meet with each person individually and tell each one something slightly different. With one, you're launching the line as is with new slightly different colors. With another, you're changing the names of your colors. With another, you're going to launch with different packaging and the same names. With another, it's different packaging and different names. And with the last, you're just launching as is, believing your fans will disregard the fakes."

"A lot of these things tend to be decided by a group of people—different groups of people for each step."

"We understand that, but after what you've told me, if you position it as though you need to make sure you're saving your company and the impending losses, and you're making an executive decision, then it should work."

I sit and think about it. It's a little out of character for me to make a unilateral decision, but I can see how it could possibly work. "Do you think that's enough for you to figure it out?"

"Possibly. We'd also put tracking software on each person's cell phone, plus their home and personal computers. When I talked to Jim, he said based on their sweep of the office computers, no one had done it from a computer in-house."

"That's another reason I'm convinced that it's not coming from in-house." I sit back, and the thought occurs to me. "You know, Tim Carpenter at Cosmetics, Inc., has been making noise to buy Metro for some years. I've always resisted the big conglomerate, figuring we're more agile to buck trends and therefore create them, but also, I don't want to work for anyone. I like being in control of my own destiny."

"We'll add him to our list and check him out. I can't imagine that if someone wanted to buy you that they'd sabotage your business."

"I know. But it is a way to get a bargain."

"It's something we should at least rule out."

"Thank you. Back to my team. What would be the next step?"

"Cybercrimes has the ability to create emails that look like they're going to others when they aren't. We'll work through a series of emails that the team will be cc'd on, then watch where they get forwarded and how, which will give us more information. If we don't find anything, you can tell everyone that you've changed your mind without telling them what you're doing."

"That might work." I don't want to commit to anything quite yet.

The waiter comes up and places a small salad in front of us. "I didn't want to interrupt, but today the chef is serving a light Caesar salad, the main course is our cioppino, and dessert is a simple lemon meringue cookie." I'm shocked since we didn't order and look up at Walker. He shrugs.

"When you reserve the single dining room, you get the chef's special. Is it okay?"

"It's perfect. I love everything they're serving, and I particularly love cioppino." I laugh. "I guess it's a good thing I didn't have much breakfast."

We go back and forth over the proposed idea, discussing the possibility of my doing this. Walker is definitely a politician, and he eventually sells me on it. He's still convinced that it's a member of my team, but I don't think so. The fire oozes up in my belly, and I want to prove to him and the rest of the team that not one of the five is guilty. I trust them all completely, and none of them would betray me.

"Caroline, I know you think we're wrong. I want to be proven wrong. Tim Carpenter at the cosmetics company is an option, but if nothing else, we're ruling them out."

"Thanks, Walker. I'll do it."

When lunch is over, I've decided I like Walker. He may be a consummate politician, but he really does want the city I love to prosper and do well.

He gives me a warm embrace. "I'll have someone contact you on your cell about how you're going to get started."

I nod. "We'll talk soon."

As I drive home, I think about what lying to my team to prove they aren't involved is going to do to the culture of my company. In the end, I feel like this is my best chance of figuring out what's happened so I can keep my company alive.

chapter

thirteen

MASON

MY MEETING WITH CAMERON IS WRAPPING UP. "When are you leaving for New York?" he asks.

"I take the red-eye out tonight."

"Are you flying commercially?"

"No, I have a NetJet along with Jim's man who's going with me."

"Any word on Annabelle?"

"Not really," I reply. "I'm hoping we can track her. Right now, I'm concentrating on Titan Software going public."

"I think we're all excited. My understanding is that Adam and Eve have been quiet."

"Yes, but they've prepared us for something big. I assume you'll be at the development site tomorrow, watching the typical happenings and making sure we don't have another SketchIt or Pineapple Technologies. Cora Perry and her team will be on site throughout the day, too."

"We're bringing all the big guns out on this one."

"Good. With their threat of something big, I want everyone to be on the lookout."

"Agreed. What are we going to do once we catch Adam and Eve?"

"After we celebrate and go through the long ordeal of a trial, we'll probably be retired."

Cameron snorts. "I hope that isn't the case, but I know the road is long and winding." He stands and heads toward my door. "Have a good night. Fly safe, and we'll look for you when the bell rings in the morning and celebrate the start of Titan Software going public. And don't do anything stupid while you're gone. Believe it or not, we do prefer having you here."

SHN always spends a half day celebrating a company going public. The stock market closes at two o'clock on the West Coast, so we usually have the television on all morning and watch the early stock price changes. Dillon typically arrives by six to watch the opening bell ring, which is why I go. Typically the launch team of that client joins him, but it depends if they're close to a second launch. Most go about their day as usual. Dillon has typically determined that we'll sell a small portion of our stock when it reaches a particular price. This allows us to get the money we've invested back out. Once the final bell rings, the entire team will stop to celebrate with champagne and drinks. Titan Software will be a good win for us. It'll be strong, not something that will swing the market one way or the other, but we'll make good money.

Gathering up my things so I can get to the airport, I pick up my phone and get a glance at a candid photo I took of CeCe. I've never done that before. In the picture, she has a cup of coffee in her hands and is looking away. The lighting is soft, and she looks angelic. I actually took the picture about a year ago on accident and never erased it. She's so beautiful. I stare at it wistfully and wish I could get her to come with me to New York, but I just don't feel it's safe.

My phone rings, the caller ID showing it's Jim.

"Hey, Mason. You got a minute?" he asks when I answer.

"Sure. We're ready for Titan to go public tomorrow."

"You have Jack Reece going with you, correct?"

"Yes. We spoke this morning, and he's all set. We're flying out tonight on a red-eye private plane heading for JFK."

"Nothing like cutting it pretty close." Jim snickers.

"I can't really say this where it doesn't sound too contrite, but I'm getting used to this. It isn't worth going in early. The jetlag won't let me sleep much the night before anyway. Plus, it's just the easiest way to approach this. There's so much going on since I've been back that I constantly feel like I'm playing catch-up."

"I understand. Will you be able to get any sleep on the plane?

"Jack and I are going to try. It'll be a short night, but it'll be worth it," I tell him.

"Great news. We'll be watching, and my team in New York will be meeting you. Jack has briefed them on your itinerary, so you should be good to go. Call me if anything comes up. Now, before you go, I have something I wanted to run by you."

"Yes?"

I hear him take a big breath over the phone. "I think Annabelle may have surfaced at her sister's."

I sit up straight in my chair and become hyper alert. "What do you mean you *think* she surfaced?"

"We've caught some activity at her sister's home down in Orange County. Someone just showed up last night, and with a hyperbolic mic, we were pretty positive someone was moving around inside the house, and that it was her."

"Are you calling the FBI? The police?" I don't know if that's good or bad. My stomach clenches.

"I think it's something worth investigating. Before we call the FBI or police, we'd like confirmation. We were thinking you could talk to her and see if you can't get her to come in on her own. It'll play better for her in the long run." Jim always did share my soft spot for her. He was protective like my team, worried she was a gold digger, but he'd spent time with her, and we weren't sure if she was involved in this mess. "How about instead of coming back to San Francisco from New York, you meet me down in Orange County. You can fly into John Wayne Airport. I'll pick you up, and then we'll head over to her sister's place in Anaheim Hills."

"Do you think we can just knock on the door?"

"I think that's a good place to start."

I think about it. I would rather her explain to me and the FBI what happened and why she disappeared. "I can meet you. I don't want a big tactical force on her. Hopefully we can talk her into getting a lawyer and talking to the FBI at the very least."

"Great. We'll see you when you can get to the OC."

"That's the tricky part. Tomorrow's Tuesday, and I'm in New York all day. I'm having dinner tomorrow night in New York and want to see a couple people while I'm in town. If I come on Thursday, will that give us enough time?"

"Absolutely. My team will stake out the house 24-7 and maybe have more of a routine."

"Okay, that works for me. Maybe we can get her to talk."

"Great. I'll watch for the flight plan and expect to see you Thursday morning. I'll also get you set up in a hotel."

"Not the Disney Hotel, please. Maybe something in Newport Beach?"

Jim lets out a hearty laugh. "Has someone made a reservation for you at the Disney Hotel before?"

"Cameron talked my admin into making the reservation there since it's the 'happiest place on Earth.' They thought I needed to lighten up."

"Mary did that? I can't see her falling for one of Cameron's practical jokes."

"Yes, it was Mary, but she hasn't done it again since. Of course, telling her that I would book her in a cheap motel the next time she traveled and make sure there were crying babies on both sides of her on the flight convinced her I was serious."

"You can be brutal. But you know Cameron was behind it."

"Of course. I got him back. I might have sent roses to Hadlee—they were newly dating, and she'd just lost her house to a fire."

"I bet that got him upset."

"It was fantastic."

He's laughing, and I know he would have done something similar. "See you Thursday. Call me if you need me."

The office is emptying out, and we need to get going. I see Jack pacing out in reception. "Jack, let me make one final call and then we're good to go."

"You're the boss."

I pull up FaceTime on my phone and dial CeCe. She comes on, and she looks stunning. I'd like to think I'm behind the glow, but she's always beautiful. I don't know how I got so lucky to land her. Every time I see her, my heart goes pitter patter. I'm so excited and ready for the rest of our lives to start; I just need this other crap to stop. "Hey, are you ready to go?"

"Getting there. I've got my schedule set. I won't be back until late Friday or maybe Saturday."

"Were you successful in getting a meeting with Angus Morgan?"

"I was, thanks to you and Greer."

"That's all Greer. Vanessa may be my PR person for Fashion Week, but she's Greer's cousin and essentially her sister."

"Meeting with him is a great way to expand our relationship since Todd from his team is on our advisory team. I'm also talking to people from several of the big financial houses who are interested in possibly taking future investments public."

"Oh." She smiles broadly. "You're going to be wined and dined."

"I am."

"Angus has told stories about strip clubs. Just so you know, you can look, but you can't touch."

I throw my head back and laugh really hard. That's not my thing. "When I have perfection at home, why would I need to look anywhere else?"

She blushes, and I can't help but fall further in love. She just doesn't understand how beautiful she really is. I know the papers have told her that for years, but she always felt like there was some other reason they were always saying nice things about her, because it was always followed by a 'but.' It'll be my mission in life to make sure she knows that she's truly a beautiful woman.

"Why are you trying to butter me up?"

I try to act all indignant because she isn't too far off. "I'm totally not buttering you up, but I'm hoping that while I'm gone, we can maybe do a little bit of naked FaceTime."

"You are funny. But if that's what it takes, I'm all in." She looks around, and then I see her pull her breast out of her scoop-neck top. She fingers her nipple. "Is this what you're hoping for?"

"Ces, you know I'm in an all-glass office, and now I have a raging hard-on."

"I miss you already."

"I'll talk to you tomorrow, and then I'll show you what naked FaceTime is."

She bites the corner of her lip, and it drives me crazy. "I may not be able to wait for you."

"You're killing me, woman."

"Just making sure you know what's here and waiting for you." She points the phone down, and I see her slowly moving her skirt up to her innermost sanctum. If she doesn't stop soon, this woody in my pants will take time to go away.

"I'm hanging up now," I warn.

"Talk to you tomorrow. Fly safe. I've got to go take care of myself now that I'm all amped up."

"You and me both. Good night, sweetheart."

"Good night." She moans just to tempt me.

Once we disconnect, I have to take a few deep breaths. I think of my mother, then my aunt, and my dick begins to deflate. I'll need to stroke it off at some point, but I'd much prefer to do it while I'm alone and with CeCe on FaceTime, not with my bodyguard in the same room.

When the bell rings at the close, I'm exhausted, but overall it was a good day. Dinner tonight is with James Patrick, the CEO of Stanley Morton, one of the largest banks on Wall Street. I'll need to pound some serious caffeine and be grateful for the time change. I'll be running from one meeting to the next for the next three days, but it does feel good to be back at work and doing what I love, knowing that when I go home at night, I have a stunning woman in my bed.

chapter

fourteen

MASON

MY TRIP TO NEW YORK WAS THANKFULLY UNEVENTFUL. I rang the bell with my client, and it was a nice celebration. In our first day, we made back our investment and then some. That's always a good sign, to watch our investment be embraced by the public.

My dinners with James Patrick and Angus Morgan were very productive. With Angus, we talked about making some aggressive moves, but having advice from him and Todd really makes me feel more comfortable with that. I shouldn't doubt Dillon. He's a brilliant financial mind.

When we take a company public, we tend to do so with the same two banks. One of them is struggling to keep up with the number of offers we have. Sara is a machine, and they have huge legal departments, but they struggle to meet their own deadlines. Stanley Morton would like to replace them. I'm not sure I'm ready to make such a big change, but it's nice to be courted. I committed to doing two deals with them next month. They make money on the shares we put up for sale, so banks are often making us promises. I'll let Sara figure out if they're a good fit, but for now, they have my blessing.

When I step off the plane in Orange County, the warmth and smell of the Pacific and orange blossoms are like a blanket. I love it here. If I could, I'd move SHN down here. The weather is consistently good, and the cost of living is a little lower for our staff. Maybe one day, but now that I have CeCe to consider, that may not be as easy.

A member of Jim's team is parked on the tarmac at the base of the stairs. I've been sitting for the last five hours, and I could walk into the terminal if they'd let us, but in the VIP section, we're allowed this perk. We discussed this on the way out, but Jack insists it's safer.

Jim and Jack flank me as they drive me to my hotel. "We've had a team of two sitting on the house around the clock since she's returned. We're listening to conversations she's having over the phone." Jim hands me a large manila envelope. "Those are the transcripts. Look them over and see if anything stands out to you. You know the players and my team doesn't."

I nod.

"Jack and I will meet you for breakfast tomorrow morning, and then we'll make our way over. Traffic will be heavy, but we should make it within an hour."

I blanch. An hour? I forget the traffic here sucks. Maybe San Francisco isn't such a bad thing. Who cares about the endless gray days when the longest you're in a rideshare is thirty minutes?

"So what's the plan? Just go knock on the door?"

"Yep. We'll knock and hope she answers," Jack says simply.

"Will we call the FBI or the police?"

"I don't want to be too aggressive with her. We know where she is, and my goal would be for us to talk her into giving herself up."

We pull into the hotel driveway, and once we've climbed out of the SUV, Jim leads me into the elevators along with three others. I look at a wall of shoulders, which is shocking given I'm a tall guy myself. I'm starting to feel a bit claustrophobic when the elevators open into the living room of my suite.

"We set you up over there." Jim points to the room on the left side of the suite. "There will be two men up and working here in the living room at all times. The other room will be used by my team."

"Thanks. What time do you want to go down and eat in the morning?" I ask.

"How about eight? I'd like to be on the road by nine at the latest."

I nod. "See you then."

I put my bag on the bed. My business suit I used in New York is worthless here in Orange County; the summer weight wool is too much for even winter here. I pull out khakis and a dress shirt for the morning, stopping to think about the shirt. I realize Annabelle picked it out. Maybe that's a good omen for tomorrow.

I try CeCe over FaceTime, but she doesn't pick up. I send her a text instead.

Me: Hey. I made it to Orange County. Nice to be in the same time zone, but I'm exhausted and going to bed. Sorry I missed you. Hope you're having a good night. Talk to you tomorrow. XOXO M.

My body clock is so disjointed after starting the week on the West Coast, working like crazy for three days on the East Coast, and then heading back to the West Coast—but not at home. Honestly, it doesn't faze me much. I've been tired since I was sick. I can't wait to get back to my presickness energy.

When my head hits the pillow, I think about CeCe for half a second and then pass out. She does appear in my dreams. Sometimes it's a seductive sex dream, and other times we're running from Annabelle. That's the part that worries me.

The following morning, I wander out of my room at eight in need of an IV of caffeine.

"Are you ready for today's gymnastics?" Jim asks.

"I'm ready as I'll ever be. Have they seen her?"

"Yes, she does a few small errands but mostly stays at the house. She talks to her sister almost daily. Her sister is working out of town, so she's by herself. What do you know about her family?"

"She has two sisters and a brother. Their father was an alcoholic and could be abusive, but I don't know much more than that. I wanted to meet them at the beginning, but she always pushed back. I figured she was embarrassed by them and didn't press it. I can't even tell you I know their names."

"Have you decided what you want to say to her?"

"You mean besides why the fuck did she disappear after I was poisoned?"

"Well, that's a start, given that she may not have been behind the poisoning."

"As you know, we broke up before it all went down, so maybe she's down here licking her wounds. Do we know if she's using her cell phone?"

"No. It may be here, but it isn't on or doesn't have its GPS chip activated."

We start the drive across Orange County, and the 55 freeway is jam-packed and slow. "How do people do this every day?"

"The Bay Area is worse."

"Yes, but if you don't want to deal with it, you can always take a train or a bus. That doesn't really happen down here."

It's almost painful that we go less than fifteen miles and it takes over an hour. It isn't even rush hour.

As we exit the freeway and head toward her sister's home, the guys who are watching the house call Jim. "She's just left. We're following her," they say on speakerphone.

We pull to the side of the road until we know at least the direction she's headed. If she's just going to get coffee or running a quick errand, we can remain here for when she returns.

"She's heading for the 55."

"Let's see where our little friend is going this morning," Jim muses.

The guys pass us going the other way, but I didn't see her. We swing around and join the tail. She drives in the same ugly traffic we were in to a huge mall just blocks from my hotel.

"This is South Coast Plaza," Jim announces.

"I think I can see our hotel from here."

"Not quite, but almost."

She parks and walks into Neiman Marcus. One of Jim's team gets out and follows her in. She lives for shopping, and I know from experience this could be a while. We park and head in to find the team in the store.

Once I'm inside, the men tell me where to find her. I'm nervous about confronting her. I don't want a scene, and I'm hoping I can convince her to turn herself in.

I spot her looking through some clothing racks of sundresses, and I walk up. "Hello, Annabelle."

She turns and stares at me, clearly startled with a look of fear on her face.

"Mason, what are you doing here?"

"Annabelle, we've been trying to reach you. Are you okay?"

"Yes, I'm fine. You can't be here."

"Annabelle, we need to talk about what happened. I was in the hospital and was in bad shape, and no one could get a hold of you."

"You broke up with me. I didn't want to return anybody's phone calls or have anything to do with you or your snobby friends. I didn't know what was going on, and I don't care." She tries to walk away from me, but I follow her.

"The police and FBI in San Francisco want to talk to you. They want to make sure you weren't part of what happened to me."

"I don't even know what happened to you."

"I was poisoned with wolfsbane. The person who poisoned me had access to my home. Please, can you take some time to talk to the FBI and the police?"

She spots Jim and begins to move quicker. She's superfast and has the advantage that she knows the footprint of the store better than we do. "Mason, go away! I'm not interested in anything you have to say to me."

Trying to remain calm, I attempt to reason with her. "Annabelle, why are you threatening CeCe?"

"I can't talk to you anymore. Go away!" She runs around me and heads to the women's restroom, quickly ducking inside. She'll have to come out eventually.

As we wait, I share our brief conversation. Jim looks over at me and asks, "What do you think?"

"Something's not right. She's glossing over her threats to CeCe. I hate to admit that I think she's more involved in this. I wouldn't say she's behind it, but she certainly knows something."

It's been a while. Jim sends one of the females from his team into the bathroom. She's gone a few moments and then comes back out. "No one's inside."

"Where did she go?" Jim gets on his earpiece. "Does anyone have eyes on her car?" He listens for a few seconds. "It's still in the parking lot?"

chapter

fifteen

CECE

"THERE'S A MISS CORA PERRY HERE TO SEE YOU."

I hadn't put her on my schedule, but I was expecting her. It's interesting that she didn't identify that she works for the FBI. "Please send her in."

Cora follows Christy into my office. She's a pretty woman. Probably has a nice figure under her bulky navy pantsuit. I've always noticed that she wears blouses with a bit of color with her black and blue pantsuits. Today she has a soft pink blouse that makes her blue eyes sparkle, her fair complexion rosy in comparison. Her short blonde hair is curly and cute. She smiles warmly as she enters. "Wow! What a beautiful view!"

I can't help but like her. "Thank you. It's pretty stunning, particularly on a clear day like today. We can see into the North Bay beyond Berkeley, and we can see a touch of Piedmont and a little bit south of Oakland."

"That's pretty spectacular." She nods as she takes a seat across from me.

"I notice you didn't identify yourself as FBI."

She smiles broadly. "Well, we don't want to show our panties to just everyone yet."

"Good point."

"You employ over five thousand people here in San Francisco?"

"We do. There are roughly a thousand in this building doing administrative and design work, and the remaining work in our factory in South San Francisco."

"That's impressive. What made you want to produce here at home and not where labor is less expensive?"

"Pretty simple, really. I wanted to be able to visit my manufacturing at any time, just like I go over to Nordstrom or other places that carry our lines and see what they look like on the shelves and watch how people respond."

"I'm impressed."

I sigh. "It would be a giant mess if this shut us down."

"It would be pretty debilitating to San Francisco as well."

I sit back and look out at the view we were just admiring. "Yes, it would be hard on a lot of people. But I will tell you in confidence that I've already decided that, no matter what, I will personally finance the company to get us through all of this. It isn't my preference, but I have the money in a trust from my grandfather. I pay well for San Francisco, but I still know how difficult it is to live here. Many of my employees live check to check, so I'd rather make sure everyone is able to cover their debts while we realign our plans."

"Not many CEOs would do that."

"No, but Metro isn't your typical company. We do our best to care about our employees."

"You do know that Walker's going to use this information."

"He's a politician through and through."

"I think he likes you."

I smile, and I know Cora could become a friend after this mess is over. "I think he likes me for what I bring to the table, not me personally."

"Don't be so sure of yourself. He's really going hard at the director of the FBI over how the White-Collar agents dropped the ball. I'm glad it wasn't my team."

"Honestly, I'm just grateful that somebody picked it up."

"Yes, me, too. I love your cosmetics and would hate to see you have to close."

I smile. "I love to hear that you like our products. We'll make sure that before you leave, you're well stocked. We don't have our latest line, obviously, given it's what introduced us, but I think you'll like what we have."

"Honestly, I shouldn't take anything for ethics' sake."

"I understand. What we have here are all free samples that we give to people and donate to homeless and abused women's shelters across the city."

"Well, nice segue into the reason I'm here. I understand you met with Walker about the plan."

I nod.

"I would like my team to formulate the emails you follow up with. Do you currently have something you routinely send as an attachment to an email?"

"Probably about a half dozen or so things regularly."

"Great. Can you forward a few to me? My team and I will go through them today and send you an email that we can have them open on their cell phones that will ghost their phones. We'll be able to track anything they do with any Metro-related email. Even if they forward it to a personal account, we will then know if it's forwarded elsewhere and where the email is opened and how often."

"What if they don't open the email on their phones?"

"We can attach it to a cat video or something they'd like. Believe it or not, it's not hard to find something that people will click."

"Good to see it's so easy," I reply snarkily.

"I'm hoping, like you, that this proves all of your staff is clean and we need to concentrate our efforts elsewhere."

I knew I liked Cora. She read my mind—or she's talked to Walker about why I think we're looking in the wrong direction.

"I understand you've worked out with Walker what you're going to say and to whom," she continues.

"We did."

"Are you comfortable with that?"

"My biggest concern is what it'll do to our company culture. I've worked so hard on building it for the last ten years."

"I can see why that's a concern, but we should know somewhat quickly what information is being moved around. My team will also be working in the background when you send emails to any of the suspects."

"How does that work?"

"The original emails will be customized to each person. They'll have the others cc'd on them. They'll get emails, and through some algorithms we set up, they will know that any email that goes to, say, Evelyn, is supposed to talk about launching, but with Angela's emails, it'll talk about a name change. That way, everyone is in the loop from a unique perspective. It may sound complicated, but it happens so quickly that most won't even notice the difference."

"If I respond from my cell phone, does that change anything?"

"Not at all. For anything that goes through your email system, there is an algorithm that makes the adjustment happen." We sit in silence a few seconds. "I understand your concern about the reaction if your team finds out you did this without telling them. My suggestion would be that once you know no one on the team is involved, you can say someone outside the company—or maybe your mother—talked some sense into you and just beg for their forgiveness. Most people understand you're not perfect."

She must read all my "fan mail" that Christy goes through. "Thank you. It'll be rough for a while, I'm sure, though if it gets out, I think they'll understand. At least I hope so."

"When are you talking to them?"

"I was planning on it tomorrow, but maybe we need to wait to send out this ghost software and the emails first."

"If you can forward me emails this afternoon, we'll be ready for tomorrow. That's no problem. My team does this quite often."

"How often do you *not* catch someone?"

"What matters is we know something quickly."

I notice that she didn't answer even remotely. The thought disappoints and depresses me that someone I trust with everything has done this to me.

"I meet with Christy every morning at about eight." I bring up my computer and look at my schedule. "Right now, I have one-on-one meetings with the rest of the team throughout the morning."

"Then we'll ghost their cell phones this afternoon."

"Thanks." I hate that we have to resort to this, but in the back of my mind, at least I know this will clear my team.

"You're going to pull this off without any problems," she assures me.

"I'm really glad you guys are here to help me."

"We want this to work. We don't want you to have to dip into your trust to keep your company alive and save this beautiful view."

"Are you from the Bay Area?"

"No, I grew up in Colorado. My father was a professor at Colorado State University."

"Really? What did he teach?"

"Philosophy."

That's shocking to me. When I think of a philosophy professor, I think of a guy with long hair and Birkenstocks, a real hippy who likes to contemplate the meaning of life. "Wow. What does he think about you being an FBI agent?"

"He's an old hippy from the sixties, and I'm the youngest of eight. He hates it, but all my brothers and sisters are in law enforcement. My oldest brother is in bond enforcement, two are lawyers, one's a police officer, one works for the Sheriff's office, plus me in the FBI."

I like Cora. She's really down to earth and easygoing, and I feel like I may have someone for her to date.

"Are you single?"

"Unfortunately, yes. Not many men are comfortable with a woman who carries a gun. Although in this town, they worry more about my working in Cybercrimes."

"Oh, I bet. So many feel they're amateur hackers."

"Exactly."

She puts her hand on my arm. "This is going to be okay. There are a lot of eyes on this."

"I appreciate all your team's help. I should warn you—I consider myself a part-time matchmaker."

She laughs. "I've been to a few partners meetings. You've pretty much matched most of the team, haven't you?"

"Not quite. A few found them on their own. I know a lot of people, so I make introductions between people who seem to work well together."

"When this is over, I'm open if you think you know someone who might want to hang out, but I'm waiting to see how your matchmaking goes for yourself."

I smile. "It's something that's been in the works for a long time, but it's a slow, slow process. I'm not pushing him in the least."

"That's fine, but make sure you take care of yourself."

"Oh, I've got myself covered, but for you, let's see if I can find somebody who's a little less intimidated by your technical and gun-slinging skills."

"Just don't make it Walker Clifton."

"God, I wouldn't do that to anyone."

She laughs as we walk out of my office. Christy has a large sack full of cosmetics ready to go. "Here you go."

"Oh my goodness! What am I going to do with all of this?"

"Wear it proudly knowing that we do not test on animals and that these samples are available in any department store, so it isn't any kind of bribe. They're fun to try and share them with any of your friends."

"Caroline, I appreciate this, and thank you. It's very kind of you."

"Of course."

I wave to her as she gets on the elevator, then return to my desk. Christy hands me a stack of messages.

"Any of them interesting?" I ask.

"Walker Clifton wants to go out for drinks tonight."

"That's not interesting—that's boring."

"Maybe it'll get Mason to move a bit faster."

"He's only been out of the hospital a few weeks, and we're practically living together. How much faster should we be going?"

"I'm ready to roll up my sleeves with your mother and a wedding planner."

I laugh. "Slow down. We are not anywhere near that."

I pick five emails and forward them with attachments to Cora.

Within an hour, she sends me the email she'd like me to send to the team. If anyone doesn't open them tonight, the team will send them something they will open that matches their interests.

I pick up my cell phone and call Mason. I just want to hear his voice.

"Hey, beautiful."

It warms me to my toes when he says that.

"Hi. I met with Cora Perry this afternoon."

"Are you all set?"

"We're close. What are your plans for tonight?" I ask.

"I'm still down in Orange County."

"That's disappointing. I miss you."

"I miss you, too. Soon, sweetheart. I promise."

"I'm going to head home shortly and take a long bath with lots of bubbles and drink some serious wine."

"Do you want me to call you later tonight? It doesn't have to be a saucy call."

"I'd like that."

"I'll call you when I get back to my hotel room, then. It's all going to work out. I can feel it in my bones."

"I know. I can, too. Cora said they do this more often than we want to know."

"That's scary."

"I agree," I say. "She also didn't tell me that it never works."

"What do you mean?"

"When I asked, she didn't deny that they've never found the culprit."

"CeCe, I know you trust each of these women like your best friends. We'll get through this together and get it all figured out. I have to admit, I'm a little jealous that you're catching your saboteur faster than we're catching ours."

A feeling of calmness overcomes me. "Thank you. That's what I needed to hear."

I hang up and finish a few more things in my office. Heading home a bit later, I do exactly as I promised: I eat a small dinner that my housekeeper left for me and then draw a bath with lots of bubbles and a lilac scent. Soaking in the tub, I mentally prepare for my day tomorrow, walking through what I'm to say and how I want to share my news.

A text message pops up from Cora: **Everyone has opened the message and downloaded the ghost software. You're good to go.**

My anxiety rises. This needs to go well.

When my bathwater turns cold, I climb out and dry off leisurely, then lay out my clothes for tomorrow, needing to do something to calm my nerves. I have a new designer who did a piece for me, a cross between business and couture. The pants are a dark forest green, wide but not obnoxious. The top matches the pants and has geometric cutouts around the zigzag collar, and the blazer is the same color in silk with a tunic collar. I have a tan pair of Manolo Blahnik mules to go with it. I always feel better in a new outfit. The green will make the gold flecks in my brown eyes pop.

I debate taking a sleeping pill but worry I'll have a hangover from it tomorrow, so I just climb into bed.

I toss and turn. I never hear from Mason, which bothers me, and I begin to wonder why he's in Orange County. I don't recall any of their investments being there. This gets my brain going, and I try to put it aside, to no avail. The clock ticks by two, then three thirty. I remember looking at the clock again at almost five.

I must have finally fallen asleep just as my alarm goes off at six. I'm not a morning person. Life sucks this early. I know people like to work out in the morning, but even just the thought gives me hives. I want so much to cover my head in the blankets and just go back to sleep.

Misty looks at me from the side of the bed. She needs to go out. Thank goodness I live across the street from a large city park, so it isn't too bad. I grab her leash and a ball, and we walk across the street. The morning is brisk and cold. She does her business quickly, even for her, and starts tugging me along back to my house. "I don't blame you, Misty."

We walk back inside, and she immediately goes to her bed and parks herself, burrowing under a blanket and looking at me like I'm crazy to go back out in the ugly morning.

"I'd love to stay and cuddle, trust me, but I have to go in today."

She tilts her head to the side as if asking me if I'm sure.

My car service will pick me up in an hour, so I quickly shower and blow out my hair. When I'm ready to go, Angela has a cup of coffee ready for me. "Would you like a quick breakfast, Miss Caroline?"

"Thank you, no. I have a meeting this morning."

"Dinner tonight for you and Mr. Mason?"

"He's traveling right now, so I'm not sure. We can order in if he comes over."

I head out the door and close my eyes, trying to meditate during the drive over. I've never really done the meditation thing, but I'm looking for anything that can help me right now.

chapter

sixteen

MASON

JIM AND I ARE EATING OUR THIRD BREAKFAST TOGETHER. This was supposed to take a half day, but now we're at three.

"My team is turning Orange County upside down trying to locate Annabelle again," Jim explains. "She never went back to her car and seemed to just disappear. We have someone sitting at the house she was staying in, but she hasn't shown up. My team breached her sister's home yesterday, and we're confident she hasn't been back."

"Have you checked any flight or train manifests?"

Jim takes a drink of his orange juice. "We have. And we've checked her credit cards, and her sister's cards. They aren't showing any transactions."

"Where could she have gone? Have you found any reason she's being so evasive?"

Jim has a mouth full of scrambled eggs and simply shakes his head.

"This isn't good."

"We'll continue to watch her sister's place, and we'll step up on her friends' places in San Francisco."

"I'm going to return to San Francisco," I tell him. "I have too much to do to sit here and wait for her to resurface."

The fifty-minute flight back to San Francisco was shorter than the ride from the airport to my office. I miss those heliports that New York City has. When I finally get to the office, many are out at lunch, which is almost a welcome reprieve; I'm able to start up my computer and do a few things before the line forms out my door.

Cameron comes in and places a cup of coffee in front of me. "How was New York?"

"Productive. I had some good meetings afterward. I go back again next week."

"We should get an apartment in New York so you can leave clothes and toiletries and just get on a plane."

"Not a bad thought. It would be a decent investment, and a possible perk for the employees. But that's not why you want to talk to me."

Cameron shrugs noncommittally. "I guess I'm looking to get an update on Annabelle."

"Did you know that I left New York on Thursday and flew to Orange County?"

His face is a combination of surprise and confusion. "No. Does anyone know? Did you see her?"

"I talked to her for a minute and then she disappeared."

"Disappeared? How did she do that? She's half your size. I would think your long legs would be able to keep up with her."

"She ran into a bathroom, and we waited. When one of Jim's team went in the bathroom a few minutes later, she wasn't there."

"Was there a second entrance?"

"Nope. We don't know what happened. She's in the wind."

"She's showing she's not innocent."

"I agree."

Cameron slaps his hands on his thighs with a loud clap. "Finally!"

"I never disagreed with anyone. I liked her but decided she was so intent on being in my space that I'd rather keep my enemy close."

"Do they know anything else?"

"Nothing. We're back to waiting."

"Got it."

Cameron stands to leave. "Oh, before I forget, in that pile of paper on your desk is a copy of the notes from the interviews of the hackers that was sent over by Cybercrimes. They want us to look through it and see if we recognize anything."

"I'll do it. Thanks."

"Welcome back."

I spend the afternoon immersed in my work, trying to catch up between what feels like a thousand interruptions. When they finally stop, I look up and see only a few people are left in the office. It's dark outside. *Where did the day go?*

I had put aside the Cybercrimes report earlier, but now I can start to go through it. It's a stack of paper about an inch thick. The beginning describes the location where they grabbed everyone. From there, it leads into each of the thirty-five people—twenty-three men and twelve women—who were arrested and their interviews.

As I read through, I notice the hackers come from all walks of life; a few are immigrants, but many grew up here in the States. There is an overall theme of hate of the 1 percent.

As I'm making my way through the specifics of each interview, one of the names looks familiar to me. I can't help but wonder if I've met this person before. Thomas Van der Wolfe. It stops me because it's a three-name last name, and I don't see that often. I do a query in our system where we track all our contacts. He doesn't show up, but there's a thread in the back of my brain that I can't quite unravel. I finish going through the report, but nothing else sticks out to me.

How do I know Thomas Van der Wolfe?

When I close up, it's after eleven. I put in almost twelve hours at the office, and I'm exhausted. I call up my car service and let them know I'll be ready in ten minutes, then tuck the Cybercrimes report in my bag. Maybe it'll come to me.

chapter

seventeen

CECE

I ARRIVE AT THE OFFICE RIGHT ON TIME. Evelyn leaves me a message that she's running behind and suggests we meet for drinks after work at the Fairmont. That's fine. She's the one I'm least worried about. Christy gives me a few minutes to get situated and then joins me in my office, bringing in two coffees and a bear claw.

"You know me too well."

She smiles. "I know life is stressful right now."

"I like to bury my stress in sugar and carbs. Who doesn't?"

We walk through my schedule for this week and the next. "I may end up heading to New York," I tell her. "I'll keep you posted."

"Tim Carpenter from Cosmetics, Inc., wanted to meet you the next time you were in New York. Would you like me to tentatively set that up?"

Not a chance. Plus, I'm more afraid he'll look at my negative P&L and not want Metro. I'd rather live with the notion that he wants Metro than learn that this speed bump is his idea of a stop sign. "That was before this mess started. I have a feeling we need to be a little stronger financially."

"He knows you're a diamond. Don't let this mess convince you otherwise."

"I'm considering launching the line we developed with a few changes."

"You know the business. Just let me know if I can help in any way."

Her quick answers and unwavering support prove to me that she's not involved. "I don't know what I'd do without you."

"You probably have a better social life since I push everyone away." She winks at me and smiles.

"You do exactly as I ask. You know I keep my circle small."

"I know things are slow with Mason, so maybe a side date with someone else will get him moving."

"Cora said that yesterday. I'm really okay with slow."

"I want to plan a wedding before I retire."

"You know the R-word is a bad word around here," I warn.

"It's on the horizon. Not super close, but Fred is talking about buying a Winnebago and driving all over the US and Canada."

Fred is Christy's husband. They met when they were a little older. He had kids from a previous marriage, so they didn't have any of their own, but they have several four-legged furry ones that go almost everywhere with them. "You can take the summer off. I'm good with that."

She smiles. "You have a meeting with Becca in a few. Can I get you anything?"

"No, I'll return a few emails. Just send her in when she arrives unless I'm on the phone."

"Let me know if you need anything."

I write a quick note to Cora and let her know the change with Evelyn, but all is on track.

It seems like time passes quickly, and then Becca walks in. I don't even realize she's in my office until she's sitting across from me. "Hello," she says enthusiastically.

"Hey." I stop composing an email and give her one hundred percent of my attention. "How are things going with Jeremy and his team at Accuracy Communications?"

"It's slow right now, but we see the light at the end of the tunnel. Some people will never be convinced that we don't test on animals. They've read about it on the internet and seen some horrible pictures, so it must be true."

I sigh. "I've been dealing with those people almost my entire life. A gossip rag reported I married the actual Devil—I could never convince them otherwise. I'm having a secret love affair with my brother—besides the ick factor, they still believe it. I've been matched with Mick Jagger. I've been matched with most A-list actors—both married and single—because I talked to them at a party. No one ever believes that I'm not nearly as exciting as the press makes me out to be. I get it."

She giggles. "I guess it could be worse. You were matched with Lucas Dreams."

"That's true. After it came out, he did ask me out. But he was a dud. Despite being one of the most handsome men in film, he was short and incredibly vain. He didn't like me wearing heels because it made me taller than him. One of my worst dates ever."

"I bet his publicist set that up so he could use it as an excuse to call you."

"That's what I thought he had done, too, but I politely went on our only date and left him at the table when some woman sat in his lap." I'm getting off track in my avoidance of bringing up my sticky subject. "Anyway, so I don't throw off your calendar, what else do you have to do?"

"I think we're almost done. Right now, Accurate is throwing most of the work my way. We'll have some stragglers, but I think we're almost done."

"Great. I've been thinking, when I look at the P&L, it's pretty ugly. Honestly, we're negative over six million dollars on this." I can see her getting nervous. "I think I want to relaunch the line."

She isn't a good poker player. Her face contorts in a puzzled look, and she's trying to make sure she's heard me right. "What do you mean?"

"Well, I think we launch the same color palette. We can change the names, but all the packaging and merchandising are ready to go. As you pointed out, our clients are loyal to us and will buy our authentic product knowing there's a fake out there," I say with much more confidence than I feel.

"Are you sure? Accurate seems to be thinking otherwise."

"I have to do something. The six million in red on our P&L is devastating, and if we don't do something, we're going to shut our doors for good."

"Oh… okay… yeah…."

I can tell she thinks I'm ready to step in a big pile of sticky poo, which I would be if I were actually going to do this. Bringing out my best acting skills, I continue. "You've already done all the public relations for this. I'm not expecting that it would take anything else planning-wise from you. We'll figure out a way to make it work."

"I understand. I guess we should launch so we can save all the jobs associated with this."

"Exactly." I must be able to sell ice to an Eskimo.

We wrap up our meeting, and after she leaves, I shake my head. I can't believe I just lied to her. I could see the disappointment on her face when I told her what the plan was. She knows better than anyone that this is a bad idea. The PR blowback is only going to get the animal rights people more inflamed. This only confirms why the idea that it's anyone on my team is wrong. I hope this is a good plan.

I'm immersed in some spreadsheets when Christy buzzes me. "Jordan is here."

"Perfect. Send her in."

Jordan enters, giving me a run for my money when it comes to clothes. She's got a good benefactor, but so do many women here in San Francisco with all the tech billionaires. "Hello. Does this time still work for you?"

"Yes." I put my computer to sleep and give her my undivided attention. "How are things going now that the fall line isn't as heavy on your plate?"

She fidgets in her seat. "I wish I could say that I had so much work I was overwhelmed, but I don't, so for job security's sake, I'd love more to do."

"Good. I may have that for you."

She sits back, and what seemed like anxiousness was probably just nervousness. "I've been wrapping things up on the line we're launching for women of color."

"How is that progressing?"

"I should have ad slicks for you in a few days."

"We didn't use the same fall colors, right?"

"No. We used two that overlapped, a blue-black and a black-black, but the rest were more vibrant for olive and darker skin colors."

"Great. I signed the contracts for the models. Quite the coup to get Anna Martinez and Beyond to represent our line. Did they have any problems after the animal rights issue?"

"As soon as we knew, I went to both their publicists. They knew it was a smear campaign. They're an A-list actress and a singer, so they've experienced that before."

"That's very comforting."

"Everything will wrap up in the next two weeks, so I'm anxious to get going on whatever my next project will be. I've never seen anything like this."

"That makes two of us. You did a really outstanding job pulling the fall line together, getting all the focus groups ready and helping to procure names and advertising."

She sits forward, and I can tell she's upset. "I can't tell you how pissed off I was with that stupid Chinese company. I helped to design and develop an amazing line with stunning colors, packaging, and advertising. I know everyone lost out, and I hate to whine, but I was the only person one hundred percent dedicated to this launch, and now they have something to show for it and I don't."

I can't decide if she's working me or if she truly feels this way. "You were a dynamo, and quite honestly, when I look at the P&L and the loss of six million dollars to our bottom line, I think it's too much to waste. I've been talking to a lot of people, and the feeling is that we launch with new names and different packaging."

She stops what she's doing, sits up straight, and cocks her head to the side. "What do you mean?"

"We're going to use the same palette that we developed and designed, but we're going to give it a new name and new packaging. We don't need to bring together any focus groups;

we can just go with the second choice in both cases," I tell her, laying it on pretty thick.

"Okay. I think I can pull some of that together." I can see her mind going through what the second choices were. "We did a lot with the packaging, but the second choices were quite a bit down the list from the first choices."

"I think that'll be okay. At the very least, I think that's probably a great place to start. Maybe we can meet in the next few days to go over everything. Look at my calendar and throw something on it. Just keep it between us right now, if you don't mind."

She nods vigorously. "I'll have those for you in a few days."

"Of course, we want to keep the circle really small on this, as we don't want it to get back to the Chinese cosmetics company."

"I totally understand." She hesitates a minute. "You do realize there could be some major backlash with this."

"Unfortunately, the other major backlash is if we don't do this, we might as well close our doors and let everyone go."

"I understand. Thank you, Caroline."

As I watch her go, I'm not fully convinced she's my mole, but I'm not unconvinced either.

I can't talk to Scarlet, Evelyn's assistant, until I've talked to Evelyn, so I'll wait and grab her in the morning. As my day wraps up, Christy knocks on my door. "Do you need anything else?"

I smile at her. She's always so accommodating. "No, I'm good. I'm heading out in ten minutes to meet with Evelyn. Did she ever make it in today?"

"No, but she was online, so she was working from home."

A few minutes later, I head out of the office. Taking a rideshare across town, I think about the conversations today. I'm not sure that I did much to confirm where I stand with my team. After this, it'll be up to Cora and her team. Before I realize it, the Fairmont's doorman is opening the car door for me to step out.

I walk into the Tonga Room, which is a tiki bar. It's a little cheesy to be in the middle of Union Square, where the best shopping in the city is steps away, but the bar's décor is right out of a Disney set with tiki lanterns and bamboo furniture, and most drinks come with an umbrella—just what I need today.

I'm seated for barely a moment when I feel a tap on my shoulder. "Caroline! What are you doing here?"

I turn and see Janice standing in front of me. She's dressed to the nines and looks really good. I can tell it's an outfit from Jennifer. "Meeting a friend. What about you?"

Michael is eagerly standing with her. "When do I send wedding invitations out?"

My eyes must bulge out of my head. "Janice, Mason and I just started dating. I know we were friends for a very long time, but this is still a little new for us. I think Mason is still trying to get his feet underneath him after his illness."

"Oh, nonsense." She waves at an imaginary fly. "That man never knows what's best for him, but I do, and you're it."

"That's very sweet of you." Evelyn crosses the room and takes a seat next to me at the round cocktail table. "Can I introduce you? This is Evelyn Stevens. She is my right hand and oversees all the operations at Metro Composition." I turn to Evelyn and plead with my eyes to help us move on without the intrusion. "Evelyn, this is Mason's mother, Janice Sullivan Harris."

Evelyn nods so as not to invite any conversation. Hopefully it's enough to get Janice and her date to move on so we can talk. I don't want to talk about company business in front of Janice.

"You look familiar to me," Janice says to Evelyn. "Have we met?"

"I don't think so. It's nice to meet you."

With a lot of dramatic flair, Janice pulls her date up close to her, and they lock their arms. "I won't interrupt. I just wanted to introduce my boyfriend, Dr. Michael Frieman. He's a urologist here in San Francisco. Isn't he just the cutest?"

He turns bright red.

"It's great to meet you, Dr. Frieman," Evelyn says politely.

"Good to see you again Michael." He turns to me. "Maybe another time, you and Mason can join us for dinner."

"That sounds lovely. Enjoy your evening." I smile as they walk away, relieved that they aren't trying to join us.

The waiter takes our drink orders of two mai tais, and we settle in for a chat. Most of the time, our conversations out like this are mostly social, but we always get a little bit of business in.

Evelyn leans in. "That's Mason's mother?"

"That's her."

"Wow, she's nothing like I'd expected. He's so reserved, and she's so… not."

I shrug. "You can't pick your parents."

"Are you dating him?"

"I guess you could call it that. I'm pretty crazy about him and have been for a very long time."

"I thought he was living with someone?"

"They broke up. And Frederic and I are no longer together either."

"Does this mean you're officially off the market?"

"I'd like to think so, but it's still early. We're just trying to figure life out. He's got a lot going on. Plus, we have our own mess to contend with, so things are kind of crazy right now for me, too."

"Oh my goodness, here I was hoping it was the prince who would come through for you, but Mason Sullivan means you stay here and don't move to some tiny European country. That's a great thing." Our drinks arrive, and we toast. "To living in San Francisco," Evelyn says.

I take a healthy drink. "Let me tell you, a deserted island in the South Pacific sounds more and more delightful every day."

"Oh, I hear ya."

"I understand you worked from home today. Is everything okay? That's so unlike you."

"You won't believe this. Last night I put my unmentionables in the washer, and the drain got clogged with one of my bras. I woke up to water everywhere."

"Your bra did that?"

"I know. The itty-bitty-titty holder was small enough that when the water drained, the bra went with it, but it didn't fit in the actual drain, so it got clogged."

I can't help but laugh. "I'm sorry. I can just see your face when the repairman shows up and plucks a bra out of the drain."

"You have no idea. I was mortified. This guy's butt cheek cleavage was better than my regular cleavage, so it was the worst. I had repairmen coming and going all day."

"I'm sorry. Will your homeowner's insurance cover it?"

"Thankfully, yes. But it's a time suck right now."

We talk for a time about a few things going on, and when it comes time to talk about what's going on, we finish our first drinks and order a second round. I want to sleep tonight, and I'm hoping this helps.

I decide to dive right in. "I've been thinking about what you said about the fall line."

"Which thing I said?"

"I've been looking at the P&L. If we don't have a fall line, we'll be six million in the red, and I may have to make some major changes."

"I know. What are we going to do?"

"I've given this a lot of thought. I think what's probably best is that we work on releasing the same line with a different name in the same packaging,"

I watch her reaction carefully.

"Wow, that's a big deal. Are you sure that's what you want to do? I thought Vanessa said it was a really bad idea."

"She did, but she's not looking at our P&L. If we don't get this figured out, I may have to close the company my mother built and let over five thousand employees go."

"Couldn't you get a loan? Surely your personal assets would secure it."

She knows me too well to think I'd just walk away. "Everyone is telling me it's a bad idea to personally finance the company."

"I understand it's a lot of money, but it's also five thousand employees." She sits back and refuses a third drink. "I'm sorry. I think I'm just being selfish. I love Metro and all the people we work with. I'd probably do what I could to try to save it, too."

Okay, I'm feeling better. She likes our culture and the family we've built at Metro. "I didn't sleep at all last night worrying about this. I can't help but think we can save the company by doing this."

“I agree,” she says firmly. “No one will say we didn’t at least try to save the company.”

“Thanks. I spoke with Jordan, and she’ll have mockups for us in a few days. We can pick back up with most of our advertising and marketing plans. The machines can easily be recalibrated to accommodate the change in packaging. We might have only lost about a month of production.”

“That’d be huge.”

“My thoughts exactly.”

I pay the bill, and we walk out of the hotel. “We’re going to get this figured out,” she assures me and gives me a big hug. We both call up rideshares, and mine arrives first. “I hope to see you tomorrow.”

“My fingers are crossed.”

I don’t pay attention to the car other than to match his picture, license plate, and car make and color. A girl has to be safe, after all.

chapter

eighteen

CECE

"WHERE ARE YOU GOING? My house is in the other direction. I live in the city, not over the Bay Bridge in the East Bay."

I try the door handle, but it doesn't work. I push my shoulder into the door, hoping it's only stuck. I push harder, putting my whole weight into the door. It doesn't budge.

"I know where you live," he sneers. "We're going for a ride."

"What are you talking about? Take me back! Stop the car! Let me out!"

He ignores me and doesn't respond. When my panic levels out to an even terror, I begin to think clearly. The app documented my ride. My friends and family will look for me. I stare down at my phone.

I can call 911.

I dial.

Nothing.

I look to see how many bars are on my phone, and instead it reads "No Service." My heart races faster than it ever has.

I see the driver hold up a contraption that looks almost like a garage door opener. "This is called a cell phone jammer. No cell service for you."

My blood turns cold. I try the door again. I finally realize the child safety locks are engaged. I don't know what to do.

Holy crap. What did I get into?

I verified everything when he drove up.

What has set this guy off?

I look frantically around me. People are busily going about their day, heading home for the evening, driving over the Bay Bridge and heading east away from San Francisco. No one looks at other drivers, too busy concentrating on the narrow lanes of the bridge and five lanes of traffic.

My pulse quickens, and I begin to sweat. I'm breathing too quick and start to hyperventilate. My mind is racing.

I think of Mason. I know he'll turn over hell to find me.

I think of my brother and desperately wish that my twin telepathy actually worked for once.

I think of my three best friends.

Emerson. I've known her since our freshman year at Stanford. She was so busy with the golf team and her classes that she hardly paid attention to my drama, but she quickly became a steadfast friend.

Hadlee grew up next door, and when her mother died, her dad left her to be cared for by nannies as he searched through three more wives looking for a replacement. She essentially moved into my room.

Greer's mother is sick. Her father plied Greer with money so she'd stay and take care of her mother while he started a new family. Now she has a wonderful husband, and I'm sure she'll be pregnant any minute.

I don't know what to do. I don't know how to stop this. Even though we're going over the bridge in heavy traffic, moving well below the speed limit, if I could open the door, what use would it be? We're going too fast and the traffic is moving too quickly for me to get out.

An evil, maniacal laugh comes from him. "Face it, you're mine!"

I sit back in my seat, knowing I need to think, not dwell. I close my eyes and hear the rhythm of the bridge. *Bu-bump, bu-bump.* I take a big breath and hold it for a count of three, then purse my lips and blow out. I do that again and again as we pass over the bridge. We head north on 80 toward Sacramento. The traffic begins to thin, and his speed increases.

I need to get him talking. I need him to see me as a real person, not someone the newspapers and gossip columns have made up. "What did I ever do to you?"

"You have no idea," he growls. "I know who you are and where you work. I know all about you and your little group of friends at SHN."

Holy shit, this guy is a stalker. How did he manage to get my ride? How is it even possible?

He exits the freeway and takes a four-lane road through the Contra Costa mountain range. I'm trying to keep talking while I pay attention to every turn we make.

"I know all about them. Dillon thinks he's so smart. He's not. Cameron thinks he's so great with computers. He's not. Mason never liked me; he always thought he was smarter than me and that he had better business acumen. Well, I showed them."

We transition to the 680 and begin heading south on the other side of the mountains in the hot central valley. It's almost like we're doing a circle. Maybe he's going to rant and rave for a while and then drop me at home. I decide to keep him talking. "How do you know Dillon, Cameron, and Mason?"

"I've known them since we went to school together."

"When did they go to school together?" Duh. They all met at Stanford.

He glosses right over my question. "We met then, too. You were all high and mighty. Mizz Caro-line Are-no. La-tee-da with your French last name and your big trust fund. You've never had to work a day in your life."

I need to direct him to share more about himself and not add to his craziness by defending myself. "I don't recall meeting you. When did we meet?"

"Oh, we've met lots of times," he says snidely.

He doesn't elaborate and begins to mutter a little bit to himself. I try to listen to what he's saying, but I can't make it out. I don't think he's drunk, just mad. Mad as a hornet.

"You guys and your little clickie-club. No one is ever good enough for you. You snub anyone who tries to break into your little group. Oh, I know all about you."

I stare at the side of his face. He doesn't look familiar.

We slow as we enter some of the larger towns on the other side of the Contra Costa mountain range. I keep watching my phone, waiting to see if I get any bars.

Nothing.

It's dark now, and all I can see are headlights of the oncoming cars. It's getting stuffy in the car. "Can we crack the window?"

"No."

I begin to do my breathing exercises as we approach San Jose. I look in my bag for the water bottle I always keep there and my keys fall out. I push them out of the way as I search and then notice the safety hammer attached to my keyring.

Of course! The hammer is made to break a window!

We have to get off the freeway at some point. He'll need gas eventually. I can wait. My anxiety begins to ebb.

Suddenly he explodes. "Dillon is a giant pussy. He's all about any slut who waves her snatch in front of him and then forgets everyone else around him. He goes wherever a pussy leads him."

I might as well engage him. "I don't know if you know this, but he's happily married and has a little boy."

He bangs his hand on the steering wheel. "Yes, I know all about the skank he married." He looks at me in the rearview mirror. "You know, I got a piece of that once. She was begging for it."

Then it hits me. I know who he is. "You're Dillon's friend Adam!"

"Of course I am."

He's Adam Reeves, and he's bad news. He's the guy who put drugs in Emerson's drink and then date-raped my best friend.

My heart sinks into my stomach. My pulse quickens and sweat breaks out all over my body. This guy is not safe. There's something wrong with him.

When I focus on him again, he's talking about Cameron. "...isn't even good technically. I can't believe they didn't ask me to be their technology partner. I had the opportunity to show them what they were missing when I played with their little investments. I destroyed their portfolio so companies avoided them, then took down Pineapple Technologies. Man, they were the easiest ones of all. I played in their system for months and they didn't even know it. Then I strategically destroyed them."

Holy shit, he's behind all the misery SHN has been dealing with over the last five-plus years.

He's not just Adam Reeves. He's Adam MacIntosh.

"What you did was theft, and you destroyed a good company and a lot of people who worked hard on it."

"It was easy. I'm part of the Robin Hood Party. We take from the rich and share it with the world so everyone can grow from it. We advocate for intellectual property reform. We want privacy protection—"

"Protection? You invaded their privacy."

"Yes, we want protection from people gathering our information and profiting from it."

"Isn't that what you did?"

"We showed them their vulnerabilities. We want privacy for everyone and everything, and then it all becomes an open book. We want network neutrality and government openness," he rants.

"How does taking Pineapple Technologies' and all the other companies' information and disseminating bad information get you what you want? It doesn't make people feel safe. It does the opposite."

His laugh is evil. "You don't know how easy it was to recruit people for the Robin Hood Party. There's so much inequality of wealth in this country. A one-bedroom apartment in San Francisco starts at $4,000, and those are all dumps. While all the 1 percent get wealthier, the 99 percent are getting poorer. Mason, Dillon, and Cameron are part of that 1 percent, and so are you."

As he goes on and on about the Robin Hood Party, I can't help myself. "The FBI arrested your band of thieves."

He exits the freeway, and I watch for my move. I can't just hop out as he's driving down the road. I can't see myself doing an effective tuck and roll. It would be more like a belly flop, and I'd end up getting squished by another car.

There are traffic lights everywhere. We'll get a red light at some point.

I have my purse strap over my arm and the hammer in the other. It fits in the palm of my hand, but it's metal and heavy, and the head has a subtle point.

"I know they arrested my 'band of thieves,' but they didn't give them any information. Everyone kept their mouth shut and just denied knowing me."

Finally we pull up to a busy intersection close to the university. It's time to make my move.

We come to a stop behind another car at a red light. He's playing with something, but I can't tell what it is. Taking a deep breath, I pull my arm back and swing with all my might. The glass breaker easily shatters the window. I quickly reach out of the car and open the handle from the outside. Adam tries to accelerate but can't go anywhere.

I jump out and yell, "Fire! Fire!" Pedestrians surround me. The wheels squeal and he speeds away. I collapse to my hands and knees, breathing heavily.

"Are you okay?"

"Hey, lady, is everything okay?"

"Where's the fire?"

Someone helps me stand. I try to collect what little dignity I have. "I'm fine. Thank you."

"Oh my gosh, that was scary."

"Did a bullet break that guy's window?"

"Why did he speed away?"

I look at my phone and see I have all the bars again. I can call 911 and report what's happened. People go back to where they were going, and I sit down on the sidewalk and dial.

"Nine-one-one, what's your emergency?"

"I'm at the corner of"—I look up at the large green street signs—"Market and Santa Clara. I was just kidnapped. My name is Caroline Arnault, and my rideshare driver picked me up in San Francisco and drove me around for the last two and a half hours."

"Are you okay?"

"A little shaken. He drove down Market Street. I don't know where he went. The back-right passenger window is shattered." I look around, but I don't see Adam or his car. "I don't know where he went," I repeat.

"Keep talking to me. I have police on the way."

Knowing this call is being recorded and will end up in a court case, I keep talking. I describe where he picked me up. I pull up the rideshare app and give the operator the make and model of the car he was in. "He drove north beyond Berkeley on 80, headed east on 4, and then went south on 680. Then I remembered I had the silly window-breaker on my key chain that my mother insisted I needed." I hear the sirens before I see them. "If you could, please call Detective Lenning at San Francisco PD, and he should call his contact in the FBI. Tell them it was Adam McIntosh. They'll know what that means. I'm hanging up now. The police are here. Thank you."

"Good luck, Miss Arnault."

The two police officers approach me carefully. "Miss Arnault?"

I collapse into tears. Big, ugly, wet tears. They wait patiently while I pull myself together, which takes a few minutes, and then I begin answering their questions.

More police cars drive up, and a few stragglers who stayed are interviewed. Out of the corner of my eye, I see a man in a brown corduroy blazer and jeans approach. It's Detective Lenning, and Agent Perry and Marci Peterson are right behind him.

Lenning and Perry flash their badges at the policemen who are helping me, visibly surprised to have two more join our party.

"Miss Arnault, are you okay?" Detective Lenning asks.

I nod.

"I called Cameron as I drove down. He's on his way," Cora shares. "He's the only SHN partner I had on my speed dial."

I immediately begin explaining what happened. "I didn't get a bad car. I got into the car that was identified and verified the license plate number. He knew all about me and my friends. At first, I thought he was a stalker. Then he started talking about Pineapple Technologies. He said he was the head of some Robin Hood Party—it's a 'steal from the rich and give to the poor' thing. He kept contradicting himself."

I start to cry again. Cora rubs my back to soothe me. "You did just fine."

"You gave us a lot of information. We should be able to catch him," Detective Lenning says. "Not often do we get descriptions and license plates. Did he say where he was taking you?"

I shake my head.

The San Jose police officer steps in. "How did you break free?"

I hold up my keys with the little hammer. "I've had it on my key chain for easily five or six years. I was thirsty and started looking for my water bottle in my bag and moved my keys. I'd forgotten they were there. I knew he'd have to get off the freeway and stop for gas at some point." I look down and hold the mini hammer in my hands. "My mother gave me this silly thing years ago. I can't believe it saved my life."

I hear Dillon's voice and turn around to see him and Emerson trying to get beyond the police tape that's been put up. "If you don't let me in there to see her, I'm going to rain hell down on this place. She's not a suspect. She's a victim, and she deserves to be handled with kid gloves."

I see Detective Lenning motion to the San Jose police officer to let him in.

Dillon and Emerson come running up. Emerson has tears running down her face, and she launches herself into my arms. "Oh my God, are you okay? What's going on?"

"I had drinks at the Fairmont with Evelyn and called a rideshare home. The driver was your friend Adam."

Emerson and Dillon exchange looks. "Adam Reeves?" Emerson questions.

"Yes. He—"

"How did he know you were at the Fairmont?"

"He knew a lot about what was going on at SHN. I'm fairly certain he's been stalking me. But he's Adam MacIntosh, our hacker."

Dillon's face turns white. "Are you sure?"

"He admitted what he did with Pineapple. But think about it. It all makes sense. He's the guy you didn't hire."

Dillon bites at the corner of his lips as he processes the new information. "No, he had a job, but it wasn't a startup. He didn't have the money to invest. He was busy doing his thing, and we were three guys with money burning holes in our pocket."

"But you didn't hire him."

"No. He and Mason didn't get along," Emerson adds.

Everyone is listening closely to our conversation. "Oh, don't even get me started. He spent a lot of time telling me about how Mason never liked him," Dillon laments.

"He's a shit," I declare.

"I only liked him because we played football together at Stanford and had something in common, but after what happened with Emerson, I cut off all contact with him."

"That's a big piece of the puzzle," Cora shares. "We can work with that."

"This move places him squarely in your crosshairs. He had to know that," Dillon states.

"Agreed."

Suddenly all of my friends and family arrive, and of course, they all start to talk to me at once. Unexpectedly, I see Mason racing up in his Tesla. He runs it up the sidewalk and parks it illegally, leaving the door open as he hops the police tape and comes running over. "Are you okay?" Pulling me into his arms, he holds me tight and we kiss. I feel calm and safe again.

A clapping sound starts, and we break apart to see all of our friends are clapping and celebrating. We hold hands, and I giggle. Looking up at Mason, I see he has a grin as wide as mine. "I guess we should tell them."

"Oh, we already knew when he left the hospital and moved into your place, but you two were playing it so cool," Hadlee exclaims.

Everyone congratulates us, but it's very short-lived as they want to know what happened. I walk them through the evening's events as I did with Dillon and Emerson.

"I knew I never liked those rideshare program apps. They're just strangers," my mom chastises.

"Mom, I've taken thousands of rides. I always check the driver, the license plate, and the make of the car. This time it was different. This guy stalked me, waiting for the right moment. It's safe," I stress.

"You're not safe. You were driven around the Bay Area for the last three hours by some strange man who was ranting and raving."

"Mom, you know what saved me? It was that silly window breaker you gave me after I put my car in the creek when I was twenty-two."

"I'm very proud of you, sweetheart, and we're all glad you're okay," my dad says.

As we're breaking up to head home, Mason stops, eyes wide. "Wait! Van der Wolfe! That's it! Cora, one of the hackers you arrested. I know who he is. He was the bartender at the hotel where Emerson was assaulted. There's a connection between Adam and one of the hackers."

"Are you sure?" Cora presses.

"Yes, I remember because I always thought it was different that he had a three-word last name."

"Excuse me," Cora says as she steps away from the group. We watch her make a phone call. It's brief, and then she rejoins us. "Mason, you're right. Thomas Van der Wolfe worked at the hotel. We might be able to get him to turn on Adam with this leverage. Thanks, Mason."

I swear Mason's chest puffs up a little bit more.

"We may have found your hacker and his reason for targeting you," Cora continues.

My dad steps in. "It's getting late, sweetheart, and you look exhausted. We need to get you home."

Everyone nods their agreement.

The San Jose policemen look a little confused. "I'll get you a signed statement," Marci informs them. I don't think I've ever been so happy to have a great lawyer and so many people around me who love me so unconditionally.

As the officers start to object, Cora hands them her business card. "We've got this. If you have any further questions, please contact my office."

Cora looks at Marci. "Can she come into our offices tomorrow morning? We'd like to go through everything that happened. We should have the 911 call by eight, so maybe we can meet at ten?"

Marci looks at me questioningly. I nod.

"Great, I'll see you then," Cora tells me. "Mason, why don't you join us, too?"

"Sure thing," Mason replies. "I think I need to get CeCe home."

"Please," I agree. Everyone hugs me goodbye, each with affirmations of friendship and love. While I know that should make me feel positively elated, I'm exhausted and truly grateful to have a ride home in a safe car.

As we walk back to Mason's car hand in hand, I see Trey pat him on the back and say something I can't hear. Once we get settled in the car and are driving north, I ask, "What did Trey say to you?"

"Just that he'll cut my balls off if I hurt you." He subconsciously reaches for his crotch.

I laugh really hard.

"What's so funny?"

"The fact that my big brother thinks he could do that."

I reach over and grab his hand. "I've waited my entire life for you. I've known for a very long time that you were the one for me. We're going to be just fine. And now that we have SHN's issue figured out, we just need to figure out mine."

chapter

nineteen

CECE

"CECE, WAKE UP. We're home." Mason lightly shakes my shoulder.

Where am I? We were just leaving San Jose, but looking around, I see I'm in my garage at home. *How did I get here?* I look at my phone and notice the time. I can't believe I slept all the way home.

"Sorry, I didn't mean to fall asleep."

"You were tired. I totally understand. Don't worry about it. You need to rest. You've been going nonstop for weeks. I know you're exhausted."

I nod, still a little disoriented. I just want to curl up in my bed and go back to sleep.

Once the garage door shuts, Mason gets out of the car and walks around to open my door. "Let's get you upstairs and into bed. We're going to sleep until we can't stand it tomorrow."

"I called Jim and let him know what happened. We're going to meet him here at the house and they'll drive us over to Cora's in the morning."

I nod.

Angela swings the door open. "Miss Caroline, you're okay. I was so worried when I saw the news." She gives me a hug.

"Thank you. It was scary, but everything's okay."

"You probably didn't have dinner. What can I make you?"

I'm more alert now, shaking the sleep from my brain. "Thank you, Ang, but I think I'm going to just go to bed."

"No problem." She steps aside so I can walk upstairs. "I'll be ready to make you a big breakfast in the morning."

Mason takes me by the hand and begins leading me upstairs. "We'll probably leave about eight thirty. I'll get her downstairs at eight. She'll need protein to make it through the interviews tomorrow."

"I'll be ready," she announces.

"Let's get you in bed," he says.

"Mason, are you trying to get in my pants?" I flirt.

"Normally that would be my plan, but tonight I want you to sleep. I can head back to my apartment if you'd like."

"I can sleep in the same bed and not have sex with you."

"I know you can, but the question is, can I?"

"I need a shower," I announce. "What time did I agree to be at Marci's?

"At nine. We'll go over to Cora's from there." Mason sits on the bed to remove his socks. The light captures him and distracts me. When he pulls his shirt over his head and I see his chiseled chest, I want to forget the shower and just jump on him. I'm fully awake now, and my body has missed him so much.

"I think if we aim for leaving the house at eight thirty, we'll have thirty minutes to get the twenty-two blocks. That should be enough to get there on time. I alerted Jim's team."

"Thank you." I feel gross from spending three hours with Adam.

I start taking my clothes off as I walk to the bathroom, dropping clothes as I go figuring, I'll pick them up in the morning. "I guess what you're trying to tell me is that moving forward, Jim's team is going to be driving me everywhere."

"Yes, with everything going on and after this mess, it's the smart thing to do. Ces, I can't tell you how worried I was when I got the message. I don't know what I would have done had he done anything to you. And he won't be the last. We need to recognize that for a while, if it isn't me driving you, then it'll be someone from Jim's team."

Before today I would have fought and made a scene that I didn't need a constant companion, but now I know differently. It isn't just Adam, though. Someone is gunning for my company, and I can't give up and let them win.

I turn on the shower and let it heat up before I step in. As the hot water rains down on me, I have the pressure at the highest I can stand. I want to wash away any scent of Adam. I remember back to when I got the call from Emerson that morning. She woke to find herself in a hotel room; Adam drugged her drink and took advantage of her. I wanted her to go to the police so badly, but she had already showered and was angry and embarrassed that she got herself in the situation.

I kept trying to tell her that she shouldn't be angry at herself, she should be angry at Adam, but it was incredibly private. I didn't understand, but I wasn't going to push it. She's a lawyer, and she knew they always seem to blame the victim in those kinds of cases. She was also worried what the guys at work would do. We now know they would have hurt

Adam badly, but together Dillon and I did something that may have started this.

I lean my head against the shower when it hits me.

Shit.

It may be my fault that Adam went after SHN.

Getting out of the shower, I remember he let it slip that he had taken pictures of Emerson while he hurt her, and we knew there were others. I talked to the district attorney, but he couldn't do anything, so I asked for Dillon's help, and we found some black hat hackers to erase Adam's cloud server. We had a pickpocket go after his phone, and we dumped all his electronics in a deep bath of saltwater. It hurt Adam. And now he's taken his revenge. One bad deed begets another.

Walking into my bedroom, I see Mason propped up, fast asleep with some reports on his lap. Apparently I'm not the only one who's exhausted. He looks so peaceful; I don't want to disturb him. I put the reports on the side table and kiss him lightly on the forehead. Grabbing a T-shirt from the drawer, I pop it on and crawl between the sheets, snuggling in close. Half asleep he pulls me in and we spoon, and I fall right to sleep.

I roll over and look at the clock next to my bed—4:00 a.m. My brain is spinning. *Why did Adam go for me now? Who's trying to kill my company? What will I do if Mason decides the world I live in is too much?*

Then it hits me. Since we went after Adam ourselves, that explains why he'd want to hurt SHN, and it could be why he went after me. But even though he didn't mention Metro, could he be behind the problems we're having as well? What about Liam? Could a defenseless little baby be at risk to get back at Emerson and Dillon? What's going to happen today?

Am I at risk of going to jail if I admit what Dillon and I did? I can't go back to sleep. Running away seems like a good idea.

"Are you okay?" Mason asks, still half asleep.

"I'm sorry I woke you. I can't go back to sleep."

"I'm sorry. Do you want me to hold you?"

"No, you should go back to sleep. I can't believe I'm going to say this, but I think I'll go get on the treadmill downstairs and work off some of my energy."

Mason's eyes spring open. "You're going to work out?"

He knows me so well. I can't help but smile. "I know, it's not my typical way of dealing with stress, but maybe this is what will make me feel better."

"Okay, sweetheart." He drifts back to sleep in a matter of moments. I wish I was more like him—able to sleep regardless of what's going on around him.

With my earbuds in, I put on an audiobook I've been listening to and get on the treadmill. I set it at a fast walking pace, and I walk for the next twenty-five minutes. It's probably been three years since I was in this room. Working out isn't really my thing. By the end, I'm out of breath, my face is bright pink, and I feel sweaty and gross, but I head upstairs feeling better. I have the energy to meet the day. Maybe this workout thing isn't such a bad idea, but I don't want to get ahead of myself.

I take a quick shower and get ready, including blowing my hair out. Going in search of my Christian Louboutin black pumps, I look over at Mason, who's still sleeping. We promised to meet Marci early today. I can go without him, though he'd be upset with me if I did. But he's clearly exhausted himself; so many things have come to fruition so close to one another.

I sit down next to him. Leaning in, I softly kiss him on the lips. "Hey, sleepyhead. If you're going to join me this morning, you need to get up."

Mason kisses me back, his tongue pressing against my lips for entrance. "You smell so good. I thought you were going to work out."

"I did." I nod toward the clock. "Look at the time. We agreed to meet Jim's team in a little over a half hour."

"Wow, I didn't realize I was so tired."

"What would you like for breakfast?" I ask as I stand up.

"I think I'd like you for breakfast." He looks at me, his eyes hooded.

"That's incredibly tempting, but I hate to make so many people who are coming in on a Saturday morning wait for us."

"You're right. I hate that you're right, but"—he takes my hand and guides it to his hard cock—"this is all for you."

"And tonight we'll see if we can make it fall off."

He throws his head back and laughs. "I'm game if you are." Throwing the covers back, he starts to get out of bed. "I'll take a quick shower, and then we can head downstairs together. Angela should have breakfast ready for you."

While I wait, I look through my PeopleMover page and check emails. I'm not even done when he comes out looking good enough to eat. How is it that men can get ready so quickly and look amazing in under ten minutes?

He extends his hand, and together we walk downstairs and into the kitchen. The simple gesture makes me feel special.

"Good morning, Miss Caroline and Mr. Mason. I see you're on the news this morning." She points to the television in the corner of the kitchen.

I look at it and realize someone caught everything on a cell phone camera. They captured me standing at the crime scene, talking to the police, and all of my friends arriving, including Mason rushing up and wrapping his arms around me, followed by a passionate kiss.

This is not good. My stomach drops to the floor. "I hope you're ready, because the paparazzi now have you in their sights," I tell Mason.

"I can manage." He scoops a bite of eggs that Angela placed in front of him and winks at me.

"Tell me when you're done with their mess."

"Done with their mess? They'll get bored with us just like they did with Trey and Sara."

"They didn't get bored with them. Trey and Sara go out of their way to not be seen and work hard at their privacy."

"And we'll do the same."

"When it gets to be too much, you just need to tell me. Please don't do what Frederic did or any of the others who dumped me publicly. I could take it from them, but from you, it would be devastating." I'm trying so hard not to cry.

Mason stands and pulls me into his arms, giving me a deep, full kiss. When we break apart, he holds my shoulders and stares into my eyes. "Caroline Arnault, I want you to know that I love you. I've loved you for a very long time. I assure you, there is nothing the paparazzi can do that will convince me otherwise."

I can't believe he just declared his feelings so directly. I'm not sure I heard everything he said correctly. "You love me?"

He nods. "Without any doubt."

I'm over the moon. "I love you, too."

He pushes his lips hard against mine, then pulls me back in for a tight hug. "Good. Then it's settled. We know the paparazzi are going to do their part to drive a wedge between us, but we don't need to worry about them. We'll manage the paparazzi, our work issues, and any other speed bump that comes our way together."

The weight on my shoulders is lifted. There's always the possibility that he doesn't understand what he's just agreed to do, but knowing we're going to get through this as a team is a surprising relief.

Angela, who's overheard the entire conversation, tells Mason, "You hurt Miss Caroline, and you better hope I don't have access to your food, because I won't use some silly plant like wolfsbane. I'll use straight-up rat poisoning, and you won't survive."

Mason holds his hands up in mock surrender. "Reading you loud and clear." He winks at her, and I know we're a unit. We can do anything as long as we're together.

Jim walks into the kitchen. "Did I hear Angela just threaten Mason?"

"No. She was just letting me know the ground rules—rules I can happily live by." Mason grins.

Angela hands him a cup of coffee, and Jim joins us at the table. "Good. Now, here's the plan. The car is in the garage. There are two members of my team waiting to go when you're ready. There's some press out front and in the alley behind the house. The Suburban has tinted windows, and we can load the two of you so they can't be sure you're in the car. From there, we'll drive to Marci's office, where we'll enter through the garage. At no time are you to go anywhere without us." Jim looks at me and waits for me to agree.

"Nowhere without a member of your team with me. I got it," I assure him.

"Caroline, you know we need to have a conversation about how you can't be picking up rideshares anymore."

"I understand. I'm not happy about it, but I get it, and we can circle back to that at a later time." I see both Mason and Jim ready to argue this with me. "Much later, after all of this is a distant memory for everyone."

"Agreed," they both say in unison.

"Marci let me know that the FBI will be at her offices since it's a Saturday," Jim states.

“I guess that means we’re heading to Marci’s office,” I say.

chapter twenty

CECE

AS WE LEAVE THE GARAGE, several cameras start flashing around us. The guys drive all over the city, trying to lose our tail of reporters. They call ahead and drive into a closed parking garage, and two of Jim's men step behind the vehicle, preventing anyone from following us into the garage. What a mess.

When we exit the car and call the elevator, a security guard uses a key card to give us access to Marci's office. "Mr. Adelson, we've got this place buckled up tight," he says to Jim.

"You have the list of those who can join us?"

"Yes, sir."

Jim goes from being our front man to blending into the background as we exit the elevator.

Marci gives me a big hug when she sees us. "How did you sleep last night?"

"Not very well."

"I totally get it." She escorts us to a large conference room with a beautiful view of the financial district and the bay. "There are coffee and donuts—I thought the sugar would give us energy."

A woman after my own heart. "That's perfect. Thank you."

"The plan for this morning is that our friends from Cybercrimes, White-Collar, and SFPD will be here in about thirty minutes. They want to go through everything with you. You'll make a statement that my legal assistant will type up and you'll sign, and then we'll messenger it down to the San Jose police department. How does that sound?"

"That's fine." I take a deep breath and pull up the courage to admit that I may be the cause of all of this. "I should tell you before they get here. It occurred to me last night that Dillon and I did something initially that may have provoked Adam."

"What happened?"

I walk her through Emerson's assault and her refusal to go to the police.

"I understand," Marci says. "The police are brutal, and it's unfortunate that they tend to blame the victim and not the perpetrator."

"Dillon and I weren't going to let him get away with it. Adam mentioned he had photographed everything. We couldn't take the chance that he'd use the pictures to blackmail her at a later date or post them to the internet to live forever." I look over at Mason, and I can see the disappointment in my actions start to take over his neutral expression. I whisper, "This entire mess may be my fault."

"What did you do?" Marci prods.

"Dillon knew some black hat hackers, and we knew some less-than-savory people, so we pickpocketed Adam's phone, broke into his apartment, loaded his bathtub with saltwater and a bottle of bleach, and then dumped all of his electronics into the water. We then had someone break into his cloud server and delete everything."

I hang my head in shame. I'm ready for Mason to unleash his anger at me, but he looks at me curiously. "You did that after Dillon returned from his forced break from the company?"

I nod.

"The hacking had been going on long before Dillon went on his break. That's part of the reason he went in the first place. We thought he was falling down on the job, so we forced the issue."

I cover my mouth with my hand. "Oh my God. I can't believe this. I've been so worried that this was all my fault."

Mason pulls me into his arms. "Is this why you got up so early and went on the treadmill?"

"Yes," I whimper into his shoulder.

"CeCe, Adam has been upset with us since long before all of this happened. He targeted Emerson as part of this mess, not the other way around."

"Well, I haven't finished telling you what we did."

Marci sits back in her chair. "I'm listening."

"Dillon's black hat friends were upset at what Adam had done, and they destroyed his credit, even going so far as to delete his mortgage payments, putting his condo into foreclosure."

"When did this happen?"

"About five years ago."

"Well, you're past the statute of limitations. I think for our statement to the San Jose PD, we can ignore this, but we should probably bring it up with Cora Perry, just in case."

I look at Mason. "Do you hate me?"

"Why?"

"Because I was so upset that I broke the law."

"You were protecting your best friend. I understand. I only wished I'd known. I would've helped or at the very least thrown a party."

The weight lifts from my shoulders in relief. "I love you," I tell him.

Marci looks at us with a smile as big as the Amazon. "I see you two have made some progress."

"Maybe just a little." I giggle.

Jim steps into the conference room. "The FBI and SFPD have arrived."

Marci looks at me. "Let's not go into the black hats today. I'll approach Cora about it without the others here."

"No problem," I assure her.

Suddenly the three of us are outnumbered as Cora Perry and three members of her team enter, followed by Agents Greene and Winters. Detective Lenning arrives behind them with a young detective who he introduces as his partner, Detective Anna Montoya.

I'm asked to go through everything from last night. Detective Lenning shares my 911 call with the group. "You were pretty smart to tell her all the things you did."

"I knew it would be recorded, and I knew it would be played at his trial one day."

"As I said, pretty smart."

"They've cast a wide net looking for Adam Reeves," Cora shares. "We've pulled his information from the rideshare company, and the address he uses is a PO Box that's disguised as a street address. SFPD and Oakland PD have the box staked out, but we're not optimistic that he'll return there any time soon. Currently, he doesn't have any credit cards or bank accounts in his name. He's pretty much off the grid. The cell phone he used with the rideshare company is a burner."

My stomach drops. "Does that mean we're back to square one?"

"Absolutely not. We know who Adam is. Now we have to figure out his sister Eve, which we're working on. Tina, can you share what you've learned with the group."

A tiny woman with her dark hair pulled back into a ponytail sits up in her chair. She's part of Cora's team. I want to peek under the table and see if her legs touch the ground, but I know that would be tacky. I still consider it.

"We pulled Adam Reeves's information. He was in foster homes growing up in Southern California. He spent his last two years of high school with a family in Santa Ana. It looks like there were other children coming and going, but the father died during his senior year and the foster kids scattered. He went up to Stanford, where he played football. He was a defensive end—I'm not sure what that is exactly—and he never played first string, but he was good enough to be there on scholarship."

"Thank you, Tina. So, we're looking for Eve?"

"Yes, we have a thread we're pulling. The Los Angeles field office has delivered a court order for the records of the kids who were with him in the final foster home," Tina says.

"Why do you think it was the final foster home where he met his 'sister'?" Mason asks.

"The profiler in our office believes the final home where he lived the longest had the biggest impact. If we don't find anything, we'll work backward from there," Cora shares.

Cora turns to me. "Last night, you mentioned that he and his merry band of thieves call themselves the Robin Hood Party. Tell us what you remember."

I walk them through his rambling. "As he talked about it, I found he contradicted himself. One minute they're out to screw the 1 percent, and the next he was upset with the founders of SHN because they didn't invite him to join them."

Cora leans back in her chair, making everyone lean in. "This doesn't make sense compared to what they're trying to do. Of course, since when do criminals make sense? This does fill in a lot of holes for us. They're robbing from the rich to supposedly give to the poor."

"They really aren't robbing the rich, only the almost rich or the rich on paper, and they're making a lot of people poor in the process. And they really aren't doing much to give to anyone but themselves. They're more out to destroy than anything else," one of the FBI team interjects.

"You're right. Posting confidential information on the internet isn't getting anyone rich, but it is robbing them of their hard work." She's silent a few moments. Tapping her pen on the table a few times, she looks at the timeline. "So why call themselves the Robin Hood Party?"

"There were so many reasons I didn't feel he was a good fit for us. Now he's validated my opinion, of course, but at the same time, I wonder if we'd still be in a mess had we hired him. We talked about it, and I was the one who put my foot down. He was the reason we said it had to be unanimous for us to agree on these issues, not just the majority," Mason explains.

"I think your instincts were right on. You would've been in trouble regardless."

The room is quiet a moment.

"Have you remembered anything else since then?" Detective Lenning presses.

"No. I don't think so." I'm really glad he's asking and not Cora, because lying to the FBI is a federal offense while lying to the SFPD is not.

"Why do you think Adam went after you?"

"I've been part of the group since the beginning. Emerson came to my father and me when they offered to buy her company. We went through the contract together and agreed it was a good idea. I was added as an advisor less than a year later. And I'm involved with Mason, the founding partner who Adam sees was the reason he wasn't asked to join the company."

"Did he know you were involved with Mason?"

"He didn't say as much, but since Mason was released from the hospital, he's been staying at my house. If Adam's been stalking me, then he most likely would've seen Mason there at some point."

"Did he mention Metro Composition?" Agent Greene asks.

"No, unfortunately, he didn't."

"All right." Cora bounces her pen on the table a few times, then looks at her watch. "We've been here for over two hours. It's lunchtime. Why don't we call it a day, and then we can circle back in the few days?"

Cora, Mason, Marci, and I make polite conversation until the room empties. "I didn't want to ask in front of all the men, but tell me more about Emerson's assault. How did it happen?"

I walk her through what I know and the link between the bartender and Adam.

"You guys didn't do anything to get back at Adam?"

"My clients will stipulate that they may have commissioned a crime, but it's past the statute of limitations, and this supposed crime happened after the espionage began at SHN," Marci interjects.

"So stipulated. What did you do?" Cora looks at Mason.

He steps back and holds his hands up. "I didn't know anything about it until today."

"I did it," I admit. "Adam assaulted my best friend. She was sure it was her fault because she trusted him enough that after ordering a drink for herself, she went to the bathroom."

"We know that, since the bartender was implicated, her drink would've been drugged regardless of her going to the bathroom," Marci adds.

"We know that now, but she really did a number on herself because of what happened."

I tell Cora the sequence of events, leaving out the most important detail of Dillon being involved.

Cora sits for a moment. "I'm not happy that you felt you had to resort to that level of crime, but between us, I'm not sure I would've done much different. These cases are awful in the justice system, and it always seems to come down to a 'he said, she said' situation. And we know that in this case, the bartender would've lied."

"Exactly." I nod vigorously.

"Who helped you?"

"I don't want to lie to you, but I'd rather not say," I tell her honestly.

"My bet was it was Cameron," she says. "He has some mad computer skills and is typically a white hat hacker, but I would bet under the right circumstances, he could be swayed to the dark side."

"I promise you it wasn't Cameron."

"He has those skills."

"Yes he does, but I promise you it wasn't him," I repeat.

"Well, then you and Dillon make a joint statement. We'll put it in the file. It's beyond the statute of limitations, yes, but I don't want his defense to come back at us for not having documented the activity."

"How did you know it was Dillon?" I ask, shocked.

"Process of elimination."

"We'll put together a joint statement from Dillon and Caroline," Marci assures her.

"Any news about the problems at Metro?" I ask.

"These two cases kept me up last night. I didn't sleep well myself," Marci shares.

"I have an update on Metro and what happened so far," Cora says.

"Great, we'd all love to hear it," Mason says.

"We got you all set." She pulls out a sheet of paper from her folio. "Here are the dates when everything kind of started showing up in the Metro Composition user groups and on the internet. We were able to deploy the Trojan horses and mirror software on your teams' work, home, and personal phones and computers. We've been watching what everyone is emailing, trying to be very aware of what's personal and what's not."

"Anything interesting yet?" Mason asks.

"We've seen a few things that are a little off, but nothing that really rises to a level of concern." She turns to me. "After you spoke to everyone yesterday, we saw a few emails go out talking about the situation, but it was nothing concrete. If possible, we'd like you to send out another round of emails that will further cement your decision and the next steps."

"Do you think it's necessary?" I ask.

"We do. We want to watch and see if anything escalates to the point of being actionable."

"What about their privacy?"

"We are reading all of their email, both personal and business. They don't have much privacy, but we aren't being intrusive and sharing it, even with you."

That makes me feel a little better. I guess I really don't want to hear if they don't like me.

"Caroline, we're close. I promise," Cora assures me.

I nod.

"You're headed to New York next week for Fashion Week, correct?" she confirms.

"Yes. We're not really doing any named shows, but my makeup artists will do the Gap show. They want their focus on their clothes, so we aren't really headlined for that one. We're not doing any displays like we've done in the past, and we've given up our suite at the Four Seasons."

"Wow. What does that mean?"

"We're not doing anything to promote the brand this time around."

"I'm sure that must be very difficult, and for that, I'm really sorry."

"Thank you."

Mason reaches for my hand and gives it a reassuring squeeze.

"I also want to assure you that we're continuing to chase several avenues to broaden our scope so that we're not only focused on your team. I'll keep you posted," Cora tells me before we all head out.

chapter

twenty-one

CECE

SITTING IN THE LOUNGE AREA waiting for my flight, we're flanked by two of Jim's men who are traveling with us.

"They're scaring all the cute guys away," Evelyn whines.

"After the kidnapping, I don't have a choice these days. I'm sorry."

Evelyn is wearing a very short skirt, and when she sees one of the guards is watching her carefully, she inches it up. Internally, I roll my eyes. He doesn't even smile. She arches her back, pushing her breasts out, and looks seductively at him, hoping it'll get at least a small smile, but nothing. "Apparently they're grumpy bodyguards, too."

"You're too much." I look across the lounge, cranky from the two weeks of little to no movement on the SHN case and the issue at Metro. I hope this trip to New York for Fashion Week isn't too disappointing.

"They're here to look after us, not serve as your date."

She pouts.

"What happened to your boyfriend?" I ask.

"We broke up ages ago. I think that's why I'm on the prowl."

"We're meeting Vanessa this evening for dinner, and she always has a habit of bringing guys who work for her husband along."

"That's great! I can't wait. I think my vagina is going to seal up if I don't find some action soon."

I smile. If it was one of my friends, I'd pull out my famous retort: "Who needs a man? If you want companionship, buy a dog. If you want sex, buy a toy. You'll be happier in the long run." But it isn't work appropriate, and despite having a close relationship with Evelyn, I do want to keep it somewhat professional.

We wait until final boarding call is announced, and then we make our way to the plane. It's the one perk I have for being a little bit well known when I fly commercially.

Jim's men board the plane and check to make sure all is well, then bring us on, leading us each to a window seat across the aisle from one another. Jim's men sit in the adjoining seats.

"Why are we going commercial?" Evelyn grumbles as we sit down.

I know she likes going by private plane, but we're flying first class. It's not like we're sitting next to the bathroom in the last row with crying babies. I try not to let it get to me. I know she's equally stressed about everything going on.

After we've leveled off and the seat belt sign goes off, I ask the guard sitting next to me, "Would it be possible for Evelyn and me to sit together? I'd like to have a conversation with her that the entire plane doesn't want or need to hear."

When Evelyn trades places with the guard, she murmurs, "These guys are super hardcore."

"After what happened, Mason and Jim are making sure they keep me on a very short leash."

"Better you than me. This would drive me crazy if it happened all the time. Honestly, you really put up with a lot of shit. My breakup with my boyfriend was incredibly anticlimactic compared to yours with Frederic."

"The worst part? Frederic and I didn't have a drama-filled breakup. We drifted, and then he went out with a porn star, and that made the tabloids."

She sighs. "I'm glad I know the real you."

"I'm really sorry about you having to deal with this mess, but I'm glad you're coming with me."

"I'm good. I'm hoping Vanessa is going to make this trip worthwhile." She winks at me, and I know she's back to discussing getting laid. "Maybe had the sex with my ex been better. He just couldn't figure out how to get me there. It's not like I'm a Stradivarius. I'm just a regular old violin, and he needed to learn to play the strings. I tried to teach him, but he thought he knew how it worked."

"I've been there," I offer. I'm not going to go into any more detail.

"Are we staying at the Four Seasons tonight?"

"Yes, we have one of the suites with the living room areas; that way, Jim's men are close by. But don't use that as your excuse not to find a date. You're a big girl, and they won't bother you."

"Don't worry about me. I'm not going to let them slow me down." She leans in and quietly says, "Although, I wouldn't mind having one of them show me something slow." She looks up at one of the guards, winking at him and biting the corner of her mouth.

"I hope you find what you're looking for in New York." *And it better not be one of Jim's men.*

"I plan to."

* * *

Once we land at JFK and make our way to the hotel, I brace myself for the next activity—an impromptu visit. We're heading to Barney's to see how our counter is doing. It's the most expensive of all of our retail space. We sell our cosmetics only in department stores and high-end cosmetic stores, and not only do we rent that space, but then we also pay a small percentage of our sales back to the store. There are established metrics in our lease, and if we aren't meeting them, we'll lose our spot. Barney's is a good gauge of how things are going across our total sales.

Our space at Barney's is front and center. When we enter the store, it's bustling with very chic women—and a few men—all in the New York City uniform of black pants, black tops, black leather jackets. But no one is stopping at our counter.

I notice our makeup artist isn't engaging anyone as they walk by. We stand back and watch for a few minutes.

"What is she doing? She's not even making eye contact with anyone."

I walk up to the counter, and she doesn't even look up at me.

"If you need anything, you let me know," she offers without really looking at us.

"Can you show me some of your mascara? Which do you recommend?"

"They're right there where you're standing, and the display explains what they do."

My spirits plummet. I'm going to give it one more chance. "So, what is it like working for Metro?"

She shrugs. "It's an okay job. Their checks cash."

"I would think working in makeup would be so much fun."

"Makeup isn't really my thing."

I'm stunned by this, and Evelyn raises her eyebrows at me, equally unhappy. This falls under her responsibilities.

Evelyn reaches in her bag and pulls out her business card. "Hi, I'm Evelyn Stevens, Metro Composition's VP of Operations. What is your name?"

She walks over and takes the card from Evelyn. "Marie." Her attention turns to me, and her eyes widen when she recognizes me. "Oh, shit."

"What's going on?" I can tell from the way Evelyn's voice is strained that she's close to blowing.

"Everyone knows we don't have a new line because of the Chinese company stealing it, and despite what you tell them, people think we experiment on animals, even though it's all bullshit." She puts her hand over her mouth. "I'm sorry. I'm not allowed to swear at the counter."

I look at her carefully as the tears pool in her eyes. "I know things are tough right now. We're working on it. Evelyn and I do these drop-bys to see how customers are relating to our products. Marie, I can see it's tough, but I hope you can reach out to people and be interactive."

"It's just hard because of what's happened."

"I get it. It's frustrating that people aren't even stopping, but when we did, you didn't pay us any attention."

"I had $250 worth of sales yesterday. Nobody's buying, but there are lots of lookers."

"I'm sorry it's so hard right now. We're working on fixing that."

"I'll do a better job," Marie promises.

"In the past, I've done events at the store. Do you think if we did an email blast out of corporate to celebrate Fashion Week that you'd be up for a flash of people?"

"Absolutely."

I turn to Evelyn. "Let's reach out to Becca and have the public relations group send out an email blast and a press release. Let's get some people into the store and get Marie busy. Sometimes if we promise my autograph with purchase, we can make a big splash."

"No problem," she assures us. I know we can't do this for every store, but I can't afford to lose this prime piece of real estate in Barney's.

Evelyn spends the afternoon with Marie and her manager, preparing for the store event which we'll do as a flash mob tomorrow. It's a rush, but it'll bring people in, and we may just save our spot at Barney's.

We make plans to meet back at the hotel and go over together to meet Vanessa and her husband for dinner. I need some time to rest a minute, so I head back with my escorts and decide to lie down and take a quick nap. Maybe I'll find the energy to be more than a lump on a log at dinner tonight. This week is going to be incredibly busy, and without the fuel that participating in the shows provides, it's going to be like pushing a large boulder up a hill.

When the alarm on my phone wakes me at eight o'clock, I'm a bit disheartened that no one from my team tried to call. I didn't want the interruption, but business needs to continue, and if they aren't emailing me, they're stagnant.

I get ready for our dinner tonight, wearing a new couture outfit that I asked Jennifer to send over. It's from a new designer based in the Bay Area, a dress that's a cross between the 50s and today. So classic and chic. I may not feel like going to this dinner tonight, but I'll look like I want to be there, at least.

I'm missing Mason. We don't always talk every day, but I wonder what he's doing right now. It's after five o'clock in California, and I can't help myself. I decide to text him.

Me: Thinking of you.

He doesn't respond. I think he mentioned he was going out for drinks with a client tonight, so I won't let it get to me. He's busy, and I don't want to be high maintenance.

I meet Jim's men and Evelyn in the living room. As I walk up, I realize I don't know my team's names. They introduced themselves so quickly when we got in the car to head to the airport, and Evelyn was so self-involved at having to go commercial, that I missed it. "I'm sorry, but can you tell me your names again?"

"I'm Jack Reece, the head of your team. Tonight Will Hamilton will be with us." He looks at Will, who nods. Both men are dressed in custom-made suits, and they look quite handsome. You can tell they're hiding stunning bodies and at least one handgun apiece. "I understand we're headed to Café Fontaine."

"That's correct."

"We've checked the reservation. They're expecting us, and we'll be sitting at a table adjacent to yours."

Evelyn comes out in a very fashionable Dolce Gabbana dress with a neckline that plunges to her belly button and a slit in the side to just above midwaist. She looks beautiful; the guys are going to love her tonight.

"Ready?" I ask.

"Yep. I'm ready. I hope this tape holds, or I'll be giving it away for free tonight." I know the tape she's talking about, and unless she gets nervous and sweats a lot, she'll be just fine. Angus's men will have hard-ons all night looking at her, and she should be able to take her pick.

"You look fantastic," I tell her.

"As do you," she says.

We're escorted down the elevator and into the car. The drive is slow despite a nine o'clock dinner reservation. Evelyn and I make small talk about what's going on back at the office. She received a few calls, but they were mostly about the event we'd planned at Barney's. "Have you mentioned your plan to relaunch the line to Vanessa?"

I haven't told Vanessa that the FBI is looking at Evelyn. I know they're wrong, but before I can tell Evelyn anything, my phone pings with a message from Emerson: **Good luck tonight. We miss you! XOXO Liam and E.** Then a few seconds later a picture of Liam appears, his face overtaken by a toothless grin. He's not even my child, but I love that little boy. I send back a heart emoji.

The car slows and comes to a stop in front of our restaurant. "Oh, look at this place," Evelyn exclaims. It looks like it was plucked right out of Paris in the 1920s and put here on a busy Tribeca street.

"Vanessa always knows how to impress," I reply, in awe myself.

We're quickly escorted inside, and I don't get to tell her about what's going on with the FBI. I have this nagging feeling that if I don't tell her first, when she ultimately finds out, this is going to cause a permanent rift between us that will be unrepairable.

Will goes in first, leading Evelyn and me into the restaurant, with Jack walking behind me.

Vanessa arrived early and is already waiting for us. Someone is standing at the table talking to her, but she thanks them and focuses on our arrival with a smile.

"Caroline!" She stands and pulls me into a light embrace, kissing both of my cheeks.

"Hello, Vanessa. So great to see you! How are you doing this crazy week?"

"Not as busy as I'd like to be with the loss of your line being showcased this week. I'm truly disappointed about what's transpired for your company."

"We'll get them next year. We'll have a new line out that will get beyond this mess. We're going to be just fine," I say, though it's as much for my benefit as it is hers.

"I know you're going to be more than 'just fine.' There's nothing but resilience in your bones. I'm grateful to be part of the ride. I'm just disappointed it's not this year. But tonight, we're not going to talk about business." She smiles. "I had Angus bring two of his most aspiring gentlemen for you to go and play with." She smirks.

"You know I'm seeing someone," I whisper, so I'm not totally rude to her other guests.

"I know you and Mason are finally together. I lost that bet, by the way; I thought you two would've gotten together ages ago. But I couldn't set up Evelyn and not bring a guy along for you. It would throw off the symmetry of my table."

"You are so like your cousin Greer."

"Our mothers were sisters, and as much as we dealt with, we might as well have been sisters as well."

I know the mental illness that she and Greer managed growing up with their respective mothers was challenging, so I don't want the conversation to dwell on that. "Evelyn is excited to meet a nice man."

Evelyn smiles wide and greets Vanessa. "I can't wait. Rumor has it this is how you introduced Todd from your team, and he's now getting married to Cynthia here shortly."

Vanessa winks conspiratorially. "That's why these guys are lining up."

Out of the corner of my eye, I see Angus and two very handsome men make their way toward our table. Angus is a tall and strapping man. In another life, he played tackle for the University of Texas and still keeps in shape today.

"Caroline." He greets me with soft kisses on my cheeks.

"Angus, it's so great to see you."

"How are you doing? I'm sorry about what's transpired for your line."

"Thank you. It's certainly a bump in the road, but we'll weather it."

"Let me introduce you to Steve Hatch. Steve, this is Caroline Arnault and Evelyn Stevens," Vanessa says.

"Very nice to meet you." I smile warmly and nod like a bobblehead doll.

"And this handsome gentleman here is Steve Kanter," Vanessa continues.

"Well, it should be easy to remember your names since they're both Steve," I try to joke.

"Please call us Hatch and Kanter. Everyone does," Steve Hatch says.

Evelyn sits down next to Kanter. I've never been very good at flirting with men I don't know, and I admit I'm a bit jealous as she talks to him in a low voice, touches her hair, and giggles like a young schoolgirl. The feeling must be mutual, because he puts his arm around her, and she snuggles in tight. It's a bit awkward to watch, but instead, I concentrate on Vanessa while Hatch and Angus talk about work. "Thanks so much for the warm New York welcome."

"I'm just thrilled you came," Vanessa gushes.

"We went by the counter at Barney's today, and we're going to do an impromptu event at the store tomorrow."

Vanessa claps her hands together. "Wonderful! What are your plans?"

I explain our email blast and my offer of signing makeup purchases.

"That will bring them out, and you'll be sold out in no time."

"We're pulling inventory from the Macy's and Nieman stores."

My cell phone pings and my heart races, hoping it's Mason.

Mason: Thinking of you, too. Missing you very much.

A sense of calm warms me like a blanket. Mason's attention means a lot to me. I try to concentrate on the conversation between Hatch and Angus, but I'm distracted by Mason. I know it's rude, but I quickly respond anyway.

Me: What would you do if I was there?

"We're being rude talking about work," Hatch says to me.

"You're fine. Vanessa and I were also talking about work."

"Are you here for Fashion Week?"

"Yes, but we don't have any shows this year. We've partnered in the past with several designers, but we've hit a few bumps and are just watching from the sidelines."

"That's too bad."

"It is." I don't want to rehash our drama, so I decide to redirect the conversation. "Are you from the Northeast?"

"Actually, I'm from your neck of the woods—California's central valley close to Sacramento."

"Really? I love the heat in the central valley. Were your parents farmers?"

"No, but my dad was a consultant for many of the almond farms."

"Wow, I'm impressed. Is he still doing that?"

"He's retired. I'd like to get back to California at some point. I understand you know Todd Wellington?"

Todd also works for Vanessa's husband and originally moved to San Francisco hoping to date me, but I matched him up with Cynthia at SHN instead. "I do, but"—I point to Angus—"he knows Todd much better than I do."

Hatch smiles. "Any help I can get to let me move closer to my family would be greatly appreciated."

The waiter arrives with a bottle of Johnnie Walker Blue, a small covered ice bucket, and glasses for the group.

My cell phone vibrates, and I can't help but read it.

Mason: I'd eat that sweet pussy of yours until you released all that sweet honey into my mouth and then start all over again.

I can't help but shudder with excitement. *Is it getting warm in here?* I'm sure my face is flushed. If he isn't careful, I'll have to go back to the hotel and take care of myself.

Another text arrives before I can respond.

Mason: What else would you like me to do to you?

Angus pours glasses for everyone, and we toast to a good week in New York.

The list of things I want to do with Mason is lengthy. We've been friends for a long time, but I don't know what he likes or doesn't like.

Me: What's your favorite sexual position?

"Hatch, how did you land here in New York?" I ask, trying to distract myself from the cell phone burning a hole in my hand.

"I went to school in Boston, and Angus made an offer that was very tempting, so I moved here to New York."

Angus recruits from Harvard, so that tells me a lot about Hatch. "But you're ready to move back to California?"

"I will admit I hate winter. I miss the weather back home. And I miss my twin sister."

"You have a twin sister? I have a twin brother."

My cell phone vibrates, and I have to look at Mason's response.

Mason: I certainly like to see your pretty eyes while we make love, so my favorite would be you lying on your back with your long legs wrapped around me while I drill you from the side of the bed.

Oh, have mercy on me. I need to fan my face. How can I concentrate on my conversation when visions of having sex with Mason are overtaking my brain? My heart is racing, and I'm afraid I'm going to have a wet spot between the legs of my silk pants.

"Wow, we're both twins, and you're from the Central Valley. It's nice and hot right now," I gush. That wasn't awkward at all.

"I know. What I wouldn't give for a couple of ninety-plus degree days with low humidity. I miss the smell of all the blooms on the almond trees."

"What do they smell like? Almonds?"

He lets out a hearty laugh that I can't help but like. "Actually, if you smell almonds, I think you're smelling cyanide. Almond blooms actually smell like honey. It's a light scent, but when you're walking through the orchards, it's strong. I love it."

"It sounds like you've spent a lot of time on almond farms."

"I worked my summers from the time I was fifteen until I finished grad school working almond harvests."

Angus leans in. "You want to know farming futures, Hatch is your man."

"Good to know." I feel my phone vibrate again. I want to respond, but I don't want to continue being rude, so I excuse myself and head to the bathroom.

Mason: I also love it when you ride me and I can finger your clit. Did you know your pussy clenches around my cock when I do that?

I lock myself in a stall, recalling exactly what he's describing in vivid detail.

Me: I did know it does that, but that's because you know my magic button.

Me: Would you consider yourself an ass or tits man?

I wait patiently as he responds.

Mason: With you, I could play for hours with both.

Mason: Do you like giving head? You're very good at it.

Me: I love it. Do you like going down on me? You're incredibly talented.

Mason: I love going down on you and would even if you didn't reciprocate.

Me: I need to get back to dinner with Vanessa, Angus, and the group. I'll text you when I leave. Just imagine me taking you deep in my mouth and massaging your balls.

Mason: You're going to kill me, woman.

Me: Well, at least you'll die with a smile on your face.

Mason: I want to know all your fantasies tonight.

I make my way back to the table just as they're serving our dinners.

Hatch cuts into his stuffed lobster and I enjoy my mahi-mahi as we make polite conversation. Evelyn and Kantor join the conversation, and we have a great time.

As the evening winds down and we prepare to leave, Hatch turns to me and says, "Vanessa tells me you have somebody at home."

"I do."

"Is it exclusive?"

Wow, he's aggressive.

"It is."

"I'm not surprised. You're beautiful, smart, and positively amazing."

I turn to Vanessa. "Are you paying him to say this?"

She starts to answer, but Hatch is quick to say, "Not at all. I just can't help but be disappointed that I didn't meet you first."

"You're incredibly sweet." I kiss him on the cheek.

Evelyn and Kantor tell us they're heading out for drinks. "Have fun." I send them off with a wave.

I get into the back of the car between my guards and immediately go back to my cell phone. It's been almost an hour, and I've been thinking about what I want to know.

Me: Lingerie or nude?

Mason: You have a perfect body. Don't hide it.

Me: Toys—good or bad?

Mason: Good and sometimes sinful. I want to know a fantasy of yours.

Me: Candles, maybe a little bit of spanking and hair pulling.

I hold my breath. I don't know if that was too much for him. He's a sweet guy, and if that isn't something that turns him on, I don't care. He's much more important than any silly fantasy.

My phone vibrates, and I look at his response. It's a picture of his hard dick.

I really wish he was here with me.

Me: I think I just came in my panties.

Mason: Show me.

Me: I'm not back at the hotel yet.

Mason: Did you pack any toys?

Me: There is a good possibility I did.

Mason: When you get back to your room, I want to FaceTime with you naked and your toy.

Me: We're just pulling up now. You'd better be naked yourself.

chapter

twenty-two

MASON

I'M COMPLETELY SPENT. Having sex over FaceTime wasn't as great as being there with her, but it was a close second. CeCe is amazing in so many ways, and we need to get this crap behind us as soon as possible. I want to look at engagement rings, but I always have a trail of photographers everywhere I go, so that would let my secret out. I need to talk to her dad beforehand, at the very least.

I hate being so far away from her. I want to feel her warm body next to mine. All day I kept thinking of her. It's nine thirty now. It's still a bit early, but I'm determined.

I pick up my phone. "Jim, this is Mason. I'm going to fly into New York tonight."

"No problem. Off to see CeCe?"

"I can't stand her being so far away."

"I understand. Jack Reece and Will Hamilton are with her, along with my New York team. I can have Patrice Newman join you."

"Thanks. I'll leave tomorrow morning at about six from CeCe's place heading to the airport. I know she has an event tomorrow at Barney's, but maybe I can surprise her tomorrow for dinner."

"I'll alert the team."

"Thanks, Jim."

I disconnect the call, feeling like I'm fifteen again with a constant hard-on and a complete fascination with everything she does. I alert the crew that I'll be looking to leave in the morning and then send a text to my friend Will Guidara in New York who owns a restaurant.

Me: I know you're a tough reservation to get last minute, but any chance I can get a table for my girlfriend and me tomorrow night?

Will: For you and Caroline? Of course!

Me: What time can you fit us in?

Will: The second seating at nine?

Me: We'll see you then. Thank you!

I smile, knowing I have reservations at Eleven Madison Place, one of the hottest restaurants in the world. I can't wait to spoil CeCe.

I send messages out to the team letting them know I'll be working remotely for the next few days but will be reachable by phone and email, and I go to bed excited. My plans are coming together perfectly.

Patrice and I land at JFK just after four. As I settle into the helicopter that will fly us over the ugly traffic driving into Manhattan below, I text CeCe. What are your plans tonight?

CeCe: I'm exhausted. I'm almost back at my hotel, and my plan is to take a bath and relax. Maybe spend some time with you on FaceTime.

My heart beats faster. No one but Jim's team knows I'm in town. I thought about alerting Evelyn, but everything was moving too fast.

Me: Sounds great. I was thinking the same thing.

The flight is less than fifteen minutes from the airport to Manhattan's heliport, and I quickly find myself in the back of a Suburban as Jim's team shuttles us over to the Four Seasons.

chapter

twenty-three

MASON

WALKING INTO THE LOBBY OF THE FOUR SEASONS with my team around me, I spot Evelyn sitting off to the side in a chair talking intently with a man. I can't make out who he is. His hair is a chocolate brown, and I can't tell if I know him.

As I look at them, I can tell they aren't a romantic couple. There are no smiles, no intimate gestures or any signs of laughter. Rather their heads are close together, and the conversation is rapid-fire back and forth. Evelyn is so involved with the conversation that she doesn't see me walk by less than ten feet away. If I thought I knew the man, I'd interrupt, but I don't recognize him from behind, so I keep moving toward the elevator. I'd rather spend my time with CeCe anyway.

The elevator arrives, and I'm greeted by Jack Reece. "Hello, sir."

"She doesn't know I'm here, does she?"

"We haven't told her, sir."

"Thank you. I want this to be a surprise."

"She told us she was in for the night."

"I may try to talk her into going out to dinner later."

"Just let us know."

The elevator opens at her suite, and I enter the living room. The view of the sun setting with Central Park in view is beautiful. "Hello?"

CeCe walks out in a black silk robe wrapped tightly around her waist. "Mason?"

I drop my bag and walk toward her. "Surprise."

She comes running into my arms and holds me so tight I can't breathe. My hand curls around the back of her neck, and I ravage her lips with all the pent-up energy of a man starved. My teeth scrape her lips while my tongue takes control of her mouth, dragging her in deeper.

We eventually break our kiss, but we don't let go of one another. "How did you get here? When did you arrive?" she asks.

"I just got here. After our conversation last night, I decided I hate being away from you. Don't get me wrong, last night's conversation was a close second, but not close enough to being with you." I lean down and kiss her softly on the top of her head.

"I can't believe you're here. Last night was pretty amazing, but I much prefer you here."

"How did today go?"

She turns professional, stepping back and withdrawing a bit. "It went well. We sold out of just about everything, which happens when you offer to autograph a piece of cosmetics. Barney's was excited about the event because store sales were up."

"Good. That should secure your spot with them, at least for the time being."

"We've already told Becca to identify our top ten locations so I can do this again. Then we'll identify the next ten. We'll keep doing this until I can't stand it, but at least it fortifies my brand for a while."

"Any conversations about animal testing?"

"No, thank goodness. Most people were just excited to tell me how happy they are about you."

"Me?"

She smiles. "Yes, you're quite popular. They love to tell me how glad they are that Frederic's out of the picture. They also ask about Trey and what's going on with Sara and when they're going to have a baby."

There's no way they know much about me, so I can't imagine it was anything more than my name—and it's probably not even spelled right. "Well, at least they're not asking you if *you're* having a baby."

"No, not yet, but they're excited about us."

I reach out and trace her nipple, which is standing out beneath the thin silk. "What were you doing when I came in?"

"I was just drawing a bath. Care to join me?"

"I thought you'd never ask."

She reaches for my hand, and I follow her into the bathroom like a dog in heat. My cock is already standing at attention. I can't wait to enjoy that sweet body of hers and hear the sounds she makes. CeCe's everything to me, and my heart beats ten times faster when I'm with her. I see the world in color now, when before I only saw it in black-and-white. She's quickly becoming my everything.

She stands in front of me, watching me in the mirror as she unties her robe and slowly slips it off her shoulders. I unbutton my shirt and drop it to the floor. I can see her slit glistening, and her nipples are perfect and begging to be touched. I can't help but reach for them and suck while she moans her appreciation.

I kneel on the hard tile floor and ignore the nonforgiving surface so I can worship the goddess in front of me. I open her legs and dip my tongue deep within her to taste her sweet honey.

"That feels so good," she moans.

I lift her leg over my shoulder, licking, nibbling, and sucking as my fingers explore. She's trembling and trying not to moan as I kiss around her, teasing and watching her get wetter and wetter. Squirming, she reaches down and pulls her lips wide, exposing herself to me. I take the hint and press my mouth against her slick slit in a deep kiss. She sighs loudly and shudders around me. My tongue snakes in and out, massaging her clit and thick, slippery slit before pushing inside.

"God, Mason…." She sighs in utter bliss, her legs writhing around me as I sit between them. "You know you've ruined me for all other men."

My response is to slip a finger inside her and stroke her sweet spot while my tongue slithers around her clit, making her shudder and squirm even more. My finger pivots in and out slowly, and I feel her squeeze me. She plays with her breasts, squeezing them and massaging them in circles.

"Okay," she breathes, her voice thick with desire. "Okay, we need to switch or I'm going to come. Please give me your dick."

I pull my mouth from her pussy and turn her to face the mirror, running my hand up and down her wetness. I finish undressing and let my pants slide to the floor, exposing my hard cock.

"I want to taste you," CeCe moans.

I shake my head. "This isn't about me; this is about you. I want you to watch yourself come undone—to see the ecstasy in your face when you reach your pinnacle."

I spread her legs wide and push into her from behind. She's tight and struggles to take all of me.

"Relax, baby." Reaching around her, I circle her clit. She holds on to the countertop, her head moving from side to side as I slowly pivot in and out, each time going a tiny bit deeper. "That's it, baby. I want you to enjoy the ride."

"Fuck me, Mason," she moans.

"I always do as I'm told." Gripping her hips, I use them as leverage as I move in and out. The wet slapping sounds of our bodies crashing into one another over and over echo throughout the bathroom. I grab her hair and pull back just enough so that her erect nipples rub against the cool marble. "Do you like that?"

"Yes," she moans.

I've never hit a woman in anger, but knowing CeCe likes to be spanked while being fucked is a complete turn-on. I slap her perfect ass and a nice pink spot appears as her pussy grips my cock like it's in a vise. *Holy shit.*

"Harder," she begs.

I fuck her faster and spank her ass again. Her pussy clamps around me so tight that I think she's cut the circulation off.

Pivoting in and out, I announce, "I'm going to come."

"Fill me."

I work her clit hard, moving in fast, tight circles. When I can't take it anymore, my cock erupts deep inside her, and I feel her pussy tighten one more time, pulsing as she moans her own satisfaction.

"Did you see yourself come?" I ask once my breathing calms down.

"I did. What a rush."

We're both spent. "Do you think the bathwater is still warm?

She nods and steps in. I see the pink marks on her ass as she moves, and my flaccid dick begins to harden once again.

I sit on the shower bench facing her. With the soap, I massage her feet, working out what little tension is left in her body.

"Caroline?"

"CeCe," she corrects me.

I nod. "CeCe. I don't know what I would've done without you. With everything going on at SHN, the poisoning, and everything else, I would've been lost without you."

"I feel the same way."

"I love you, and my world is nothing without you."

"I love you, too, Mason."

"I know this is fast, and we've got a lot of things to get settled, but I want you to start thinking about the two of us spending our lives together."

"I'd like nothing better."

My heart beats faster with my excitement. Could our timing finally be right? I don't want a fling with her—I want her, period. "I'm not proposing—yet—but I know that I've never wanted anyone else like I have you."

She leans forward. "I feel the same way. We don't have to do anything quickly. We just need to be together."

I don't want her to think I'm going to do this halfway. I want to give her everything. "I have to ask your father, and I need to make sure your brother isn't going to cut my balls off before I officially ask. I know you're worried that with the crazy press, I may change my mind, but I'm telling you this now so you know—I'm not going anywhere."

She turns a shade of pink. "Thank you."

"Tonight I have a reservation for dinner at Eleven Madison Park."

Her eyes widen, and a smile takes over her face. "You were able to get a reservation there?"

"Will and I go way back, and he was very generous to open a table for us last minute."

"I didn't think those existed for anybody."

"We can go another night if you'd prefer to continue doing what we've started and just order in room service. Our reservation is at nine, so if you prefer to stay in, I should call and cancel."

"As much as I would love to have four or five rounds of what we just did, I think we can manage both."

"I don't want to fool you, I think my record is with you, and that's four times in twenty-four-hours, so maybe a break will help me make it five." She giggles, and I love the sound. "You're so beautiful."

"I love it when you say that to me, because I know you believe it."

"I really do."

As CeCe finishes getting ready, I walk into the living room for a pre-dinner drink. To my body clock, it isn't late, but I don't want to hover while she gets ready. Men really do have it easy. Take a shower, throw on clothes, and comb your hair. If your hair is being difficult, add gel. Women have it much harder. I can get ready faster than CeCe can dry her hair, let alone style it or put makeup on or get dressed.

Evelyn is sitting on the couch, flipping through channels on the television.

"Hi," I greet her.

"Hey." She looks at me shocked. "What brings you to New York?"

I jerk my thumb toward the door to CeCe's room. "The gorgeous lady in there."

"Wow, I've never had anybody cross the continent to spend time with me."

"I have no doubt that one day you will." I pour myself a finger of scotch and offer one to her, but she shakes her head.

"I have plans at eleven tonight. The late seating at some restaurant on the east side."

Caroline comes out, attaching an earring to her ear. "With Kantor? He seemed into you."

"He was a lot of fun last night. He was able to get a dinner reservation, so I'll meet him there."

"Have fun. We're off to dinner at Eleven Madison Park."

Evelyn's eyes widen. "Wow. I remember you saying last time you couldn't get a reservation at that restaurant."

"I didn't. Mason knows the owner of the restaurant group."

"Hopefully it's everything they say it is. Enjoy your dinner tonight," I say to Evelyn as I usher CeCe to the elevator down to the car.

Patrice Newman joins us and says, "There's a small gaggle of reporters outside. We're taking you directly to the garage."

"Do they know where we're going?"

"No, but it won't take long for the word to get out."

As we exit the car, the flashbulbs pop and the yelling for our attention commences. The doorman greets us. "Mr. Sullivan. Miss Arnault. Welcome."

Walking in, the bar is too busy to sit with a drink, and the dining room is full of guests. The maître d' says, "Welcome to Eleven Madison Park."

I don't even hear the woman approach until she's standing at my elbow. "May I take your coats?"

After we shrug them off, the maître d' shares, "Will has suggested the table in the back. It offers the most privacy."

"That would be greatly appreciated," CeCe says.

The restaurant is elegant, from its taupe-covered velvet chairs to the silver bowls with flowers that adorn each table. We follow the maître d' to a bench-seating table tucked quietly in the back away from windows. "Would you prefer to sit with your back to the restaurant?" he asks. "You may be able to avoid any unwanted attention that way."

"Thank you," CeCe says. "The paparazzi seem out in full force."

"We're happy to run some interference and make sure you aren't bothered this evening. We'll monitor the crowd, and if you would like, we can also make arrangements for you to exit through a hidden door we have right here"—he points to a wall—"that cuts through the kitchen. John Paul and Francis will be your servers tonight. Enjoy your evening."

We are immediately greeted by the two servers, who pour sparkling water into our glasses. "Welcome to Eleven Madison Place," John Paul says. "We have the tasting menu of five courses. Would you care for the accompanying wine course?"

I look at CeCe, who nods vigorously.

"Yes, please," I reply.

"Enjoy your evening." He bows his head and disappears.

I spot Jim's team close by, standing close but behind a privacy wall that the wait staff uses. The restaurant has a way to allow them to blend in and few people know there is security lurking.

"You know, it'll always be like this," CeCe warns.

"You're worth it. Were the paparazzi at the Barney's event today?"

"Yes, they covered it, though I'm hopeful that we got some good old regular media coverage as well."

"Vanessa worked really hard, I bet."

"She did. As did Becca and a few others. We may not have the presence we wanted for Fashion Week, but we've made ourselves known, and maybe this will work as we combat the animal testing mess. My fingers are crossed."

"Mine, too."

"When I return to San Francisco, I have to circle back to Cora and figure out where they're at with my case. I'm a bit nervous that we haven't heard anything since our last update. My team is getting close to launching this line we don't really want to launch. If it isn't one of our team members, I'm hoping they've got their eyes on someone else."

"Agreed. Oh, I noticed Evelyn was in an intense conversation with some guy in the lobby when I arrived at your hotel. Do you know who she was meeting with?"

"What did he look like?"

"Hair about the same color as Trey's. I didn't get a good look at his face, though."

"That sounds like Steve Kantor. I'm pretty sure they spent the night together last night."

"Interesting. It didn't seem like a romantic meeting, but what do I know?"

Throughout dinner, we're relaxed and carefree. CeCe is the first woman with whom I've felt able to be my true self. I don't need to put on any false pretenses or worry she'll be looking for something from me. I like this feeling.

"I can't eat another bite! Everything was perfectly seasoned, with little taste surprises in almost every dish. The lamb, lobster, and vegetables were all exquisitely displayed and tasted great," CeCe says as John Paul clears away the fourth and main course.

"One last course left," he tells her. "Tonight is a rich chocolate truffle layer cake and delicate cream puffs with chocolate sauce."

"I have room for that." CeCe grins.

I lean in and nuzzle her ear. "I'd be happy having you for dessert."

I see Will working the room, and after a moment he comes over. "Mason, I'm so happy to see you."

"Thank you so much for the table. Have you met Caroline Arnault?"

"No. It's quite a pleasure to meet you." He leans down, but watches me. I know he's happily married, so I'm not worried when he slowly kisses her hand.

"Your food is amazing. Thank you for the table," CeCe gushes.

"I hear you're a regular at Quince," Will says.

"I am. Do you know Michael?"

"I met him once. His work is amazing. I hope you find our food equally as good."

"Without a doubt," CeCe says with a twinkle in her eyes. She knows if she tells Will it was better, he'd probably call Michael and brag to him. She's so smart.

"Have a great evening and enjoy your dessert," Will offers as he moves along to another table.

Champagne is paired with dessert, which is perfect. We need to celebrate, not only the success of her trip but also us.

"We're not officially anything, but you've had a great start to a rough week, and it's only going to get better," I promise.

We clink our glasses together.

"Thank you. Your visit and tonight are perfect." CeCe smiles broadly.

"Are you ready to go back to the hotel?"

"I am. I believe you promised me another three times tonight."

"I'd hate to disappoint you."

chapter

twenty-four

MASON

THE SLOPE OF CECE'S BACK HAUNTS MY MEMORIES and strains my pants. It was really hard to get on my plane to return to San Francisco and leave CeCe behind, but work called, and I can only do so much for so many days outside of the office. I haven't slept well since I returned. Sleeping in any bed isn't right without her. I do honestly believe my dick is chapped and about ready to fall off. I think back to the look of ecstasy she had the morning when I made her come with my tongue and my pants become uncomfortably tight. I hope it'll always be this way.

She gets home this afternoon, and I can't wait.

My phone rings and I look at the caller ID, then quickly snatch it up. "Hey, Jim, what's up?"

"We've located Annabelle. She's in Oakland."

"Oakland? Why? Where?" I question, completely dumbfounded by the news.

"She's in an apartment about two blocks away from where the hacking farm was raided. It could be a coincidence, or she's involved."

"They say there's no such thing as coincidences," I reply with disdain.

"That's how I see it, but we haven't identified whose name is on the lease of the apartment where she's staying."

"Are you going to confront her again?" Fuck! I so wanted her to not be involved with this hacker shit. I can't believe it! What am I going to do? How am I going to confront her? "Do you want me to try to talk to her?"

"We've notified SFPD, and they've looped in Oakland PD. The plan is that she'll be arrested today."

"Should I be there?"

"She'll be remanded to SFPD custody. They'll tackle the poisoning and work with the FBI for the federal crimes."

"I feel like I should get her an attorney." I can't explain why I feel this way, but while she may not be the love of my life, she was still a good friend who took care of me.

"I won't give you an opinion either way."

"Thanks, Jim. If you hear anything I should know from SFPD or your team, please don't hesitate to call. Let me know when she's taken into custody, and I'll notify the team."

"Will do." Jim pauses before ending the call. "Mason, she's innocent until proven guilty. We don't know anything yet."

"Thanks for the reminder."

After I hang up, I cross my arms, stand, and look out over the busy streets of San Francisco. I can't see water or anything from our office. Dillon can see Oracle Park from his, and we always joke that if we could open our windows, we'd hear the cheers when they play in the stadium.

Why would she do this?

What's her relationship, if any, to the hackers?

I would bet all of the money I have that she can't read code, so she can't be Eve, so what is she to them?

Why is she hiding from all of this if she isn't guilty?

Time passes incredibly slowly. Outside my office, it's a flurry of activity. We have new investments coming in and potential sales and public offerings. It's busy, and I can't concentrate. I walk to the break room and get coffee, but I'm never far from my phone. Each time it rings, I answer before the caller ID announces it.

"Mason Sullivan," I say into the receiver.

"Oh, hi. It's me." CeCe's voice is like butter melting on toast—smooth and liquid. "Everything okay?"

"Yes, why do you ask?"

"You sound like you've had a few too many cups of coffee."

I chuckle. She's good. Settling back in my chair, I decide to tell her what I know. "They're arresting Annabelle as we speak. Jim's team found her in an apartment in Oakland not too far from the hackers' location."

"Wow. How are you feeling?"

"You know how you're convinced that there's no way your team could betray your trust?"

"Yes?"

"That's how I feel about Annabelle. Maybe at first, but not after she moved in with me."

"I'll support you."

"Thanks." I then realize that isn't why she called me. "What's going on with you?"

"I'm meeting with Cora tomorrow, and we're going to go over what her team's found."

"I can probably make myself available if you'd like."

"That's exactly what I was hoping for. She wants to meet first thing, which does nothing for my current sleep habits."

"Well, I can put in a word with someone who'll let you get your rest this evening."

"Thanks. I guess while I have you, I should ask if you're up for dinner tonight over at Dillon and Emerson's."

"I have a feeling that I may be wrapped up with Annabelle, but if that doesn't happen, sure."

"Call me when you know something. And enjoy the rest of your afternoon."

After a few interruptions from the team, my phone rings again and it's Jim.

"Hey, Mason. She's been arrested and is being transported back to SFPD. Detective Lenning is working with Assistant Director Perry."

"Do I need to be there? Do they need anything from me?"

"I don't think so, but I would guess they'll reach out to you through Marci."

"Of course. Keep me posted."

Jim hangs up, and I quickly call Marci and give her the update.

"That's great news. They'll probably want to interview you again after they've had a chance to talk to her. I'll let you know when I hear from them," she says.

"Do you think it'll be today?" I ask.

"I don't. I think at the earliest, it'll be tomorrow. Are you joining CeCe and me tomorrow morning?"

"That's the plan."

"Great, we can dig for information then."

After I disconnect from the call, I send out a group text to all the partners and advisors.

Me: Annabelle has been arrested in Oakland. They're transporting her to San Francisco. We don't know anything yet, but I'll keep you posted as I hear things.

Cameron: Wahoo! Fantastic news!

Dillon: We should all celebrate. How about our house after work for dinner and drinks?

Cynthia: Todd and I are in!

Christopher: I'll be there. Bella informs me she'll try.

Greer: I'll be with you in spirit! I'm happy that maybe we can close this chapter down.

Emerson: Our house is a wreck. Bring blinders.

CeCe: Great news. I'm up for a celebration. See you about 6?

Emerson: 6 is perfect. I'll order in from the Greek place in our neighborhood. Please bring your beverage of choice.

This saddens me, but I get it. We all hope this means we're almost at the end of the tunnel regarding our mole and hackers.

Dillon peeks into my office. "Hey, you want a ride to my place?"

"Sure. Leave in ten?"

"On Mason time, that means twenty minutes."

"I'll try to make it fifteen."

As I close down my office, there are a few people still working, including Quinn. "Aren't you coming?"

"I have a closing with one of William's new clients. With Emerson still on her leave, we're shorthanded. I don't think I can make it."

"Please come, at least for a little while."

William walks up and kisses her on the forehead. "You can come in early tomorrow."

She closes her eyes and shakes her head. "Fine. I'd much rather hang out with you than review job descriptions and evaluate overlap in headcount between our investments and our staff."

As I walk up to the elevator, there are several partners already waiting. "I told you it would be twenty minutes," Dillon announces.

"The extra five minutes were convincing Quinn to join us," I explain.

"You're forgiven. It wouldn't be the same without her," Cynthia admits.

Our gathering is full of food, drink, and merriment. I'm not hungry, but I eat anyway, not even tasting what I put in my mouth. I don't want to celebrate Annabelle's arrest. I want to get to the bottom of this. I want to know if she was involved, to what extent, and why.

CeCe leans in and gives me a lingering kiss on my cheek. "How are you doing?"

I shrug.

"We'll have more answers in the morning," she assures me, and my love for her grows even more. She can tell how I'm feeling without me telling her.

"I know. I just don't want to celebrate tonight."

"Then let's get out of here and go home."

"Do you mind?" What a relief. I don't want to celebrate that I could've been fooled all along and that my friend was behind this.

"Not at all."

I walk up to Dillon and Emerson. "I think we're going to head out."

"Is everything okay?" Emerson asks.

"Yes. We're meeting with the FBI in the morning, and I'm just anxious for some answers."

Dillon puts his arm over my shoulder. "Mase, we don't know if Annabelle is behind all of our problems, but we're going to find out. We're getting closer to the light at the end of the tunnel. You've been through hell, and now you need to get some rest. Go."

"Thanks, man."

We say our goodbyes and meet up with Jim's team to head back to CeCe's house.

Holding her hand is reassuring. She brings our clasped hands to her mouth and kisses the back of mine softly. "We're going to get through this together."

Her assurance both makes my heart soar and calms me at the same time. I feel so much better knowing she doesn't blame me for getting involved with Annabelle.

Jim's men drop us off out front. The smell of wet earth and the temperature dropping signals the fog is rolling in. CeCe cinches her coat a bit tighter at her waist, and I reach for her delicate hand. Walking into the house with our fingers intertwined, we shrug out of our coats, then talk about mindless things as we go through the mail and read our emails.

"You're home early. Are you hungry? Would you like me to make up some dinner?" Angela smiles, tying an apron at her waist as she approaches us in the foyer.

"We've eaten. I think we're just going to—"

There's a sharp *ping* sound coupled with glass breaking. Suddenly the house alarm goes off, the noise hurting my ears. I'm disoriented and not clear on what just happened, but I know it isn't good.

Over the loud, frenetic siren, I hear more glass break. "Get down!" I yell.

Although it's only seconds, it seems like hours that the alarm blares, and there are thuds all around us. The Asian blue-and-white vase filled with puffy white flowers that sits at the center of the table above us shatters, spraying water all over the foyer and us.

I quickly scan the room. CeCe sits next to me, and I can see she's unsure what to do. We're being sprayed with bullets, and it's overwhelming.

As if they beam in from the garage, Jim's men suddenly appear above us with guns drawn. The sound of the alarm is deafening, and we're all covering our ears. Glass continues to break around us. I look up and see a growing blotch of red pooling at Jack Reece's shoulder. He ducks down and yells over the rapid gunfire. I can't make out what he says, but he points to the kitchen toward the back of the house and urges me to move. As the bullets whiz by over our heads, we crawl on our hands and knees to the garage. Glass is spraying over our head, and I feel a sudden slice of pain in my thigh, making me stop. The pain is searing.

Three men come in and essentially lift us off the ground and carry us into the garage.

"Get in the car!" Jack yells.

Misty comes out of nowhere and bounds into the car with us. She understands the house isn't a safe place to be.

With one eye on CeCe, making sure she's doing the same, I launch myself into the back of the car. Angela is hauled in with us. Thank goodness she's okay.

"HQ called the police. They'll meet us there." The garage door opens, and as soon as there's enough clearance, the tires squeal as we launch out of the garage into the dark alley. For half a moment, I feel a level of calmness.

Then we see someone at the end of the alley. They're in all black with what looks like a black full-face motorcycle helmet. The driver does the opposite of what I expect, pushing down on the accelerator instead of the brake. Bullets ricochet off the Suburban, but nothing happens. The driver races toward the man, and with the headlights, I notice it's not a motorcycle helmet but full body armor. My stomach drops as he pellets us with round after round of bullets. Angela is screaming and crying, CeCe is yanked to the ground, and I'm pushed on top of her with Jack on top of me.

We drive out of the alley and are thrown hard as we take a tight turn at high speed. We're hit by a car in the right quarter panel but keep driving. More gunshots hit the vehicle from behind. Hard turns jostle us as we're rocked back and forth. Tires squeal and the streetlamp reflections flicker as we race down the street. I hear sirens in the distance and have never been so grateful for them. They're close, but I can't make out what the guys up front are saying.

Angela is quiet now, and I'm scared for her. "Angela?"

"I'm here. I'm okay. Scared shitless, but I'm fine." She starts speaking in Spanish, and my guess is she's cursing at the shooters.

Jim's man continues taking hard turns, and without looking out, I have no idea where we are.

We hit a big bump, and the tires squeal on what sounds like a concrete floor. The fluorescent light bathes us as we enter an underground parking garage and then come to a screeching halt.

The doors of the Suburban are ripped open. "Is everyone okay?" Jim asks

Jack announces, "I think so. I was grazed in the shoulder and am bleeding like a stuck pig, but it's superficial."

"You'll just use the scar to pick up chicks." One of the men snickers. Knowing they can joke right now gives me great relief.

As Jim helps me out of the vehicle, I see my pant leg is covered in blood. CeCe sees it at the same time I do and screams, "Mason was hit!"

It begins to burn as the adrenaline wears off. My legs are weak beneath me, and two men grab me under the shoulders before I collapse. They assist me inside as I say, "I'm fine. Really." They lead me to a room as Jim calls someone, and then a man appears with a large black bag.

"Make sure CeCe is fine," I call out.

With a pair of scissors, the man destroys my pants in a matter of seconds. "A bullet grazed Jack, too," he announces, then says to me, "It's going to hurt for a while, but you're going to be fine."

"What the hell happened?" Jim demands.

"We got them dropped off, and someone must've been at the park or across the street. They showered the house with bullets, and a second man at the end of the alley greeted us with rapid gunfire as we fled," Jack shares.

"I saw the Suburban. It took quite a few shots," Jim observes.

"Make sure you thank Chevrolet for the bulletproofing. We'd have been toast otherwise." I watch Jack rub his temples.

"I've let the police know you're here when they're ready," Jim tells me.

CeCe nods a little too quickly. I reach for her hand, and she squeezes it tight.

"We're okay," I assure her. "Angela's okay, too."

"I've never been that scared in my life," CeCe admits.

chapter

twenty-five

CECE

"WHO WOULD HATE ONE OF US SO MUCH that they'd send a hit squad after us?" My voice breaks. I'm trying so hard not to cry or hyperventilate.

Mason puts his arm around me, and I feel enormously better. "I have no idea."

Detective Lenning is shown into the media room where we're sitting wrapped together in a blanket. The adrenaline has worn off, and we're both exhausted. "Ms. Arnault. Mr. Sullivan." He nods as he sits across from us on a deep black leather couch. "Tell me what you can recall."

Mason walks him through leaving Dillon and Emerson's house and coming home. "I heard glass break, and then the house alarm started going off."

"How did you get out?" Detective Lenning asks.

"Jack Reece and the rest of the team came in and pushed us to the floor. We crawled into the garage, and CeCe went in the back of the Suburban first, followed by me."

"Do you remember when Jack was shot?" Detective Lenning asked.

It all happened so quickly that I'm struggling to recall the sequence of events. "It was before we went down on our knees, I think."

Mason shakes his head. "I didn't even notice. I was so worried about Caroline and Angela being hurt."

"Who do you think did this?" he asks.

Mason stands, and I can tell his leg is bothering him, but he won't admit it. "We were just thinking about that, and we have no idea."

With my elbows on my knees, I hold my head. I'm so tired that I struggle to follow the questions. Everything comes crashing down on me. It's too much. My business imploding, SHN's problems, Annabelle's arrest, Mason... I just don't know how much more I can take.

Detective Lenning looks at us carefully. "You both look exhausted. Our team has the street blocked off and the press pushed back. We don't know if this is related to your outside issues, but you won't be able to return to the house tonight."

Misty nuzzles Mason as he says, "That's fine. We can go to my place." He strokes Misty's fur, and I swear if she could talk, she'd tell us she was ready to go home.

"They'll be staying here," Jim cuts in. "We haven't secured Mason's home. We have several bedrooms here, and they'll have protection."

I don't want to fight with Jim, but I can tell Mason is ready to refuse. I put my hand on Mason's arm. "We'll stay here."

Detective Lenning is led out of the room, and Jim turns to me. "We've received calls from your business partners. They know you're fine."

"I don't have my cell phone," I state.

"Neither do I," Mason says. "I hit the floor and left it behind."

"We'll see if we can get those along with a change of clothes," Jim replies.

"Are we still going to see Cora in the morning?" I ask.

"That's not a problem as long as you have our escorts," Jim says as he leads us to an elevator.

The elevator ascends, and I'm stunned when we exit and look around. "Do you all live here?"

"No, just me," Jim shares.

It's a giant loft with windows from floor to ceiling. "You're allowing us to stay in your home?"

"Yes, I have a guest room." He looks at Mason, and as if Jim can read his mind, he says, "Don't worry, it would take a Howitzer to break through the glass."

"You're very kind, Jim."

"It's not a problem."

He disappears for a few minutes and comes back with two T-shirts and an unopened package of boxer shorts. "Here, this might work to sleep in."

Mason accepts them. "Thanks, man."

We change clothes and crawl into bed, and before my head hits the pillow, I'm out.

"Ces, it's after eight. Do you want to get up?" Mason asks, waving a cup of coffee under my nose.

"No, I want to sleep for a week," I answer into my pillow.

The coffee smells so good, the scent helping my brain's synapses to connect. As I sit up, I slowly remember where I am and how I got here and why we're here. I accept the coffee he's offered and take a few sips before I can say much. "Thank you. How are you feeling this morning?"

Mason winces. "I'm fine. They ruined my favorite pants, though."

"All of your pants are khaki. You have a favorite pair?"

"Of course. They were the pants I was wearing when you told me you loved me."

"I thought you were naked when I did that."

"We were in your kitchen, and I was wearing them that morning."

"I'm impressed." And I really am. I wasn't testing him, but to know that our declarations are etched in his memory, and he even remembers what he was wearing, makes me feel ten feet tall. "I need to brush my teeth, and then I'm going to attack you."

"Angela went over this morning with Jim's team and brought you several outfits."

"That's good news. I can't see Jack going through my unmentionables and being comfortable."

He smiles. "And I'd want to knock his lights out." He leans in and kisses me on the forehead. "Though, despite his injury, he'd put me down before I could touch him."

"As long as you realize that." I giggle. Then everything hits me again. I have a big day ahead of me. "I need a shower."

I work my way into the bathroom and start the water, turning it up high. My shower does little to relax me, however; the muscles in my shoulders are still tense, and the more I think about today, the more overwhelmed I feel. Jim doesn't have much for me to do anything with my hair, but at least I have clean hair.

I walk out towel-drying it and smell bacon and crepes. Now I know why Angela wanted to get back in the house. She wanted her crepe pan. "Angela, you're amazing."

"You have a big day ahead of you, and I knew you needed a good breakfast."

I give her a big hug before taking a seat at the table. "You're amazing. How are you feeling this morning?"

"I'll admit I didn't get much sleep last night."

"I'm truly sorry you've been dropped into this madness."

"All that matters is that we're all okay," she says with so much assurance that I'm not sure if she's trying to convince me or herself.

"I've spoken with all the partners. They blew up our phones last night with voice and text messages," Mason softly says from behind me.

"Thanks for doing that."

"We're to call them after we meet this morning with the FBI."

My stomach sours. I'm dreading this morning.

Mason looks at me. "It's going to be okay. Today's the day you're going to take back your company."

"You're right," I say with more enthusiasm than I actually have. "Are Jim and his team ready?"

"They're waiting for us."

With both hands, I push myself up from the table. "Let's get this over with."

I probably look more confident than I feel. But it helps to have four members of Jim's team, Marci, and Mason all walking in with me.

When the receptionist hands me back my ID, she says, "I'm really glad you're okay."

"You're very kind. Thank you. I'm glad, too." I wink at her.

"You know where you're going?" she says to Marci.

Marci nods. "We're all set. I brought you one of these." She hands the receptionist a sandwich. "It's a little early, but I really appreciate your turning me on to the best Philly cheesesteak in the city. You were spot on with Jake's on Buchannan's."

Her eyes grow large as she reaches for a foot-long sandwich. "Girl, you know it!" She peeks inside and takes a big whiff. "How were you able to get a hot sandwich so early?"

"I called and begged. Then I asked my assistant to get it and meet us here with it. They were very kind to have it ready for me."

As we exit the elevator, Cora is standing there with a look of relief. "I'm so glad you both are okay. When I saw the news, I immediately called Detective Lenning. He told me you were fine, but I'm glad to see it with my own eyes."

"Thanks for moving our meeting back a bit." Mason says.

"Not a problem in the least," Cora says over her shoulder as she leads us to a small conference room. "We've never met in here, but this room houses your case."

"Cora, thank you. I'm very excited and anxious to hear what you've learned."

The table only seats six people, but we all manage to squeeze into the tight space.

Cora starts the meeting off. "Thank you for coming in this morning. We know you had a rough night." She grimaces. "Three weeks ago, we placed trackers on five of your employees' cell phones and company computers. We tracked every word said and every keystroke, and we've been successful at eliminating two people."

She walks to the wall. "Jordan, as the project manager, adores you. She's had three job offers from Cosmetics, Inc., each one getting progressively more aggressive, but she's claimed her allegiance to you and to Metro Composition."

A wave of relief floods me. "I knew it couldn't be her. She had a lot riding on the fall line."

"We're confident to eliminate her," Cora replies. Then she moves to Christy. "You were absolutely correct, she is extremely loyal to you. Other members of the staff have attempted to engage her in gossip, but she's said nothing to anyone."

"That doesn't surprise me. I've known her since my mom started the company when I was in sixth grade. She wants to retire soon."

Despite Jordan and Christy being eliminated, I can't help but be disappointed that after all this time, we still have three people left.

Cora hands me a three-inch binder. I open it up and see emails from the three remaining suspects from my team. They've removed all the identifying markers. "These are all the email and text messages the other three have traded. The yellow sticky notes are questionable, and we'd like your eyes to review them. We've also included a large MP3 file that we'd like you to listen to of some dubious voice mails."

I feel positively overwhelmed. I don't know where to start or how to go through it. Not only do I feel it's a violation of their privacy, but I also don't know that I want to know who hates me that much.

"Right now we're asking you to be patient. We know this is taking longer than you wanted and we'd hoped, but we feel confident that we're almost there. We're chasing down some leads, and we believe we're going to be able to eliminate one or maybe two more within the next twenty-four hours, but we need your help."

"Whatever I can do. I'm ready to put this behind me," I reply.

Marci pats me on the arm and smiles. "It's going to be okay. We see the light at the end of the tunnel."

chapter

twenty-six

MASON

WE FINISH WITH THE UPDATE ON METRO. I know CeCe must be disappointed that they could only eliminate two of the five, but I also know that if they hadn't eliminated Christy, that would have been really devastating to her. She trusts Christy with everything, and a violation like that would've put her in a black hole that would be difficult to pull her out of.

"What's your plan?" Cora asks me.

"My plan?"

"I'm curious to know what you're planning on doing once all of this is settled."

"Good question. We try not to dwell on this because it seems to extend our timeline when we do. Dillon and I were talking about it. We're hoping this gets settled through the courts, and everything else that comes up by the time we retire."

Her mouth quirks at the corners. "It's good to know you can retire early."

"I don't think this is going to be quick." I hope I'm wrong, but I'd rather be cautiously optimistic.

She throws her head back and laughs loudly. "You never know."

It's then I realize she hasn't led us back to the elevator but to a large conference room featuring SHN's case. She waves to the empty seats and waits for us to take our seats. As we sit, we're joined by the team working on our case. Sitting on the edge of my chair, I'm anxious for what I suspect will be an interesting briefing.

Tina, one of Cora's analysts, turns to me and says, "We've been unsuccessful in locating Adam Reeves to date, though we do believe he's here in the Bay Area."

"Do you think he might've been behind the shooting last night?" I ask.

"We do," Cora says. "Jim Adelson's team was able to capture the gentleman at the end of the alley, and the police questioned him throughout the night. He's admitted to working with the Robin Hood Party."

I sit back and sigh loudly, showing my discontent that Adam hasn't been found. My mind spins. First he tried to kidnap CeCe, and then he shot up her house. He needs to be caught. He's escalating, and we need to locate him before he hurts someone.

"Well, at least we have some answers from last night." CeCe bounces a pen on the tabletop. "How are you going to locate Adam?"

"He has no digital footprint at this point, so we're going through all of his known associates. We're pulling up his family members, trying to figure out how he's surviving."

"Bitcoin, I'd assume," I halfheartedly joke.

"We've watched some of the bigger Bitcoin trading, and it isn't him. That doesn't mean he isn't using it to survive," one of Cora's team members says.

"How would you be able to see a transaction between two private individuals?" I question.

"It's not as hard as you'd think. Through software, we can navigate a cryptocurrency's blockchain, which will tell us all the details we need to know, just like how we track large cash transactions. It's actually easier than cash because they have to use a blockchain to move it around. Bitcoins are extremely difficult to actually hold—not impossible, of course, but still extremely difficult."

Good to know. I'm not sure I needed all that information, or that I understand it, but it's good to know they've gotten that taken care of.

"I assume he's using a fake identity," CeCe mutters.

"It's certainly quite possible. He's a hacker, and he would know how to navigate the dark web to purchase good fake identities and bounce between multiple people's Social Security numbers and fake credit cards," she concedes.

"And how many people a year have their identity stolen?" I ask snarkily.

"Nine million," one of Cora's team volunteers.

"Can you share with us what you're doing to find him? What's Annabelle saying?" I ask.

"She isn't talking, but we can't find any connection between them, and we don't see any proof that they're working together." Cora holds out a hand to stop me from speaking. "That doesn't mean it's not there, it's just not obvious yet."

"Have you officially ruled her out?" I ask.

"No, but we've found a few conflicts which are pointing to them not working together."

All of the air escapes from my lungs. How can that be? "Have you cleared her for poisoning me?"

"No, and we think she's involved in something else as well, so she won't be released any time soon," Cora shares.

I sit back hard in my seat. "If she's sitting in holding refusing to talk to anybody, isn't she entitled to an attorney and due process?"

"Not always," Cora replies. "We feel we're close to wrapping this up, and she hasn't requested an attorney yet."

"Close? That's huge."

"In my experience, people in these cases tend to negotiate it out, so we don't actually go to court. Otherwise we have seventy days to charge her."

"Seventy days is a long time. Why so specific?"

"The law says that if we don't have enough to charge her at that point, we need to release her."

I'm dumbfounded by this news. They know she's guilty of something. How did I miss it? Or did I? "Do you think she'd meet with me?"

"No, she's refusing all visitors and hasn't reached out to anyone at this point."

"She hasn't? Not even her friend Amanda?"

"She just quietly sits in her cell. When she gets tired of sitting, she stands and stretches."

"Can Mason see her even if she doesn't want to see him?" CeCe asks.

"No, I'm afraid not," Cora says firmly.

"What about our safety?"

"We do believe Adam is watching you and your friends. We're working with Jim and his team to make sure there's protection on all of the partners and their significant others all day, every day. Of the thirty-two hackers we've arrested, it took us a while to get the first one to turn—she was young and somewhat new but from the information she gave us, we've slowly but surely had success in turning eighteen of them."

"That sounds promising," I reply.

"It has been. They haven't just attacked you and your clients. They've been hacking municipalities across the country and taking information hostage, and they've also been hacking into individuals who've committed various ethical infractions and have blackmailed them."

"What are they doing with all their money?"

"We haven't traced it all. This Robin Hood Party is incredibly disjointed, but they make sure no one knows more than what they do."

chapter

twenty-seven

MASON

WE'RE ESCORTED FROM THE BUILDING TO OUR CAR. CeCe reaches for my hand, and I feel a sense that this may finally be wrapping up. I know it's occupied my thoughts for years. It may not have been all I thought about, but everything we did as a company was a defensive move against this mess. It's now second nature to be vigilant. As much as I'd prefer to not have to do that, most likely we need to continue. This Robin Hood Party will have someone behind them waiting to do the same thing again.

"Should we update the team?" CeCe says softly, interrupting the black hole my mind is dying to jump into.

I squeeze her hand. "I think so. Should we invite them over to my place?"

"That sounds like a great idea."

"Oh, wait, what about Angela?"

"She and Misty have gone to my mother's and will stay there for a while."

"Okay, good. I'd hate for her to have no place to go and no work because of our mess." I send a group text to the team. Anyone up for two nights in a row? Met with the FBI and we got some news.

Cynthia: Are you okay? I saw the news.

Me: Yes, we're just fine. We can tell you all about it if you can make it.

Cameron: Where and when?

Dillon: I think Emerson is already on her way. Count us in.

Me: We're on our way back from the federal building and should be at my house shortly.

My text messages ping back and forth as everyone replies they can make it.

CeCe is on the phone, and I hear "Twelve large vegetable and twelve large combinations, six large mixed greens, and six Italian." She rattles off my address and gives them her credit card number. I'm stunned. She looks over at me as she disconnects the call. "I've ordered pizza and salads from that spot close to your place."

"Wow, I'm impressed. I have drinks, so we should be good."

As we pull up in front of my condo building, I see Christopher and Bella waiting in a car outside. By the time we walk into my place, better than half the partners have joined us. I'm being hit with multiple questions at a time when CeCe says, "Come on in. We've lots to tell you, but you'll want beverages, and food is on the way."

We walk everyone through what's happened in the last twenty-four hours.

"That's amazing," Quinn says.

"Was it really only a flesh wound?" Hadlee, our resident doctor, asks.

"I promise, just a flesh wound. I won't be hopping on the treadmill for a few days, but I'm fine, and Jim's doctor sewed me up. I don't think I'll scar."

"So you mean to tell me that they can't confirm whether or not Annabelle is involved?" Emerson is incredulous.

"No. Now let me hold that baby boy. He's awfully cute." CeCe reaches for Liam and bounces him up and down on her lap. "Unfortunately they can't determine exactly what she's guilty of, but they know it's something."

"I know you've thought about this, but I'm curious if there's any consideration that Annabelle might be behind what happened at Metro?"

The group quiets down as everyone waits to hear what CeCe thinks. We've all had that question in the back of our minds, and with the amount of guilt I'll have if that's the case, I'll have to spend my life making it up to her.

"That's my biggest fear of all. I think that's why I'm most anxious to hear what they're so sure she's guilty of because in my mind, she could absolutely be behind what happened at both SHN and Metro." CeCe sighs, then continues. "Honestly, I never really thought about it before the meeting with Cora, but you know she hated me. I worked hard to make sure Mason and I didn't spend time alone together."

"Yes, and look at where it got us—in loveless relationships." I snort. *Wait, did I say that out loud?*

Everyone nods in apparent agreement.

"But we know it was meant to be based on where we are today." CeCe winks at me and blows me a kiss.

"Let's think about some of the similarities between the two companies," Cameron starts. "Both have been terrorized by a mole and probably hackers."

"Yes, and they both posted false information," William adds.

"The only difference being it was against CeCe's actual company, whereas it was SHN's clients."

"Okay, what else is the same?" CeCe looks at everyone, but no one can come up with anything concrete. "Unfortunately, this kind of corporate espionage is probably more common than we think and they're not related. It's most likely just poorly timed from our perspective. This may be the new world."

We debate for a while longer, and then Trey stands up and announces, "I can tell my baby sister is exhausted. Let's let them get some rest and pick this up on Sunday night at our parents'."

The group begins to disperse. As people leave, we hear a lot of "We're glad you're all right," "Sure would be nice if this was over in the next seventy days," and "I can't wait for this to be behind us."

Shutting the door behind the last person, I turn to CeCe. "You're amazing, you know that?"

"What do you mean?"

"You're so strong. I watched how you managed everyone here tonight. I didn't think I could love you more, but I do. I know that with you, I can get through anything."

She walks toward me and puts her arms around me. "I think the exact same way about you."

Our lips meet softly, our tongues exploring. When we break apart, she whispers, "I'm exhausted."

"Let's get you in bed."

I'm immersed in a prospectus from William for a new app that, if successful, could change the way we use money in the future. Paper money and coins would become obsolete, though I want to believe that would never happen—too many people want something physical to hold.

My phone rings, bringing me out of my stupor. The caller ID says it's coming from the Federal Bureau of Investigation. It's only been a few hours, but my guess is it's Cora.

"Mason Sullivan," I say as I answer the phone.

"Hello, Mason. It's Cora."

"You're the only one from the FBI who calls me anymore. You're the only one who still loves me." I mock pout.

"That I do." She laughs. "I thought you'd like to know what we knew yesterday but were unable to prove until after we met. I have some surprising news that's comes from our interview with Tom Van der Wolfe."

"I've been curious about the man with three names."

"Were you that aware Adam and Annabelle are siblings?"

I sit back in my chair, totally stunned by this revelation. This is completely out of left field. "I had no idea. Absolutely none."

"Did you ever meet any of her family?"

"No. She said her father was abusive, but otherwise she never mentioned anything about them except that she grew up in Orange County. Does this mean she's Eve?"

"We don't know yet. We need to sit down with her, but he let us know this bit of information. As I said yesterday, there are some instances where we feel confident that she wasn't a part of the hacking, so we aren't sure what the connection means quite yet. Tom doesn't realize he let that tidbit out, so we're playing it close to our vest, but I wanted to find out what you know."

"Apparently nothing. I don't know what to say. I am completely and utterly shocked by this."

"I've been thinking about your volunteering to meet with Annabelle. I *may* take you up on that."

"Whatever you need. I'm not going to tell anybody this information yet. I need to talk to her first. Are you okay with that?"

"Mason, you're the keeper of the information. I'm fine with you withholding information from your colleagues. I'll follow your direction regarding this because it's your company, but I haven't decided if you can talk to her."

"Thank you. It's not solely my company, of course, and maybe I'm going to get in trouble by doing this, but I need to talk to Annabelle first before I tell everyone. Otherwise they're going to storm down there with me wanting to rip her heart out."

"Come by at four this afternoon. I haven't decided for sure if it's a good idea for you to meet with her, but I'm thinking about it."

We hang up, and I turn to look out the window behind me. How could I have missed something so big? How is it possible that they're related? They look nothing alike. I realize Trey and CeCe are fraternal twins, so they look somewhat alike. Dillon and his sister, Siobhan, don't look exactly alike, but they still have enough similarities that you could pick them out as siblings.

Adam is a former linebacker for Stanford. He's a big guy. Annabelle is petite.

Adam has dark brown hair. Annabelle is a blonde.

Adam has pasty white skin. Annabelle has an olive tone.

I just find it hard to believe that they're siblings. Not to mention I'm one hundred percent positive that Annabelle doesn't know the first thing about coding. She knows purses, designers, and who's who on the *Forbes* list, but not the difference between a string of Java code and even basic HTML. There's no way Annabelle can be Eve.

So who is?

William sticks his head into my office. "Hey, boss. Have you got a sec?"

"Of course. Come on in. Your timing is perfect. I was just going through your latest proposal."

William sits down opposite me to walk me through the issues with the company, then attempts to tell me how it's still a good investment.

I just can't concentrate at all.

All I can think about is Annabelle and Adam being brother and sister. *Holy fuck. How did I not see this?*

"Hello? Mason? Anybody home?"

"I'm so sorry, William. I really am. I just got some really odd news and I'm... I'm still reeling a little bit, frankly. Forgive me, tell me again what you need?"

"It looks like Newsprint wants to go public sooner, and they don't need another round of funding. Is that going to be okay?"

Newsprint? When did we get on the subject of Newsprint? They're one of the companies in our portfolio that we invested angel and first round in. They have a tremendous idea of how to use artificial intelligence to scan for real news without any political or biased news. It would impact the stock market greatly, which is why it fell under William.

"We have early shares, so whatever they want to do; it's perfectly fine if they want to pop early. We'd land really well if they were successful in an early IPO. Get with Sarah, and she can work on a date for you and get everything taken care of. Let me know what I can do to help, but the idea of not giving them another round of funding and being able to cash out even sooner is amazing news."

"Great. I'll keep you posted." William stands to leave.

"Can you shut the door on your way out, please?

"No problem."

I need to tell someone, and while I'd like to call CeCe, I know she has a board meeting going on right now.

I call Marci instead and am put right through to her. "Hey, Mason. What's going on?"

"Are you sitting down?"

"Yes, what's happened?"

"I got a call from Cora Perry this morning with some surprising news."

She gasps. "Do tell."

I take a big breath. I can't believe I'm going to say this out loud. "Annabelle Ryan is Adam Reeves's sister."

"Shut the front door," Marci says in obvious shock. "I am absolutely stunned."

"Me, too."

Marci goes into lawyer mode instead of just being my confidant. I take great pride in having such a shark for a lawyer. "There was no indication when you were living together that you knew they were related?"

"None."

"Did you know she had a brother?"

"Yes, I knew she had a brother and two older sisters, but they all lived down in Orange County. As far as I knew, she was very distant from them. They had a really rough childhood. Annabelle told me stories of being abused by her father and said she didn't have much of a relationship with her family. I asked to meet them several times, and she always declined. I had no idea."

"Wow, that's really stunning. So, what's the plan?"

"Well, I guess they haven't told her they've uncovered this bit of information yet. I've asked to meet with her and see if I can get some information out of her. She isn't talking to anyone, and they have seventy days to bring about a court case."

"When will they decide?"

"I think soon. Cora seemed to like the idea but wouldn't commit when I talked to her, though Cora wants me to come by at four this afternoon. I think she's going to let me talk to Annabelle."

"Okay."

"How about you consider making a couple thousand dollars this afternoon and join me?"

She chuckles. "Mason, I wouldn't miss this for anything. Do you want to meet here first or at the federal building?"

"See you in front of the Federal Building about three forty-five? That way we're walking into the building together and through security and able to meet Cora upstairs."

"No problem." Marci hesitates, then asks, "How are you doing with this information?"

"I'm completely caught off guard and dumbfounded. In the short time I've known, I haven't been able to think about anything else. This came completely out of left field."

We hang up and I try to work, but my mind returns to many of the conversations I had with Annabelle.

I remember her telling me she wasn't close to her family.

She and my mother didn't get along, but I didn't put too much stock in that given each of them wanted to be the center of my universe.

She was born in Utah and moved to California when she was three, so she considered herself a native.

Her parents couldn't afford to send her to college, so she tried attending on her own, but she didn't know what she wanted to do, so she dropped out.

What did her father do? I can't quite recall. Her mother was a homemaker.

I remember asking her when we first started dating to introduce me to her family, but she pushed me off.

Now I wonder how much of what she told me was true.

Did she not tell me she was Adam's sister because we didn't get along or because she was up to no good?

My cell phone pings, alerting me that Jim's team has arrived to drive me over to the Federal Building. I pack up my things and head for the door.

I'm going to get some answers out of her if it kills me.

After meeting Marci and getting through security, I'm escorted to a small room. Cora sits opposite me. "I can only imagine how upset you are. I want you to think about this before I bring her in. Are you sure you want to have this conversation with her?"

"Without a doubt," I tell her. "I want to know why she did this."

"All right, then you can try talking to her. Have an open mind and figure out what she needs to tell you. Get her to talk to you, because all we know is that she and Adam are brother and sister. She's not implicated herself in any way."

The pressure is on, but I can do this. "I understand."

Cora gets up and walks out, returning in a few minutes with Annabelle. I'm a bit stunned by her appearance. She's in a gray and white striped prison uniform, and her hands and feet are shackled. Her typically well-coifed hair is pulled back haphazardly into a ponytail.

Her usually sparkling gray-blue eyes are missing their sparkle; the circles under her eyes are dark, and her cheeks are concave. She doesn't acknowledge me until they remove the shackles and handcuff her to a bar at the table. When she finally looks up at me, she doesn't say anything, but I watch her pupils dilate and hear her breathing quicken in the small room.

"Annabelle."

She just looks at me, her eyes glazed over.

"How are things going here?"

She cocks her head to the side and squints at me. "I'm in fucking jail. What do you think?"

"You can tell them what they want to know."

She looks to the door as if someone is going to rush in any second. "I don't know anything."

"I think you do, and so do they."

She gives me the evil eye. "What do you think you know?"

"Your brother is Adam Reeves, and he goes by the hacker name Adam McIntosh."

Her eyes grow large for a moment, but quickly she controls herself.

I want to keep her off balance, so I decide to share what I know. "Adam is the head of the Robin Hood Party, and they're behind the obliteration of Pineapple Technologies and the attempted destruction of about a dozen other start-ups SHN has worked with. Plus, we believe Adam is behind the attempted poisoning of me with wolfsbane and the attempt on my life as well as CeCe's last night when they shot up her house and the car we were driving in."

She seems surprised—I don't think she knew the last part—but it's quickly replaced by a sour look. "Sounds like you've got it all figured out," she replies snarkily.

"Maybe, but what I'm unclear about is why you did it. Why did you want to go after me so hard and destroy so many lives, then try and poison me?"

I realize that what I first saw as defiance may actually be fear.

I lean in. "Annabelle, let me hire you the best attorney in San Francisco to get you out of this mess. But please tell me, are you scared of Adam?"

Tears pool in her eyes.

"Please, Annabelle, tell me what he's doing."

"I can't," she whispers.

"Yes you can. I'll make sure you're okay."

I see the hesitation in her eyes, but I push on.

"I have two lawyers we can call to work out a deal. Just tell me something that will convince me you were trapped or blackmailed into participating."

"I didn't have anything to do with the wolfsbane poisoning. When I moved out of your place, I left my cell phone behind and moved down to my sister's in Anaheim Hills."

A rush of relief flows through me. Not only were my instincts on track, but it shows she's talking.

"Tell me about your brother."

"Foster brother. We met in a home when he was thirteen and I was ten. He lived there for five years and was kicked out on his eighteenth birthday. He didn't care, because he'd worked hard to get his football scholarship to Stanford."

"You must've kept in touch over the years."

"He kept in touch with my older foster sister. When I dropped out of community college, I was lost, and she convinced me to move up to San Francisco, with a promise he'd help me find a job."

"How did you end up at SHN?"

"I'm not sure. I interviewed for a receptionist job, and I got it. It was great for the first few months. We'd meet each night for dinner, and he'd ask me questions about all of you. I didn't think I was telling him anything super confidential. He'd ask simple questions like 'What kind of company is SHN looking to invest in this week?' I'd blather on and on, not realizing I was feeding him information. He encouraged me to go out with Dillon. I actually thought he was setting us up, but once I shared that he was tight with Emerson, the new partner, he encouraged me to pursue you instead."

"When did you realize he was going after our investments?"

"When he went crazy mad after I asked him if he sold information about Page Software to other VC firms. He was verbally and physically abusive to me."

"Why didn't you come to me? Why didn't you tell me this was going on?"

Her eyes glisten. "Because I realized I'd been the mole and had been giving him company secrets. I didn't do it on purpose, but I didn't think anyone would believe me."

"Annabelle! You shared my bed. Why wouldn't I believe you?"

"Because we had a relationship of convenience. We liked each other, but we didn't love each other. Don't get me wrong, I wanted to marry you, but you offered a great escape from Adam. I worked hard to keep you both apart."

I can't tell if she's being honest with me, so I feel the need to ask, "Annabelle, are you telling me the whole truth?"

"I am. I swear I am."

"How did Adam get SHN's research and send it around to our competitors?"

Silence.

"Annabelle, you need to be honest with me. We can dig you out, but only once we know the truth."

"He made me."

"What do you mean, he made you?"

"When I confronted him about being the mole, he blackmailed me for more information, said he'd call the FBI and tell them I was behind everything." She looks down at her lap and begins to weep.

"Are you Eve Ambrosia?"

Silence.

"Who is Eve Ambrosia?"

"I don't know."

"Really? Adam McIntosh and Eve Ambrosia are brother and sister. Wouldn't a sister of Adam's be a sister to you?"

"Not necessarily. It may be someone from a different foster home."

"When would he have met her?"

"I don't know."

"Annabelle, I promise I'll contact an attorney for you. We're going to do what we can, but you're going to have to be honest with me, and if at any time I feel you're working against me, then I'll pull my funding of the attorney. Do you understand?"

Annabelle's shoulders are shaking. She's full-on crying now.

"Do you understand?"

"Yes."

I get up to leave, then turn back to look at her. "Who do you think poisoned me?"

"It might've been Adam, but I'm not sure."

"How did he do it?"

"I only learned later that they had a key to your apartment, put the wolfbane into your toothpaste for a slow poisoning, but it was too slow, and they added more to your salad the night you got sick." Annabelle looks up at me with desperation in her eyes. "When I moved out, I left San Francisco and moved down to my sister's. It wasn't me. You were my best friend. I couldn't do that to you."

I leave the interview room and walk back to Cora's office feeling dejected. I can't believe I could've lived with someone who didn't think I'd protect her against an abusive brother.

"Mason, that was amazing," Cora says when I enter her office. "You got more information out of her than we ever could have."

"We still don't know who Eve is, so even if we cut the head off the snake, Eve could continue to run the organization."

"Do you think Annabelle could be Eve?"

"You know, I'm not sure," I reply honestly. "I'm almost positive that she doesn't have any coding skills. I lived with her for over two years, and while there was plenty of code lying around, she just glanced at it at most. I don't even think she can read HTML."

"Well, she gave us several threads we can unravel, nonetheless. You really did a great job. We're close."

"I'm going to call her a lawyer to help negotiate a deal for her, and then I think I'm going to go home and take a nap for the next five years. Wake me up when this thing goes to trial."

"I think we'll be done a lot sooner than that." Cora pats me on the back.

chapter

twenty-eight

CECE

I GLANCE THROUGH THE EMAILS, TEXTS, and transcribed voice mails that Cora handed me. They've pulled conversations they're questioning. I can tell some of these are from Becca and someone on Jeremy's team at Accurate Communications. Those are fine and above board. That's a relief.

I settle myself in my library where I can put my feet up and read through everything. It's nice to be in my own house. I know Mason and I will have to figure out where we're going to live, but I hope it's here at least part of the time. I love this house, and it's a perfect place to raise a family.

As I read through some of the printed materials, there are some that seem off. They're talking about previous seasons but not saying things correctly. For instance, Prussian was the blue in this summer's line, and the message reads "Prussian is too pink to sell well." Not only is it more of a purple-blue, but it's also off the market by the date this conversation took place. That doesn't make any sense to me. I highlight multiple passages that are off just like it.

The words on the pages begin to blur, so I take a break from reading and do some listening instead. I open the MP3 player on my computer and see there are seventeen tracks. I start with the first, sitting back, putting my feet up, and just listening.

"I'll bring that flower drink with me the next time I come. It has quite the bang." I recognize Scarlet's voice and know she's talking about an alcoholic drink she makes. I get why they flagged it—wolfsbane is a flower, and "bang" could have other connotations—but she's fine.

"Why are you calling me at the office? You know I can't talk here." That's Evelyn's voice. I've never been strict about personal calls unless they become overly excessive, and Evelyn worked her way up at Metro because of her dedication.

"I need your help. He found me," the woman wails on the phone.

"You know what you're supposed to do. Don't bother me here at work," Evelyn tells her sternly.

"I don't have any money on me to pick up my go-bag." Go-bag? Isn't that what spies use when they've been found out? Do people really have those?

"Figure it out and call me when you get here."

"Fine. You're no help." The call ends. I hear something I can't quite place, so I listen to the conversation again. And I'm almost convinced. I listen to it one more time, and I think it might be a voice I know.

I decide I'll come back to it and move on to the next conversation.

"You know I hate this job, right?" I recognize Becca's voice. "This isn't what I signed up for. I want happy things, not this shit we're dealing with. And now she's talking about walking us into a deep shit storm, and my life is going to be miserable."

"Just hang tight. If you can weather this storm and whatever else comes your way, I know you'll have plenty of other opportunities." I don't know who Becca's talking to. I think she's just complaining about her job. I don't blame her.

I listen to a few more messages. Every once in a while, I hear bitterness toward the company and me. "She has the money, and she's the one who fucked up. Maybe if she were around a bit more, we wouldn't be in this mess." It isn't the words but how it's said; this message is more menacing than it is factual. Yes, I have money, but why does that play into how the fall line was stolen? I didn't sell it. Around more? I work harder than most of my staff. Maybe I do run off in the middle of the day for a three-hour lunch or walk in at eleven, but I still put in on average ten- to twelve-hour days.

I take a deep breath and remind myself that I can't take this personally.

I sit back and look at my notepad. There are seventeen messages. Roughly half are Evelyn's and half are Becca's. Scarlett had one, but I'm able to discount it. As I look them over, the pit in my stomach grows. It's time to talk to Cora.

Mason walks in and kisses me on the head. "Hi, beautiful. How was your day?"

I sit back hard in my chair. My jaw hurts from clenching so hard, and my head is pounding. "Can you listen to this?"

I play the message.

"Who is Annabelle talking to?"

Holy crap! That's exactly why the voice seemed recognizable. It's Annabelle. "I'm listening to the questionable recordings from the FBI with my staff."

Mason stops, turns, and looks at me. "Play it again."

I turn up the volume and we listen to the recording again.

"Who's she talking to?" I can hear the excitement in his voice. This is a big clue that Annabelle and Evelyn are talking.

"Evelyn."

"Evelyn who?"

"Evelyn Stevens in my office. The VP of operations."

"Are you sure?"

I definitely don't want to be wrong, because this is huge if it is Annabelle, so we listen to it three more times.

"It's Annabelle. I'm sure of it," Mason confirms.

"We need to call Cora."

"I know." But I also know that once I make this call, my world is going to change. If Annabelle is related to Adam and there's a connection to Evelyn, then I've been betrayed by my closest confidant at work. I feel like my heart is being ripped from my body, thrown to the floor, walked on, and then driven over. I look at my hands, but I don't see them. The tears begin to fall.

Mason reaches out to me and pulls me into a hug. "It's okay," he repeats while rubbing my back.

"Why would she do this?" I've always been a good boss. She was promoted quickly, paid well, and had plenty of opportunities to take us down. Why wait until now?

"I don't know, but I'm sure we'll find out."

"And this tells us the hackers are related." The bitterness of the sting of deception rings through my words.

"Let's call Cora. Her team needs to know."

I gather up my notes, and Mason calls from his cell phone and pops it on speaker between us.

"Hello, Mason. Long time no talk."

"Hey, Cora. I'm here with Caroline."

"Hello," CeCe volunteers

Suddenly I'm no longer hurt, I'm fucking pissed off. She's violated not only all the confidentiality statements she's signed and our friendship, but the biggest thing of all is she violated girl code. I trusted her with personal details of my life, and she shared pieces of her own personal life. Evelyn needs to be arrested. "I've gone through all the printed materials. There are about a dozen that don't make any sense. For example"—I flip to the first email that I question—"on page 23, it says our distributor is Callahan, but actually Rockwell is our distributor. I have no idea who Callahan is."

"This is good." Cora's put us on speakerphone on her end as well. "I'm pulling this call into the conference room, and I'd like to have the team join us. Can you hang tight a moment?" I hear some rustling, and then she repeats what I've just shared. "What else doesn't make sense or doesn't work?"

"I've highlighted them all and made notes. There are about a dozen similar instances." I walk them through each one and answer questions posed by the team asking for some direction on why the possible misdirection. "I can't be sure, but I've made some notes on the document. I'll give them to you next time I see you."

"Perfect." I can hear more excitement in Cora's voice. "How did you do with the MP3 messages?"

"The first track is Scarlett talking about a drink she makes. We've all had it. It's one of those that's pretty strong, so you can only have one or you're feeling it for a few days. I feel confident she's off the list."

"Good to know."

"The tracks from Becca are more about her unhappiness in the office, or she's talking to our crisis communication team in New York. I don't know who she's talking to, but it's relatively benign. Might be her sister or best friend. I feel comfortable eliminating her."

"We do, too," Cora shares.

"So you knew it was Evelyn after all?"

"We suspected," she hedges, and I appreciate that she didn't tell me outright and let me figure it out. I would've had a tougher time believing her unless I heard it from Evelyn's mouth rather than from Cora's.

"Did you catch the conversation between Evelyn and Annabelle on track three?"

"What?... No!... Are you sure?"

"I lived with her for almost two years, I've heard her cry more than once. It's her," Mason assures her.

I can't let it go that they knew and didn't tell me. "If you knew it was Evelyn, why didn't you just tell me?"

"We were 80 percent there. We needed your thoughts, but we also didn't want to taint you or disrupt things if we were mistaken."

"I was so convinced it wasn't her that I almost told her several times, but something always interrupted me."

"I'm glad you didn't. She most likely would've run. But honestly, I knew you wouldn't say anything. Your business means too much to you, and you wanted to be sure we caught the right person," Cora impresses upon me.

"Now what? I want her arrested and put in jail!" Anger envelopes my words.

"I'll come get the notes from you now, and then we'll draw up the warrants. I can arrest her at the office in the morning, or I can do it beforehand. Your call."

"Do you have her under surveillance?" I want her marched out of our offices in front of everyone. I want my whole company to know who tried to take it all away from them. But I also want to be smart. I'd rather her be caught than give her time to get away.

"We do. If it looks like she's going to run, we can act quickly."

"I hate to sound spiteful, but I think I'd like her arrested at the office. I want everyone to know who's behind this mess we're in."

"I'll meet you at your place at seven, and I'll collect the materials from you. Then my team and I will begin working on the warrants for her arrest."

"We'll be here," Mason assures her.

He hangs up the phone, and I look at him pleadingly. "Why would she do this?"

"I don't know, but we'll find out." I love his confidence. I sure hope he's right. The last thing I want is for her to deny it, because then it looks like I'm using her as my scapegoat.

Mason holds me for a few moments while I truly come to grips with the betrayal I feel. "We should call Jim. I want to look at the deep dive he did on Evelyn."

Mason leaves to make the call, and I'm left to rethink every conversation I've had with Evelyn. I always kept it professional, but we traveled to Fashion Weeks all over the world and spent time talking to one another. I knew about her love life, and she knew about mine. We talked about our goals for the company. She knew I was an advisor for SHN.

I hear the doorbell sound, and Angela knocks on my door. "Miss Caroline, Cora Perry with the FBI is here to see you."

"Thank you, Angela. Bring her in."

Cora arrives, and I start to cry. "I can't believe this."

She puts her arms around me. "I'm so sorry."

I sob for a few minutes. When we finally break apart, I feel a bit better. "I'm sure you don't have to comfort too many of your victims."

She shrugs. I'm so grateful that Cora took over my case. If Agents Winters and Greene had dealt with this, I don't believe it would be at this point.

I walk over to my chair and pick up the emails. "I've highlighted the strange conversations. Hopefully your team can figure out what the mistakes mean."

"We knew they were somehow off, but without the institutional knowledge, we couldn't pinpoint anything." She thumbs through the book and sees all the notes I've written. "This is incredibly comprehensive. It'll help a lot."

"Thank you."

"When does Evelyn come into the office?"

"She's usually in by nine."

"We've already located her at her condo in the East Bay. We'll be following her wherever she goes beforehand and then into the office in the morning. I'll plan on coming in and being there when my team makes the arrest."

"Thank you. I'd like to be there, too," I tell her without asking.

"I certainly understand. Not a problem."

"I'll work with my team to make an announcement to the press. May I tell Becca and Christy, since once this breaks, the press is going to go wild?"

"That works, but make sure they don't tell her. It would be ugly if they did."

"I'll let them know. Thank you."

She leaves, and I call Jeremy. It's after eleven in New York, but part of what I pay him for is to be available when things go sideways. When he answers, I let him know what I've learned.

"We'll have a press release ready to go as soon as you give us the word. Do you want a notice to go out to your employees?" he asks.

"I'll meet with the management team, but since she'll be arrested at the office, we'll want to address this company-wide."

"Sounds good. I do suggest you bring in Becca. She'll be fielding calls."

I breathe in deeply. I agree, but I also don't want to tip my hand. She'll know in advance, but I'm just not sure how far in advance. Once I get it all figured out, I text her. Can you meet me in the office at 8?

Becca: I'll be there. Can I stop and bring you a cup of coffee from Andytown Coffee Roasters?

I love that she's offered. Andytown is out in the Sunset neighborhood and really out of the way if you can't just stop by on your way to work.

Me: You fly, I'll buy.

Becca: A Snowy Plover?

A Snowy Plover is a cold drink composed of Pellegrino, espresso, and brown sugar syrup over ice, topped with homemade whipped cream. It sounds perfect.

Me: Please. Feel free to pick out a few bakery items, too. We have a big day tomorrow.

Becca: See you in the morning.

Mason returns. "I just talked to Jim. He's agreed to meet us here at seven tomorrow morning."

"I'm meeting Becca at the office at eight."

"Could this mean this mess is almost over?" It just doesn't seem possible. How could it be?

"Gawd, wouldn't that be nice!"

"Angela has dinner ready. Then let's go to bed early."

"Deal."

When the alarm sounds in the morning, Mason rolls over. "Did you sleep at all last night?"

I read, I watched the clock change, and I went to the bathroom a dozen times. "No, not at all."

He puts his arms around me. "Today is going to be a good day."

I know he's right. One way or another, we're closing this chapter. Let's just hope the next one is less stressful. "I hope so."

I've been up thinking about Annabelle's involvement all night. "After what we learned, do you think Annabelle was truthful?"

"I do, but I'm positive she knows who Eve Ambrosia is, and I'm not sure she's as innocent as she projects."

"Eve could be short for Evelyn," Mason suggests.

"It can, but I'm not sure Evelyn would know HTML from Java. I know I wouldn't."

"Jim will be here shortly, and then he can drive you in to meet with Becca. I've already told him that I want someone with you at arm's length all day."

While I do feel that's overkill, I won't argue. Not today.

Walking into the kitchen, I see it's a beautiful day outside. Jim has already arrived. He looks well rested, and yet I know when we called him last night, he had a lot of work to get done.

I page through his deep dive on Evelyn. Her birth certificate is there, showing she was born in Utah. There are police reports of domestic abuse by her father, and it looks like her mother ran to Southern California to be with a sister.

She was twelve years old when she was moved into a foster home with her sister Anna due to neglect. There are notations about keeping the girls together because Anna was extremely vulnerable. Their father was an alcoholic drunk who couldn't be found. The mother died, and the aunt wasn't sending the girls to school, leaving them to fend for themselves when she went to work. They were always kept together, and they lived in the final home for six years. Adam lived with them for the last five.

Various pictures from her childhood are included in the file. They confirm that she and Annabelle are sisters, and that they lived with Adam. "How did you get these pictures?" It's not a real question, more astonishment that he has them at all.

"You'd be amazed at what people share on social media. Throwback Thursdays are a treasure trove of information."

"There are pictures of me from some of my most awkward ages in newspaper and magazine archives, and they show up now and again, I don't understand why people share so much online."

In an interview, the foster mother didn't have a lot of great things to say about Evelyn, mostly that she was trouble, and she was promiscuous with other foster kids they had. "It sounds like the foster home was full of kids."

"It would seem so. I think it was relatively clean, but there were a lot of kids." Jim looks at his watch. "If we're going to get you to your office for your eight o'clock meeting, then we need to leave pretty quick."

"Okay." I take a deep breath to steady myself. "Let's get today over with."

I sit in the back of the Suburban and watch the people heading into work and enjoying their day. Like Evelyn, they have a very different idea of how their day is going to unfold than it actually will. They may think they know, but life always throws us curveballs. In Evelyn's case, she's going to be going where the fashion is a gray-and-white-striped uniform and live with at least one other person in a five-by-five cell.

Becca is waiting for me in my office when I arrive. My cell phone pings before I can enter.

Jim: She's just left her house and is taking a route that would lead us to believe she doesn't suspect anything and is heading to your offices.

Now I'm getting really nervous.

As I shrug out of my coat, Christy asks, "Is everything okay?"

"Why don't you join me in my office for just a moment."

She nods, and Becca stands and smiles at me when we enter. "Here's your Snowy Plover and an apple pastry."

I take a nice gulp of the drink. "Mmmm, it tastes divine. Thank you."

In a low voice, I lay it all out to them. "You two are the only ones who know this in advance. If it gets out, you'll be in serious trouble. With the theft of our fall line, the FBI has been investigating our company. Against my better judgment, they loaded ghost software and keyword trackers on five employees' work and personal phones and computers. While I was convinced that there was no way we'd have anyone in our midst who would trade our secrets for anything, the FBI proved me wrong. In less than two hours, they'll be here to arrest one of our colleagues for selling our secrets to the Chinese competitors."

"Did this person also orchestrate the shooting at your home?" Christy asks.

"Well, if they didn't, they know who did." They don't need to know that we already know it was Adam who was behind that debacle, but Evelyn could've been involved. That will eventually come out in the news, most likely. "I'm telling you both because Accurate Communications will be sending out a press release once this person is apprehended, and you'll both be fielding a lot of calls."

Becca looks at me, clearly puzzled. "Someone we know did this to us?"

"It would appear so, yes."

"Caroline, I don't mean to be disrespectful, but I'm not sure I can be objective. They've made my life and yours a living hell for the last three and a half months. I know I'm pissed, but I can't even imagine that you're less so."

I really hope Becca sticks around. She's just the kind of person I want on my team, but if she thinks she needs to move on to something bigger and better, I'll help her get there. "I'm pretty upset myself."

"Is this why you decided to reverse your decision about launching a fall line?"

She's a smart girl. I nod. "I'm sorry I put you through everything, but we needed to watch to find out who was involved."

A look of terror crosses her face.

"Don't worry," I tell her. "My plan is not to launch any fall line. We'll take the six-million-dollar loss, and I'll personally cover that so no one loses their job with Metro or can't pay their bills."

"That's incredibly generous," Christy says.

"Yes, it's very kind of you to do that. I'm just grateful you're not launching a fall line. I just knew our animal rights activists would come out in full force and make my life positively miserable," Becca laments.

"You can't say anything," I warn. "The FBI is watching, and while you might like someone or have a juicy bit of gossip to share, it isn't worth getting caught up in the middle of this mess."

Becca shakes her head vigorously. "No way. This person's ruined my life. My boyfriend broke up with me because I was too busy to go out with him. I want to see this person rot in jail."

"Not an issue in the slightest," Christy assures me. "I'm very sorry you have to deal with this, but I'm Italian, and I think an eye for an eye, thank you very much!"

I chuckle. Once she hears the whole story, I'm sure she's going to want more than an eye. "Christy, you're amazing. And you, Becca. Thank you both."

"I need to talk to Jeremy's team. Where would you suggest I do that?" Becca asks.

"You can do it here on my phone." I turn the landline around to face her, and she jumps on a call.

Christy stands to leave, and I walk with her to the door of my office. "I'm disappointed someone we trusted did this to us," she says.

"Me, too."

"We'll see better days after this." Christy pats my arm in a motherly way.

"I agree."

She gives me a warm embrace and heads for the door. "Let me know if there's anyone you want to talk to; otherwise, I'll deflect them to Accurate Communications."

"Sounds perfect."

She walks out, closing the door behind her.

Now I need to wait. I can't sit, but I can't just stand either, so I pace around my office. Back and forth, back and forth. I'm sure I'm wearing a permanent path in the carpet. I must check my cell phone every three seconds. I know they mentioned it would be about ten, but I'm still anxious.

Christy buzzes me. "There's a Miss Cora Perry here to see you."

I jump. "Let her in."

In my head, I keep repeating, *Please don't let this have gone sideways,* over and over again.

Cora walks in wearing her black pantsuit and a stunning pastel green silk top.

"Is something wrong?" I ask her.

"Nope, I just thought I'd give you an update. We followed her here this morning, and she's just arrived in her office across the hall. We're ready. Are you?"

I take a deep breath and blow it out. "I guess so."

"Let's do it." She pulls on a windbreaker jacket that clearly says FBI and speaks into her earpiece. Then we walk across the hall to Evelyn's office.

Cora knocks on the door. Scarlett begins to object, but I shake my head and she sits down, watching as a half-dozen men with FBI-labeled attire spill into the admin area.

"Evelyn Stevens, I'm with the FBI, and I have a warrant for your arrest," Cora announces.

Evelyn looks at me and gives me the evil eye. She doesn't protest her innocence, nor does she yell or scream any profanities. She's handcuffed and led out of her office. I hit Send on a text to Jeremy letting him know she was arrested. Less than a minute later, there's an email delivered to my entire company telling them about the arrest of one of our own for selling us out.

I send a text out to my friends.

Me: Evelyn Stevens, my VP of operations, was arrested a short time ago for corporate espionage and trafficking. It appears she may also be known as Eve Ambrosia. We're unclear if she was involved in the assault on Angela, Mason, and me, but we're confident that we'll have more answers shortly.

Cameron: I'm really sorry it was someone you were close with, but I'm glad you're putting this behind you.

Dillon: Great news.

Emerson: Feel free to come over and join me for a drink if you need one. Door's always open.

Greer: Love you!

Mason calls a bit later, just after the dust settles. "How are you doing?"

"Not too bad. Most people are pretty pissed at Evelyn around here."

"As they should be. If they didn't have such a generous boss, they'd be unemployed."

"I don't know, I think many business owners would've just secured a loan to cover it."

"Maybe, but I think even more would throw in the towel and walk away."

I still can't concentrate enough to work. Christy's been fielding calls all morning, keeping them away from me. Finally, she buzzes me to tell me Walker Clifton is on the line.

"Hello, Walker," I answer.

"Hey. Evelyn spilled the beans rather quickly. We know where Adam is, and he'll be in custody within the hour."

"Do we know what motivated them to do this?"

"More will come out in the days ahead, but really it was Adam's vendetta against SHN for not including him when they started the company. She said something about you trying to ruin Adam's life, and he got her her job at Metro and then he pushed her to do things."

"That's it? All of this because of her foster brother?"

"They have a very weird relationship. He really has done a number on her. She vented about your 'perfect family,' your 'perfect friends,' and your wealth which was given but not earned but much of her hurt and anger seem to stem from a misplaced loyalty to him. Adam placed her at your company and told her how she could maneuver herself to get into your tight circle."

Looking back I remember she really wanted to do things with me outside of work, and I always rebuffed. "I don't mix my personal life and my professional life."

"Caroline, she has some real issues that have nothing to do with you. He did a number on her and we believe did a real number on Annabelle. They got her a job at SHN and then pushed her into a relationship with Mason when they couldn't get a relationship going with Dillon. This was a multipronged assault all started by Adam, and both Evelyn and Annabelle were manipulated into doing his bidding.

"I see."

"Do you know what he's talking about when she says you tried to ruin Adam's life?"

"I do. You can reach out to Marci for my sworn statement."

"I see. Was it consensual?"

"No, and as a lawyer, she knew she'd be the one prosecuted and vilified, not him." I will go down defending Emerson about what Adam did to her. No woman should ever feel bad when she trusts someone.

"I wish I could say that wasn't true, but we know better."

"When she poisoned him, she was hoping Mason was going to die and it would cripple you while she destroyed Metro."

"What would she gain from Mason's death? That just doesn't make sense to me."

"Sweetheart, her reasoning is incoherent. Just be grateful she's going to jail."

"What else did she say?"

"She had Annabelle's cell phone and was the one leveling the threats at you via text. We'll hold her on that initially while we confirm the rest of what she shared."

"Did she even admit to selling our fall line to the Chinese competitor?"

"She ranted and raved once we got her into custody and inadvertently admitted it. Chances are she'll roll on Adam and we'll negotiate."

"May I tell Mason that Adam will soon be in custody?"

"He's going to be my next call."

"Then I'll let you give him the good news."

Walker pauses a moment. "Are you and Mason serious?"

"Yes, we are."

"He's a very lucky man. I know you always thought I liked you for your money and fame, but the reality is I like you for your brains, poise, and the fact that you're a stunningly beautiful woman."

I don't know what to say to that, so instead I respond with "I know the perfect woman for you when you're ready."

"I think I let the perfect woman fall between my fingers."

"Let me know when you're ready, but don't wait too long. You'll find you may miss a great one."

chapter

twenty-nine

MASON

I PICK UP MY RINGING PHONE. "Hello, Cora. Please tell me you have news."

"We've located Adam, and he's currently in custody."

I can't help but be jealous that I couldn't have been there. I often think about what I'd be doing if I weren't head of one of the largest venture capital funds in the Bay Area, and these days I think I would've been in law enforcement. A lot of what I do centers around solving puzzles, and with this case lasting over five years, a small part of me will be missing it. But only a small part. "That's fantastic news. What can you tell me about it?"

"Once Evelyn was arrested, Adam went underground. We'd learned he had a very expensive drug habit, so we tapped our resources with SFPD and Detective Lenning to see where he was buying, and thankfully we found him."

"Drug habit? Given when we knew him, he was in great physical shape, that's actually surprising."

"It was painkillers. They're a nasty group of drugs."

"So I've heard."

"We negotiated with Annabelle's attorney. She went in wired, and he admitted to setting her up and bullying her."

"I'm really glad to hear that."

"We're releasing her in the next few days."

"What?" How can that be? She stole from us and handed over confidential information that was shared with all our competitors.

"Mason, before you get too upset, I want you to know that Adam didn't target you exclusively. He was part of a much broader network. With his help, we're going to take down over a hundred different people across the US who are blackmailing and destroying companies."

"You mean the Robin Hood Party?"

"Partially. We were able to connect Adam to over fifty open cases we have across the bureau."

"What about the poisoning?"

"That was actually Evelyn. She had a key to your place and knew your housekeeper's schedule. She'd been gaining access to your condo and when the toothpaste was taking too long, she began doctoring your food."

I sit back hard in my chair. "I can't believe this."

"I know it's tough, but I'm happy to say we're packing up the big conference room and moving another case in for us to concentrate on."

"I'm sorry you have to do that."

"I guess it's job security. Is that too tasteless?"

"Um, just a little."

She laughs. "Mason, you've built a great company, and you're full of compassion and smarts. Now go marry that woman of yours and enjoy all that life has to offer."

I grin. "That's my plan."

chapter thirty

MASON

CONCENTRATING AT WORK HAS BEEN REALLY DIFFICULT today. Last night, I waited for the master jeweler at Harry Winston to arrive with engagement ring options. I know what CeCe would love—tasteful and conservative—and I want a huge rock on her hand so it's obvious to every man who thinks he can look at her that she's taken.

My phone rings and the caller ID tells me it's my mother. I'm not sure I want to talk to her; I don't want her to put a damper on my excitement. As soon as it rolls to voice mail, it begins to ring again. It's her signal that it's an emergency.

I pick up the phone with a sigh. "Hello, Mother."

"Mason, my love, what are your plans today at lunch?"

"I'm not sure I can get away for lunch today, Mom. With everything that's going on with our hacker and everything else, it's crazy busy here."

"Sweetheart, Michael and I've decided to get married, and his friend who's a judge has some free time at lunch. Do you think work could wait a few hours and you join us, then we head to lunch afterward?"

"You're getting married?"

"I know we've only known each other for a few months and it seems sudden, but I can't help it. Michael's the one for me. We really click."

"Mom, I don't know anything about this man."

"Mason, you know I love you. You know you were the center of my universe, but I also know that as you get more and more serious with CeCe, you don't need me as much. Michael needs me. He's been widowed for a long time, and we're ready to settle down. We love each other dearly."

I just hope he's not going to take her for a ride. "You're getting married today?"

"Yes. If you can talk CeCe into joining us, we'd love to have you there."

"Mom, I love you. I'm going to do everything I can to be there. What time is your meeting with the judge?"

"At twelve o'clock, when the judge recesses from his trial. He's Michael's childhood friend."

"I'll be there. I wouldn't miss it for the world. I can't speak for CeCe, though. No promises there."

"I love you, sweetheart."

"I love you, too, Mom."

I disconnect the call and then call CeCe. "Hey, I know you're waist deep in crap with everything that's going on, but my mom just called, and apparently she and Dr. Frieman are eloping at noon."

"You're kidding."

"Nope. She's crazy about him, and I just need to hope he isn't after her for money. Would you like to go to a wedding with me today?"

"I'd love to. Noon? Where are they meeting?"

My cell phone pings. That's timing. "It looks like it's with Judge Thomas Garcia at city hall, room 29E."

"You're kidding. I know Thomas. He sits on our board at the women's shelter."

"Great. Come see your friend from your volunteer life, and we'll be witnesses to my mother's ceremony."

"I look forward to it." In a low voice, she says, "I'd prefer a lunch sometime that maybe includes an up close and personal look at that marvelous third leg of yours."

"We can do that any night you're up for it."

My mother isn't the best with finances, so I'll still give her a small allowance so she has some money she can spend without her new husband freaking out. I'll try to accept that she has someone who might look after her and keep her company.

I remember Jim emailing me his file, but I haven't looked at it with everything going on. Opening it up now, I look at Michael's background check. Nothing really comes back as strange. He's as he said, a urologist here in San Francisco. He has a thriving practice, some decent money in the bank, and owns his home outright in Pacific Heights. Maybe this isn't such a bad thing for my mom. Maybe she's right—I don't need her anymore, and she wants somebody who needs her.

I'm wrapping up my morning, getting ready to leave, when my cell phone pings with a text from CeCe.

It's actually a picture, and my eyes almost pop out of my head when I open it. She's dressed in a white merry widow negligée with thigh-high stockings. Her hair's covering her face, but I know it's her. Holy crap is she beautiful.

CeCe: I thought maybe I should wear this to the wedding today.

Me: I hope you're planning on wearing something else over it.

CeCe: Yes, but maybe later, you can unwrap it yourself.

Me: I fully intend to.

CeCe: See you in a moment.

Me: You know I'm going to have a raging hard-on at my mother's wedding, right?

CeCe: Okay, I'll go back to my normal panties and bra.

Me: Don't you dare. I plan on unwrapping you later.

The ceremony is really quite lovely. Judge Garcia tells everyone how he remembers CeCe tirelessly working on behalf of women who are homeless with addictions or running away from abusive relationships.

"It's a group effort," CeCe reminds him.

Then he tells us how he met Michael when they were awkward fourteen-year-olds.

"The girls wouldn't look at us twice in those days," Michael shares.

"They look at you now?" Judge Garcia ribs him.

"I got this beauty to look at me, and somehow I convinced her to marry me, so hurry up before she changes her mind," Michael jokes.

"I'm not going anywhere, but I'm afraid my son is important, and I want him to be able to see this. I've only loved one other man in my life, and that was his father. You're making me the happiest woman in the world today." Mom gives him a big kiss on the cheek, leaving a giant red lipstick stain. It's perfect for today's event. I've never seen my mother so happy.

Judge Garcia performs a very touching ceremony. CeCe is in a dress that looks like it's from the 50s with a formfitting top and a full skirt that goes below her knees. I lean in and whisper, "Are you still wearing what you sent me earlier?"

"You'll have to wait to find out," she says with a mischievous grin.

Michael motions me aside. "I know we don't know each other well, but I love your mother very much. I'm so glad you could be here, Mason."

"I wouldn't miss this for the world."

"I promise I'm going to make your mother very happy. I know she gets an allowance from you, but if you want to stop that, you certainly can. I have the means to keep her in the way she wants to be kept."

I'm taken aback by the offer. "She has expensive tastes," I warn.

He shrugs. "I bought into Sandy Systems on the day they went public. I also bought in on Oracle and Salesforce. I may not be as wealthy as you, but I think we'll be just fine." He kicks at a spot on the floor with the toe of his shoe. "I was saving it for my children, but my Elaine and I weren't lucky enough to have them. And since you don't need any money, I can spend it all on your mother."

I pat Michael on the back. "Don't let her know too much. She doesn't budget well."

"I want to give her whatever she wants."

"Honestly, I'm really glad she's going to be close. I plan on proposing to CeCe before too long, and we want kids, so you both can enjoy them—that is, if you want grandkids."

"I adore kids. And nothing would make me happier than being a grandfather."

Maybe my mother has finally found the guy who's perfect for her in every way. She deserves a happily ever after, and I believe Michael Frieman is hers.

chapter

thirty-one

CECE

THERE'S A KNOCK AT MY OFFICE DOOR. Mason walks in with my favorite lunch—clam chowder in a sourdough bread bowl. "I have a feeling you haven't eaten yet."

"Have I told you how I feel about you recently?"

He nuzzles my neck, "No, but you can show me." He brings my hand to his hard rod, and I stroke it through the fabric of his pants.

"You are a man of many surprises." My mouth finds his, and our tongues do their aggressive dance until I'm dizzy with lust and desire.

"I have a surprise for you at home tonight," Mason promises.

"Should I wear anything special?"

"I'd say with what we're doing, clothing is optional."

"I can't wait." The idea of Mason naked and above me, below me, in front of me, or even behind me sends jolts of excitement straight to my core.

When I finally arrive home, Angela has set a beautiful table with candlelight in the sitting room off my bedroom. Dinner is covered and waiting for us. I spot the chocolate raspberry cake, and I can't help but dip my finger in the frosting. Mmmm, it tastes so good. I can't wait to dive in.

Mason messaged me that he was leaving about the same time I was, and Jack Reece told me they weren't quite home yet. I run into my closet and pull out the white merry widow outfit that I took the picture in. It'll be just the two of us, and while I'm not sure it's the most becoming, he seemed to like it.

I hear him arrive and yell, "I'm upstairs."

I pose like I think a Victoria's Secret model would and wait for him to find me.

Walking into the bedroom, he stops short. "Fuck me."

"I think that's the plan, isn't it?"

He nods. "You look positively stunning, and I'm going to undress you slowly and fuck you hard tonight."

"Promise?"

I see a tent in his pants, and I can't wait to take him in my mouth. "We're going to eat first. It's going to be hard watching those nipples straining behind that corset, but we need to celebrate in more ways than just sexual." We head into the sitting room, and he uncovers a plate of oysters on the half shell. "Come sit down. I want to feed them to you."

I sit down at the table with only the candlelight flickering. He seductively kisses me before licking my lips, and I quiver with anticipation. Dipping his hand into the corset, he plays with my nipples. "Lean your head back."

I do as I'm told and he tips a raw oyster into my mouth. A little bit of saltwater runs down my neck, and he licks it away. I watch him feed himself an oyster. "Do you want another one?" he asks.

"Please," I breathe.

He rubs his fingertips against the outside of my panties as he tips the oyster in and then nuzzles my neck. "You're already wet."

"I'm wet for you," I moan.

"I want to cool you down, because we do have a few more courses to enjoy before I fuck you senseless."

He uncovers a plate of balsamic glazed chicken with asparagus. Picking up an asparagus stick, I move it in and out of my mouth, sucking all the juices away, and he moans. If he can torture me, then I can torture him—though he's still dressed, of course.

We only half eat our meal. My foot is between his legs, massaging his balls and rubbing his swollen cock. I know he's trying hard to concentrate on his meal, but I can't take it anymore. Getting down on all fours, I crawl forward, slowly licking my lips and concentrating on what's hiding in his pants. "Pretty please," I beg.

His answer is part moan and part groan. I unbuckle his belt and pull his pants open. He stands and lets them pool at his ankles, and I help him remove his shoes and discard his pants. His cock is standing at attention and I shudder with delight, my panties soaked. I want that cock in my mouth, and I want it now.

I flick my eyes up at him as I press my tongue flat against his base before slowly dragging it up the full length.

"Jesus," he gasps.

I trace over the slit at the top and then twirl my tongue around the entire head before starting again, licking up the front and swirling around the ridge on the underside, teasing him, making him wish he was fully in my mouth. I use my saliva as a lubricant and then gently pull his flesh up and down with my hand until I finally dip my head, stretch my jaw as wide as it will go, and take him in my mouth. He lets out a deep moan in response.

Slowly I lower my head, taking him in inch by inch as his fingers dig into the hair at the base of my neck. Knowing I have him so hot makes me want to give him more. With one hand following the motion of my mouth up and down his now-slick cock, I gently cup his balls with the other, moving them slowly toward his body. They tighten under my delicate touch, and I loosen my grip.

My main work is done with my mouth, though, and I savor every taste, keeping my lips and tongue firm against him, releasing only to lick him at the tip. He's such a delicious treat, more satisfying than a chocolate raspberry cake could ever hope to be. Each time my head dips down, I take more of him in my mouth, marveling at how loose my throat has become, that it can take much more than I ever imagined.

"God, CeCe," Mason groans, his fingers fully tangled in my hair as he takes over, guiding my head at the pace he wants. I move a little faster, my mouth stretched wide as I moan at the feel of him deep in my mouth. I pause and pull back, giving his dick quick kisses up the side before taking it back in as deep as I can, Mason's hand gently pushing the back of my head for me to continue. His breath comes in gasps as I quicken my pace, one hand still holding him firmly.

"Don't stop," he gasps, but I wouldn't even if the house was on fire. "I'm going to come," he announces.

I rub at my center, wanting a release when he sends warm ropes of cum deep down my throat. His grunts are hardly contained as we both climax, his hand falling from my head to my shoulder before he braces himself on the arm of my chair, panting for air.

I slip him out of my mouth and wipe my thumb across my lips.

"You're going to pay for that," he warns.

"I can take whatever you give me."

"We'll see about that." He smiles. "Let's finish our dinner and find out."

We continue our meal as we talk about our days and various things going on as we attempt to return to normal in our work lives.

When he places the chocolate cake in front of me, I lick my lips. "I can think of a few things we can do with this cake."

"You're going to be punished. Just eat your cake."

When I take a bite, my teeth hit something hard. It's round, heavy, and has some sharp points. I take it out of my mouth and look at the engagement ring covered in chocolate raspberry cake.

He shrugs. "I told you I had a plan. Then you had to go and be your sexy self, and it derailed me."

I giggle. "Well, what am I supposed to do with this?"

"Caroline Michelle Arnault, when I met you almost six years ago, I fell absolutely in love with you. You are beautiful on the inside and outside. It took us almost five years to find ourselves together, and in that time we became great friends, which only made my love for you grow. I'm hoping we can spend the next sixty years together. I promise to love you despite the paparazzi, our crazy lives, and my overbearing mother. Will you marry me?"

I'm so happy, I can't contain myself. "Yes, I will marry you, Mason John Sullivan."

His kiss lights me on fire, and I can't stop the excitement.

"I'm going to make you pay for ruining my plans."

Taking me by the hand, he leads me over to the bed. He sits on the edge and I stand between his legs as he runs his fingers along the edge of the cup of the corset. My nipples are so hard they hurt. "You're very beautiful in this, but I think you're more beautiful naked." With a flick of his wrist, he unhooks the corset, and it falls to the floor. Suckling my nipple, he bites and pulls aggressively, and I moan my appreciation.

He hooks his fingers in the sides of my thong and slips it over my hips, then moves me to the bed beside him. His touch never leaves my skin as he gets me on all fours and then stands behind me.

His cock nudges me, finding me slick. "You're ready," he says on a groan. "Always ready for me." And then he's inside me, pushing my walls apart, opening me, waiting patiently until my body can accommodate his size. My mouth opens on a silent cry. He feels so good inside me.

He swears under his breath, holding himself inside me. "Yes, you're going to be my wife. But right now I want you to enjoy this." His hands dig into my hips, fingertips bruising.

That's the only warning before he slams fully into me again so hard that I let out a shriek of surprise.

He withdraws and then pushes in again, completely focused on his own wild pleasure. He slams into me again and again, rubbing at my special spot inside. The teasing from before, the pain right now, it all blends together in a whirlwind of sensation.

I can't hold it any longer, and I shatter completely. My orgasm comes suddenly, making my insides bear down, my hips bucking back against him. He shouts as his cock pulses fresh heat into my sex. He draws out his orgasm and mine, pushing his still-firm cock into my slick heat with lazy thrusts, every slide sending a new wave of sparks shooting behind my eyelids.

"Harder," I whisper, though I'm not sure who I'm saying it for, him or me. I don't think it matters; we're the same being when he's inside me, moving toward one goal.

He pulls back for a brief moment of respite, and then he's deep inside me once more, his invasion thorough, his cock pulsing in pleasure. I release a pent-up sound of ecstasy, fisting the sheets as my second orgasm rips through me.

Mason speeds up, fucking me with rough intent, every thrust pushing me deeper into the bed, marring my makeup and loosening my hair. My nipples are hard and sensitive from the repeated raking across the sheets. Every sensation inside me is on fire, and I don't want it to burn out.

It swirls ever higher, tighter, sharper until I'm mindless on the end of his cock. "Please," I whisper.

"Promise me," he grunts.

"Anything," I moan. I'll promise the moon so long as I reach the pinnacle I'm so desperately searching for.

His voice is harsh, roughened by sex but determined. "Promise you won't give up on us. You won't let outside forces drive us apart."

My mind is drenched with need. It's hard to think, hard to speak. It feels like I haven't spoken in a thousand years. My mouth struggles to form words. "I promise."

With a final push, he comes undone, and we collapse and lie in each other's arms, catching our breath. I finally take a moment to look at the ring. It's beautiful, with a large center stone and a band of pavÉ diamonds.

"Do you like it?" he asks.

"It's absolutely perfect. It's not too big and ostentatious. I love it." I stare at my hand and think about our evening. "You know, we're going to have to come up with another story about how you proposed."

"No way. I was a fucking porn star. We can tell them everything."

I look at him quizzically. "Really?"

"Okay, not a chance. We need a G-rated version. Only we'll know the truth."

"I love you."

Ainsley St Claire

Holiday Heartbreakers

Gifted

A Preview

chapter

one

KATE

FORTY KIDS WON'T HAVE A CHRISTMAS, and it's all my fault.

Almost two hundred kids from middle schools across the city and county of San Francisco—from some of the most at-risk areas—met the requirements for our contest, and I'm forty donor/mentors short for our upcoming celebration. At two hundred dollars apiece, I don't know what I'm going to do. How do I break a promise I made to these kids on the first day of school? Go to school for seventy-five days, don't be absent, don't be late, and get a passing grade. If you accomplish all that, you'll get a two-hundred-dollar shopping spree at Bullseye.

Some people think "paying kids to go to school" is a bad thing. But we get paid to come to work, and some people play solitaire on their computers while they sit there. How is that not paying you for showing up? In a lot of low-income areas—

in San Francisco and elsewhere—over half of the students that complete middle school never walk into a high school, and less than ten percent of those who do will go on to graduate. Life isn't easy for these kids, and going to school every day is not easy with so many distractions. But with some incentive, we see improvement.

I've got to figure out how I'm going to fund these last few students and find mentors to spend the day with them while they shop. I've tapped my network, and it's pretty dry. But I can't disappoint these kids; they've had enough disappointment in their lives.

I open the app to my bank account: three hundred dollars. I was going to use that money for my rent next month, and, you know, to feed myself. Right now there's no man in my life to make sure I get at least an occasional dinner. I check the account for my Visa card, and I can squeeze out maybe two thousand dollars to cover ten kids. But that still leaves me with over thirty more, and still no mentors. *Crap!* What am I going to do?

Tess walks into my office. "Isn't this great? We've never had this many kids, ever! This could mean we have at least a hundred more kids graduate, and fifteen of those will go on to college, and sixty will go on to trade schools. This is amazing. Are we going to be ready?"

I force a smile. "I hope so. We're short a few donor/mentors."

"In this town, people spend two hundred dollars on dinner without a second thought. We should be able to find a few that will give to a good cause."

"I hope so. I've reached out to our board members and asked them to check with their network."

"How many donors are we short?"

"About forty. I can leverage my credit card for ten of those, but I'm not sure how we're going to be able to make this work."

"Kate, if anyone will get this figured out, it's you. Last year we had barely one hundred kids complete this project. This year we have over two hundred. You need to celebrate that."

"I will when I lock down the rest of the people we need."

"Well, then don't be shy. Bug those board members."

"I will."

But I've asked them, and they're in the same boat I am. We've tapped out our network. Somehow, I need to reach beyond my friends and get into some of the big players.

"What about your new board member?"

"That's Stephanie Paulson, and she seems pretty well-connected. She must know a few people that can help us."

I've asked her a few times during our meetings, but I need to try again in writing. I don't think my board members realize how tough it is to compete without grants in this city.

I craft a carefully worded email to remind Stephanie of our remaining need and the looming deadline, trying to sound just the right amount of desperate. We're only a five-year-old nonprofit, and we're making a difference. I can feel it in my bones. But if we can't make this happen for all the kids who earned it, we may not recover.

This is what keeps me up at night.

After just a few minutes, an email pops up.

To: Katherine Monroe
From: Stephanie Paulson
Subject: RE: Brighter Future Christmas Party

I'm sorry I kept forgetting. Thanks for the email reminder. I've forwarded your note to everyone in my contact list with your information. We should be able to come up with more than forty donors. We're only asking them for $200 and a Saturday morning, for goodness sake! The party on Christmas Eve is a bonus! Let me know if you don't hear from enough and I'll rattle the cages, but at the very minimum, I'll send over a check for $5,000 you can use for holiday decorations.

Keep up the good work.
XOXO
Steph

That lets me breathe a little easier. This guarantees I have the money. But ultimately, it's more than the financing we need. These kids need mentors, and spending the day with adults who've accomplished something means a lot.

The ringing of my phone interrupts my thoughts. "Kate Monroe."

"Hello, Miss Monroe? This is Jamal Jenkins."

"Hey, Jamal. How are you?"

"I'm doin' real good. I just wanted to make sure you saw that my name was on the list again this year."

"You better believe I saw your name. I'm very proud of you."

"Jose made it, too. And we have four of our friends who made it this year. Once they learned they could get two hundred dollars of stuff for just going to school, they were joining us."

"I can't wait to see you guys on Christmas Eve get all your gifts."

"Just make sure the Santa you get this year is a little more realistic."

I laugh. Last year's Santa was our CPA, and he's tall and really skinny. "I'll see what I can do."

"Great. See you at Bullseye next Saturday."

"I can't wait."

This is exactly why I do this. I worked as a teacher for five years, and it's the hardest job there is. Not only are you responsible for educating the next generation, but many students have so much going on in their personal life that you end up being their mentor, friend, confidant, and sometimes parent as well.

chapter

two

SITTING BEHIND MY DESK and doing mundane things like answering emails is my least favorite activity. I'd rather sit in the rain, soaked to the bone for eight hours, than sit behind a desk.

Today I've got two hundred and sixty unopened emails. I know some of them are unopened because I don't feel like looking at them, but others I should manage. But not today.

I need someone else to start managing these emails. Ever since we made the national news for helping with an international crime ring while protecting a client, we've had more inquiries than we can handle. I don't have the bandwidth to keep expanding. My security firm has only been in business for about eight years, and I have more clients than I know what to do with and a team spread throughout the U.S.

Scanning the emails, I delete the junk mail without opening it, but Stephanie Paulson's email entitled "Help" stops my scrolling.

I click it open. She sits on a nonprofit board that's looking for forty people to go shopping with a middle schooler next Saturday and cover a two-hundred-dollar shopping spree.

Interesting concept.

Their goal is to keep kids in school. Thinking back to my own childhood, I'm reminded how opportunities came to me. I was more trouble for my mom than she could handle. When I was seventeen, I landed in front of a judge and he gave me two options: jail for two years or join the Marine Corps.

I didn't expect to be in the Marines long, but once I got there, for the first time I felt like I belonged somewhere, and I loved the structure the service gave me. I ended up giving them two tours. During my last tour, my commanding officer was a Naval Academy grad. While in school he'd developed an app that moved artificial limbs to a new level that made them behave like actual limbs. He created a multi-million-dollar business, and his son was kidnapped by some less-than-savory characters in a local Chinese gang. The police and FBI were overwhelmed, so he reached out to me as an intermediary and some security. We got his son back, and that was the start of my own security firm. After that, additional work fell into my lap, and I've always felt incredibly lucky. Sometimes it takes unexpected opportunities to change the path of a child.

There's literature about the nonprofit attached to the message, and I open the director's message about her passion for kids and the importance of education. I can't help but relate.

I peruse their website, looking it over carefully. I do a background check on the director and founder to make sure everything is on the up and up. Katherine Monroe immediately piques my interest. There are some candid pictures of her on the website, and I open up her PeopleMover page to learn more about her.

She has all her privacy settings on high, and that impresses me. Using my super-secret backdoor password, I'm still able to look at her account. She has pictures of travels and friends. Her status says she's single—I'm not sure why, but that seems important. She has pictures at an Oakland A's game. She must be a glutton for punishment if she likes the A's. Also, she's stunning—chocolate brown hair with deep auburn highlights, green eyes that I get lost in, and curves in all the right places. I find my pants are tighter than they were before I looked at her pictures, and I very much want to help her cause.

I have a very high-end clientele. I'm sure I can help her get her forty donors. I know exactly what these small gestures mean. I want to make sure that some of my clients make this a priority. Usually they are asking for something from me, but now maybe I can ask them for something. I start with one of my bigger clients, SHN. Mason Sullivan is the managing partner of one of the most successful venture capital firms. He has his hands in the pockets of some of Silicon Valley's best companies.

Before the call even rings, Mason answers. "Hey, Jim. What's up?"

"Mason, glad I caught you. I just sent you a message and I wanted to make sure you saw it at the top of your list. One of my other clients, Stephanie Paulson, needs some help and it seemed right up your alley." I walk him through what I know. "I thought maybe it might be something you and Caroline wouldn't mind getting involved in and maybe pulling in Dillon and Emerson and a couple of the other partners to help out these kids."

Mason is quiet for a few moments. "I think that's something we can definitely pull off. That shouldn't be an issue at all."

"That's great news. You think all four of you would be willing to commit?"

"I will check everyone's calendars, but there are nine partners and their significant others I should be able to drag along. I'll commit to twenty donors. It'll be good for us to do something for the city who hosts us."

"I like it. Send me over a list of names and I'll pass it along."

I hang up and call the man who created my business. Nate Lancaster's working on his third successful startup and has more zeros in his bank account than Bill Gates.

"My man Jim. How's it hangin'?" he says as he answers.

"Hey, Nate. What's going on?"

"You know, living the dream. Every day is a holiday."

"Yeah, in your case that's probably true."

"Hey, man, how did you know you were on my list to call today? Cecilia wants to know if you can stop by for dinner this weekend."

"I will commit to dinner with you and the family if you'll consider a favor for me." I walk him through the nonprofit and their need. "Can you help me out?"

"Of course. So…can I tell Cecilia you will be bringing a date this weekend?"

I don't have time to date. When I have an itch that needs scratching, I have a few women I can call, but nothing serious. Women aren't patient with the lifestyle my job creates. I have to be flexible at all times.

"No, it'll be just me."

"She wants to fix you up with one of her friends." In a low voice he adds, "I know who she's thinking of, and I like her, but don't even consider it. Marnie is sweet, but *high-maintenance* doesn't even describe her adequately."

"Well, you also know my work schedule. No woman is in for this lifestyle."

"The right one will be."

I need to change the subject. "Well, in your email box is the information. We need another ten people, so if you know of any others, please ask. Send me a note with who can come."

"You need ten? I can probably come up with at least five—one will be Marnie."

I groan internally. "You just said she was a train wreck."

"I still think she'd enjoy this."

"Great, confirm and let me know."

I check my email and find a message from Mason. He has twenty-six people from SHN and a few of their clients. Then I see an email from Nate pop up with the five he's promised. That leaves us short nine, and I know my team will cover the nine and then some.

To: Katherine Monroe
From Jim Adelson
Subject: Donor

Hi, Kate,

Stephanie emailed me about your need for 40 people to take some kids shopping. I've come up with a list of 42 just in case some flake out. And I know I can easily talk a few more people into participating, if needed. Let me know if you have any questions.

Jim
Jim Adelson

CEO Clear Security

I attach a sheet of names with emails and phone numbers. I'm actually looking forward to this. Now I just need to hope my Saturday doesn't blow up and make my time with my award-winning student rushed in any way.

THANK YOU!

I really hope you enjoyed the final book in the Venture Capitalist series. I appreciate your help in spreading the word, including telling a friend. Before you go, it would mean so much to me if you would take a few minutes to write a review and capture how you feel about what you've read so others may find my work. Reviews help readers find books. Please leave a review on your favorite book site.

This is the hardest thank you to write. I started this journey with the support of my amazing husband. He urged me on and continues to do so. He's my muse and my happily ever after. He's read each of the books and loved them. I'll admit he's asked for some of the things my characters do, and I patiently explain that we're married and have a bed and two little kids that always seem to wander when we try. Poor guy. I also had the support of my BFF who listened to me talk about the first in the series and he pushed me to make it better but also helped me to define the overall story ARC. Steve died suddenly this past January at the age of 47. I so wish he was here to celebrate the end of this amazing series.

There are many others behind me holding me up and urging me on. My editors are amazing and over nine books, they helped me grow so much as a writer. I see myself as a storyteller and they make me into a fine writer.

My amazing friends…Gayle, Christie, Michelle, Nicole, Helene, Steven, Erin, Bree, Ivy, Michael, Jean, Elinor and Caroline. You all have listened to me talk about my stories and pretending to enjoy the process as much as I do. You've all been amazingly supportive, read all or parts of my books and cheered me on from the sidelines. Thank you all for being my posse. I love you all.

And finally to all of my readers, without your support and encouragement there would be no Ainsley St Claire. Thank you so much. I love your e-mails, your reviews, sharing with me what you like and don't like; I do listen and adjust. Please tell your friends if you like my stories. Getting the word out is what allows me to keep writing.

Ainsley

HOW TO FIND AINSLEY

Don't miss out on New Releases, Exclusive Giveaways and much more!

www.ainsleystclaire.com

Join Ainsley's **newsletter**

Follow me on **Bookbub**

Like Ainsley St Claire on **Facebook**

Follow me on **Instagram**

Follow Ainsley St Claire on **Twitter**

Follow Ainsley St Claire on **Goodreads**

Visit Ainsley's website for her **current booklist**

I love to hear from you directly, too. Please feel free to email me at ainsley@ainsleystclaire.com or check out my website www.ainsleystclaire.com for updates.

ALSO BY AINSLEY ST CLAIRE

The Venture Capitalist Series
Forbidden Love (Venture Capitalist Book 1) **Available on Amazon**
(Emerson and Dillon's story) He's an eligible billionaire. She's off limits. Is a relationship worth the risk?

Promise (Venture Capitalist Book 2) **Available on Amazon**
(Sara and Trey's story) She's reclaiming her past. He's a billionaire dodging the spotlight. Can a romance of high achievers succeed in a world hungry for scandal?

Desire (Venture Capitalist Book 3) **Available on Amazon**
(Cameron and Hadlee's story) She used to be in the 1%. He's a self-made billionaire. Will one hot night fuel love's startup?

Temptation (Venture Capitalist Book 4) **Available on Amazon**
(Greer and Andy's story) She helps her clients become millionaires and billionaires. He transforms grapes into wine. Can they find more than love at the bottom of a glass?

Obsession (Venture Capitalist Book 5) **Available on Amazon**

(Cynthia and Todd's story) With hitmen hot on their heels, can Cynthia and Todd keep their love alive before the mob bankrupts their future?

Flawless (Venture Capitalist Book 6) **Available on Amazon**
(Constance and Parker's story) A woman with a secret. A tech wizard on the trail of hackers. A tycoon's dying revelation threatens everything.

Longing (Venture Capitalist Book 7) **Available on Amazon**
(Bella and Christopher's story) She's a biotech researcher in race with time for a cure. If she pauses to have a life, will she lose the race? He needs a deal to keep his job. Can they find a path to love?

Enchanted (Venture Capitalist Book 8) **Available on Amazon**
(Quinn and William's story) Women don't hold his interest past a week, until she accidentally leaves me a voice mail so hot it melts his phone. I need a fake fiancée for one week. What can a week hurt?

Fascination (Venture Capitalist Book 9) **Available on Amazon**
(CeCe and Mason's story) It started when my boyfriend was caught in public with a girls lips on his you know what. People think my life is easy - they couldn't be more wrong. As my life falls apart, can we make the transition from friends to more?

Clear Security Holiday Heartbreakers
***Gifted* Available for Preorder on Amazon**
(Kate and Jim's story) Forty kids are not going have a Christmas and I don't know how to fix it. I send out a call for help and my prince appears and that's when the wheels really

fall off this wagon. Can he help me or am I doomed to fail all these deserving kids?

Stand-alone Women's Fiction

***In a Perfect World* Available on Amazon**

Soulmates and true love. They believed in it once… back when they were twenty. As college students, Kat Moore and Pete Wilder meet and unknowingly change their lives forever. Despite living on opposite sides of the country, they develop a love for one another that never seems to work out. (Women's fiction)

COMING SOON

House of Cards (Tech Billionaires Book 1)
February 2020

ABOUT AINSLEY

Ainsley St Claire is a Contemporary Romantic Suspense Author and Adventurer on a lifelong mission to craft sultry storylines and steamy love scenes that captivate her readers. To date, she is best known for her Venture Capitalist series.

An avid reader since the age of four, Ainsley's love of books knew no genre. After reading, came her love of writing, fully immersing herself in the colorful, impassioned world of romantic suspense.

Ainsley's passion immediately shifted to a vocation when during a night of terrible insomnia, her first book came to her. Ultimately, this is what inspired her to take that next big step. The moment she wrote her first story, the rest was history.

When she isn't being a bookworm or typing away her next story on her computer, Ainsley enjoys spending quality family time with her loved ones. She is happily married to her amazing soulmate and is a proud mother of two rambunctious boys. She is also a scotch aficionada and lover of good food (especially melt-in-your-mouth, velvety chocolate). Outside of books, family, and food, Ainsley is a professional sports spectator and an equally as terrible golfer and tennis player.

Made in the USA
Las Vegas, NV
21 December 2020